UNLEASHED

SARA HUMPHREYS

sourcebooks
casablanca

Published by Sourcebooks Casablanca, an imprint of Sourcebooks, Inc.
P.O. Box 4410, Naperville, Illinois 60567-4410
(630) 961-3900
FAX: (630) 961-2168
www.sourcebooks.com

Printed and bound in the United States of America
RRD   10 9 8 7

"Whatever you do, or dream you can, begin it. Boldness has genius and power and magic in it."
—Johann Wolfgang von Goethe

For my sons, Ian, Leo, William, and Jack.
Always follow your dreams, and never, ever give up.

Chapter 1

"SAMANTHA," HE WHISPERED IN HIS DARK SILKY VOICE. *Sam's skin tingled deliciously with just one word from him. A smile played at her lips as she waited for him to call her again. Her silent prayer was answered as he murmured her name. "Samantha." That same delightful rush washed over her like the warm waves that rippled by her feet. She stretched languidly on the sandy beach, and her eyes fluttered open. She was home.*

She sat up and glanced at the familiar seashore of her childhood home. Sam knew it was only a dream. It had become a familiar one. The ocean glowed with unnatural shades of blue as if it was lit from beneath. The sky swirled with clouds of lilac and lavender. She stood up and relished the way the soft, pebble-free sand felt on her bare feet. A gentle breeze blew Sam's golden hair off her naked shoulders, and her long white nightgown fluttered lightly over her legs.

She closed her eyes and breathed in the salty air. He was near. She could feel it. Her blood hummed, and the air around her thickened. She'd come so close to seeing him many times, but she always woke up just before she found him.

Not this time.

This time she would stay on the beach and call him to her. It was her dream after all, and she was getting tired of coming up empty-handed. Eyes closed, she tilted her face

*to the watercolor sky and waited. Her heartbeat thundered
in her ears in perfect time with the pounding waves.*

"Samantha," *he whispered into her ear. She stilled,
and her mouth went dry. He was standing right behind
her. How the hell did he get there? Where did he come
from? Why couldn't he stand right in front of her where
she could actually see him? This was supposed to be her
dream, her fantasy. Jeez. Can you say intimacy issues?*

*Sam jumped slightly and sucked in a sharp breath as
large hands gently cupped her shoulders. She should
open her eyes. She wanted to open her eyes, but the
onslaught of sensations to her body and mind had her
on overload. Samantha shuddered as he brushed his fingers lightly down her arms leaving bright trails of fire in
their wake. He tangled his fingers in hers and pulled her
back gently. Sam swallowed hard as his long muscular
body pressed up against hers. He was tall, really tall.
She sighed. If he looked half as good as he felt, she was
in big trouble.*

"It would seem that you've finally found me," *he
murmured into her ear.*

*Sam nodded, unable to find her voice amid the rush
of his. She licked her dry lips and mustered up some
courage. It was a dream after all. Nothing to be afraid
of. She could always wake up. But that's what she was
afraid of.*

"Why don't you ever let me see you?" *she said in a
much huskier tone than she'd intended. She pressed her
body harder against his and relished the way his fingers
felt entwined with hers.*

*He nuzzled her hair away from her neck and placed
a warm kiss on the edge of her ear.* "Come home," *he*

whispered. His tantalizing voice washed over her and he seemed to surround her completely. Body. Mind. Soul. Every single inch of her lit up like the Fourth of July.

"Please," she said in a rush of air. Sam wrapped his arms around her waist and relished the feel of him. It was like being cradled in cashmere covered steel. Leaning into him, she rubbed her head gently against his arm. He moaned softly and held her tighter. The muscles in his chest rippled behind her, and his bicep flexed deliciously against her cheek. "I need to see you."

Eyes still closed, she turned in his arms as he said softly "Samantha."

—⁓—

Sam tumbled out of bed and landed on the floor with a thud. Breathing heavily and lying amid her tangled bedclothes, Sam stared at the bland white ceiling of her soon-to-be former apartment.

"Talk about a buzz kill," she said to the empty room. "Typical. I can't even get good sex in my dreams." She puffed the hair from her face and pushed herself up to a sitting position. Sam grabbed her cell phone off the nightstand and swore softly when she saw the time. She was going to be late. Crap.

—⁓—

The steamy August air swamped Samantha the moment she stepped foot onto the cracked New York City sidewalk. On any other day the stifling summer streets of Manhattan would drive her crazy—but not today. Sam smiled. Today was her last day of work. No more horrid tourists with even more horrid tipping skills. No

more nights spent fending off her married and truly unfortunate looking boss. No more waitressing at T.G.I.
Friday's in Times Square. Thank God!

Sam let out a large sigh, a mixture of exhaustion and
relief, and slipped her aviators on with a cursory glance
up to the towering buildings. She squirmed slightly as
sweat began to bead on her brow and trickle down her
back. Adjusting the heavy backpack, she wove her way
through the pedestrian-riddled city and nestled the small
iPhone ear buds snuggly into her ears. She hit shuffle
on the slim iPod. A familiar tune filled her head; she
couldn't help but walk to the beat as she wove her way
through the minefield of tourists. Samantha mumbled
the occasional *"pardon me, excuse me"* as she navigated
the slow-moving gawkers in Times Square. Why did
they feel the need to stop and look at every skyscraper?
This was another part of living and working in New
York City she definitely would *not* miss.

Sam trotted down the steps into the subway station
and pushed her sunglasses up onto her sweaty head.
She swiped her card in the turnstile and slid through
the narrow gateway toward the platform. Stealing cursory glances at the various subway-goers, her attention
was captured by a young woman who was clearly fresh
out of college. She reminded her of herself—about ten
years ago. Sam smiled and shook her head as the train
screeched its way up to the platform. The hot air blast
that accompanied it actually provided momentary relief
from her sweaty state. She pushed her way into the
crowded train with the rest of the subway rats, and her
gaze wandered back to the young co-ed. She sat almost
expectantly on the seat across from her, as if her lifelong

dream may come leaping to life right in front of her at any moment.

Sam vaguely remembered that feeling. She had moved to the city right after college graduation. The moment she had that BFA in hand she packed it all up and moved to the Big Apple. As a young artist with age-old dreams, the city seemed the only logical place to go. It held the promise of excitement and glamour, a far cry from the sleepy seaside town she grew up in. Clearly promises were made to be broken. The young girl glanced up and caught Sam's eye. She delivered a quick, shy smile before looking away. Sam couldn't blame her. No woman in her right mind would maintain eye contact with a total stranger on a city subway.

The train shuddered to a stop in Grand Central Station, and Sam made a speedy escape into the muggy, bustling crowd as she switched trains for SoHo. She had one more loose end to tie up before she could officially leave NYC.

Gunther's Gallery.

Sam exited at the Spring Street station and hustled along the narrow side streets, grateful that the pedestrian traffic wasn't quite as crazy here as it was in midtown. She turned onto Thompson Street, and the small, but sweet gallery came into view. Sam smiled, and her heart gave an odd little squeeze, knowing that this was really *it*.

She opened the heavy black lacquered door with an audible grunt and stumbled into the refreshingly cool gallery. The heat made the wood swell every summer, and a body slam was commonplace to open the damn door. She was instantly greeted by a shrieking Gunther.

"Kitten," he squealed and pulled her into a vigorous

hug, which was immediately followed by a kiss on both cheeks. "You're late…" He released her with a playful shove. "I can't believe you're leaving me here all alone in this big bad city." He stuck out his lower lip in a dramatic pout, crossed his delicate arms across his chest, and stamped his foot.

Sam chuckled and dropped her backpack onto the black leather bench by the door. "Oh, please." She rolled her eyes. "You've got Milton to keep you company. He is the gardener to your flower, isn't he," she teased.

"Bitch." Gunther stuck his pierced tongue out at her, turned on his heels, and huffed back to the reception desk. "You're just jealous because my boyfriend is cuter than that douche you're dating."

Sam held up both hands in protest. "Excuse me, douche I *was* dating. I broke up with him like a month ago." Sam leaned onto the reception desk with her elbows and placed her chin in her hands. "We can't all be gorgeous and in high demand like you Gunther," she said, batting her eyelashes dramatically.

Gunther patted her on the head. "That's true, kitten." He sighed and brushed a stray lock of hair off her face. "Maybe if you gave yourself as much attention as you gave to your artwork, you'd find a hottie too."

Sam glared at him through narrowed eyes. "Now who's being a bitch? Besides, my experience with Roger is just the latest example of how bad my taste in men is." She let out a sound of defeat. "I give up."

"Sounds to me like someone needs to get laid," he said with haughty confidence.

Sam slapped his cheek playfully. "Gunther, not all of us think with our libidos. You know me well enough by now to understand that a man has to get me here," she said pointing to her heart, "before he can get me here." She punctuated by grabbing both of her breasts.

"Honey, you just haven't met the right man. Trust me, the right guy will get you here, there, and everywhere," he said with a flourish.

Sam laughed and shook her head doubtfully. "I don't think so, honey, at least not for me. I'll take a good book and a hot bath over sex any day."

"Clearly, you've never had good sex." He sighed and made a tsking sound.

Sam opened her mouth to protest but stopped before she said anything because the cold hard truth was that he was absolutely right.

Sam pushed herself away from the desk and turned her back on him. Worried he'd see right through her, she pretended to admire the artwork that currently occupied the tiny gallery.

Sam stopped dead in her tracks at the sight of various brown paper-wrapped pieces leaning against the back wall. Her throat tightened, and tears pricked at the back of her eyes. She stuffed her hands into the pockets of her khaki pants in an effort to get control over her conflicting emotions.

"Hey, you don't have to leave you know." Gunther's gentle tone matched the comforting arm he wrapped around her.

Sam laid her head on his shoulder and sniffled. "Well, no one can say I didn't at least give it a shot." She lifted her head up and planted a kiss on his ridiculously smooth cheek. "You gave me lots of shots. Thanks, Gunther."

Gunther snapped his fingers. "Honey, my family

owns this building in which I live and work. If I can't occasionally share these luxuries with my friends then what the hell good is it? Am I right? Yes," he said, confidently answering his own question. "I am."

He smacked her on the butt as she walked away from him toward the back of the gallery.

Sam smiled and wiped at her eyes. "I'm going to miss you." She took a deep breath, hoping to steady herself. She ran her fingers along the smooth brown paper and took a mental count. One was missing, and she could tell by the sizes that it was her favorite one.

"Gunther," she said in a slightly panic-laced voice. "Where's my mother's portrait?" *Woman and the Wolf.* It was her favorite and most personal piece. The woman and the wolf stood side by side looking out over a stormy ocean. Her mother's hand lay gently upon the massive head of an enormous gray wolf, long golden hair blowing in the breeze. Although a storm and the ocean raged around them, both the woman and the wolf exuded serenity amid chaos.

Smiling broadly, he clapped his hands. "I was wondering how long it was going to take you to notice that piece was missing."

Sam tilted her head and gave him a confused smile. "Well, don't keep me in suspense. Where is it?"

"I sold it," he said proudly.

"Sold it? When?"

"This morning," he said with obvious satisfaction. "As soon as I opened, this guy came in and bought it. Boy, oh boy, what a hottie too." He fanned himself dramatically.

Sam shook her head. "I don't get it? If you had the pieces all wrapped up, how did he even see it?"

"Well, I know it's your favorite, but it's mine too. I was really, really hoping you'd let me keep it here. It would've been like having you with me all the time. So I had it hung behind the gallery desk." He gave her a self-satisfied smile and brushed past her to the front desk.

Sam stared after him with a dumbfounded look on her face.

He glanced over his shoulder at her. "Kitten, you look like you're catching flies."

Embarrassed by her obvious shock, Sam snapped her mouth shut.

"Here's your check," he said holding an envelope out to her. "Minus my commission, of course."

Sam took the envelope from him. She rubbed the paper between her fingers. She should've been happy, thrilled in fact, but it was sad too. That portrait had been the most personal piece she'd ever created, and it tugged at her heart to know she'd never see it again.

"I really did adore it, but I do have one question though. Why the wolf?" He placed his hands on his slim hips. "I mean, I get that it's your mother and the beach where you grew up and all of that," he said quickly. "But why the wolf? You don't see a lot of wolves at the seashore."

"No," she said absentmindedly. "You don't." She'd always had an affinity for animals, wolves in particular. They had haunted her dreams for years, but when she moved to the city the dreams had stopped—at least until recently. "I dreamed about them a lot as a child. They were never scary though. The wolf was always protective. I don't know." She sighed. "Like a talisman or something."

"Talisman? Sounds hot!" He wiggled his eyebrows at her.

Sam gave him a slap on the arm. "No, you horn-dog, it wasn't like that. They were comforting and peaceful." Her thoughts went back to her painting and she could practically hear the waves. "Just like the ocean," she murmured. "Wild and free, but somehow comforting at the same time."

The phone rang, interrupting their conversation, and Gunther rushed over to answer it. As he chattered away with one of his buyers, her thoughts wandered to the evening of her thirtieth birthday. It was a memorable day simply for the milestone it was, but it was more. That night, for the first time in over ten years, she dreamed of the wolf.

Only this time, she *was* the wolf.

Gunther hung up and let out a loud exasperated sigh. "I hate dealing with new buyers. They always call up and ask such stupid questions. *When are you open?*" He mimicked with a grimace. "I mean honestly. What in gay hell? Haven't they heard of the Internet? We have a website for a reason people!"

His rant pulled her from her memories. "Thanks for everything, Gunther," she said with a small smile. "I'll give you a call in a couple of days about where to send the others."

"That's another thing. I think we should keep these for a while. If we hang them up here, there's a chance they'll sell. Sitting in Nonie's garage… ain't nobody gonna buy 'em. Now come over here, and give me a hug." He pulled her into his arms and planted a big wet kiss on her cheek. "You take care of yourself, kitten.

Don't forget to come home and visit Milton and me once in a while."

"That's just it," she said quietly. "This city was never home for me." Her thoughts went back to the portrait. "Tomorrow I'm going home."

———✺———

Malcolm stood stone still on the balcony of his family home. He overlooked the predawn ocean, which stretched endlessly before him. As he breathed in the cool, salty air, he closed his eyes and willed himself to relax. His hands gripped the railing, turning his knuckles white. He was beyond edgy, full of anticipation for the days ahead. He had waited years for her to arrive, and tomorrow she would finally be here. He shoved himself away from the railing and paced back and forth, mirroring the beast caged within. She would be here in just a few more hours.

Malcolm Drew was the last in his family's branch of the Eagle Clan. His family was one of ten animal clans among the Amoveo, a powerful, ancient race of magical shapeshifters. Malcolm was a Golden Eagle, and more than anything he wanted to keep his clan's bloodline running, but he could only do that with his mate. Without her, he was doomed to a painful, solitary existence, and eventually death. Malcolm had heard stories about those who went unmated. He shuddered at the images those nightmarish tales conjured up.

Finding female company was not a problem. He'd had many women before, but they were merely a momentary amusement that left him unsatisfied and lonely. Like all Amoveo, his uncommonly large eyes were his most striking feature. The women he dallied with always seemed to comment on them. His were an unusually light brown, and in the right light gleamed yellow. He never worried himself too much with his appearance. He considered clothing an annoying necessity and barely ran a brush through his long, shaggy hair.

He felt anxious, not just for her arrival, but for her safety. For generations his people had been hunted by the Caedo family, a fanatical group of humans who had discovered their existence. They had not lost anyone to a hunter in many years, but the threat always loomed. He shook his head in frustration and stood with his arms crossed tightly over his chest. So many obstacles lay before them.

His thoughts wandered to his parents. The story of their courtship and mating had been the stuff made of legends. Growing up he'd observed their obvious love for one another with intense curiosity. Given that mates among their people were predestined he often wondered if the love grew over time, or was it a lightning bolt, an instantaneous connection? They claimed that the bonding was immediate, but secretly he had always doubted it. He scoffed audibly at the very idea of it with no one but the gulls to hear him. He'd encountered several females, both human and Amoveo, but he never came close to feeling anything that resembled love. Lust? Sure. Love? Not a chance.

However, that all changed in a flash the second he found Samantha. His body warmed at the mere memory of that moment, and he closed his eyes in an effort to recapture it. Last night's connection in the dream realm had helped solidify their bond even further. However, his brow furrowed, and tension rippled up his back as one intruding thought returned. What if she refused him? His eyes snapped open, and he let out a low growl at the one thought that nagged at him relentlessly. Malcolm had heard that occasionally, a female would refuse the match. He shook his head at the futility of refusing. Why refuse what was imbedded in their souls? His skin suddenly felt two sizes too small as that question continued to beg at the back of his mind. His human form had become a prison from which he abruptly required release. He needed to fly. He stretched his arms wide, tilted his face to the twilight sky, and visualized his eagle form. Silently, he uttered the ancient word "verto" and shifted.

Instantly, he soared high over the crashing sea. He loved the feel of the salt air along his feathered body. His binocular vision spotted schools of fish as they moved through the waters below. The cool, early morning air caressed him and carried him along. His mind, body, and spirit relaxed. His tense muscles loosened to some extent. Malcolm closed his bright yellow eyes and reveled in the freedom and simplicity of the moment. He extended his wings to almost the brink of pain and rode the current with practiced ease. The image of his mate slipped into his mind and warmed his heart.

All too soon, he was torn from his revelry as an enormous muscle spasm tore through his feathered body. He wobbled midflight and struggled for control as his energy began to slip away. His body shuddered, and he knew the shift was coming. He struggled to maintain his clan form and immediately turned back toward his house. Malcolm strained against the shift and flapped his leaden wings with every ounce of energy he had. In a blinding flash of pain and frustration, Malcolm shifted just before he got to the deck of his home. He gritted his teeth, and in a flailing mass of arms and legs, he landed with an audible thud on the wooden planks. He lay there for a moment in a heap. Nice, he thought, very dignified.

Breathing heavily with sweat trickling down his spine, he stood and straightened out his clothing, thinking how nice it would be to have all of his abilities back. At full strength, he could shift smoothly and easily. He had recently passed his thirty-second birthday and was losing strength by the day. There was only one thing that could help him rejuvenate—being with his mate. Samantha. He had known who she was for many years. He'd dreamed of her since his adolescence. Under normal mating circumstances, she would've dreamed of him as well. The mate connection was always made in the dream plane first. If she had been a typical Amoveo female, she would've been looking for him as well. She would've recognized him the instant their dreams connected. His mate, however, was anything but ordinary.

Samantha was a hybrid and the first of her kind. Her mother had been a human. Her father had been the last of the Gray Wolf Clan, and they had been almost completely exterminated. Now that he was gone, she was the last. The most difficult part was that she didn't know it.

After a record long good-bye with Gunther, Sam hopped the "4" train and picked up the "R," which took her right into her Park Slope neighborhood. Well, according to her it was Park Slope, but there were many people who would've debated her on that. Once she moved to Brooklyn, Sam learned that the neighborhood lines were up for discussion. Where Sam lived was known by locals as anything from Park Slope to South Slope or Sunset Park or Windsor Terrace. In other words, it depended on which realtor you spoke to, but Sam didn't care. She loved the neighborhood and would miss it— but not enough to stay.

She took her time walking back to her apartment on Prospect Avenue. After all, this was the last time she'd be doing it. Tomorrow she was going home. Back to Nonie and the beach.

Home.

The very idea of it made her smile. Sam fished the keys out of the side pocket of her pack, lost in her own reverie. As a result she didn't see what was waiting for her on the building steps. Startled, she found herself face-to-face with what was quickly becoming the biggest mistake of her life.

"I've been waiting here for a God damned hour!" Roger's contemptuous tone brought her to a screeching halt. "Where the hell have you been?"

Roger Van Dousen, a trust fund baby who never grew up, was the ex-boyfriend from hell. They had only dated for about a month and had been broken up for about as long, but apparently Roger didn't get that memo.

He seemed like quite the catch at first. Wealthy, educated, polite, and handsome. However, his true nature became glaringly clear after just a few short weeks. Roger was a controlling, self-indulgent asshole with an overblown sense of entitlement. He should be the poster child for how-not-to-raise-your-child-if-you-have-lots-of-money. Essentially, he was a forty-year-old toddler.

His face, almost purple with anger, was covered in sweat. His perfectly coiffed salt and pepper hair was slicked back against his head. Sweat had seeped through his starched shirt, and his hands were stuffed into the pockets of his dark suit pants. She had heard the expression *seething with anger* but had never actually witnessed it until just this moment.

Sam removed the ear buds of her iPhone and looked him up and down through narrow eyes.

"Well, Roger. I'm really sorry to hear that," she said in the most calm and condescending tone she could muster. "I'm not quite sure how you can be upset about waiting for me since I didn't even know you were coming over. Besides, we broke up over a month ago."

He made a loud scoffing noise and crossed his arms over his chest. "Oh really? What about our conversation last night? I told you I was coming to see you and that this breaking up nonsense had to stop."

Sam cocked her head slightly and rolled her eyes. "What the hell are you talking about? Our conversation consisted of me hanging up on you after telling you—for the one hundredth time—that I never want to see you again."

He loomed over her and moved down one step closer in a clear effort to intimidate her. He blocked her path up to the door of her building, and his face, quivering lips and all, was just inches from hers. She couldn't believe that she'd ever been remotely attracted to him. Oh, he was handsome. No one would argue with that. The guy looked like he just stepped out of a Tommy Hilfiger ad. Perfect clothes, strong jawline, suntanned, and well-manicured from head to toe. However, his short fuse and sense of entitlement had quickly made him the most unattractive man she'd ever met.

Sam wanted nothing more than to back away and put some physical space between them. Her heart was beating a mile a minute, and the sweat trickling down her back was no longer from the heat. She stood her ground. He'd never hit her, but Sam suspected it was only a matter of time before he did. If people really could smell fear, she probably stunk to high heaven.

Sam didn't take her big blue eyes off of his. She swallowed hard before she spoke and prayed her voice wouldn't quiver and betray her growing fear. He was a bully, plain and simple. The worst thing she could do would be to let him know that he scared her. Like all bullies, fear only fanned the flames of his perceived power.

"Get out of my way, Roger," she said in a low and surprisingly deadly tone. "You and I are over, and if you don't stop harassing me, I'm going to file a restraining order."

Mustering up her last shred of courage, Sam attempted to shoulder past him to her door. Before she could get by and make an escape into her building, he grabbed her arm and yanked her against him. His fingers dug mercilessly into her bicep, and his alcohol-stained breath blew hotly on her cheek. Sam winced away from him.

"Don't you dare try and walk away from me," he seethed. "You think you can get a restraining order against me? A Van Dousen? My family is hooked into everything in this city."

She glanced around, frantically hoping to spot someone, anyone, who might be walking by but only the occasional car sped past. Her predicament going completely unnoticed was a cold, hard reality of this city. Another thing she would not be missing.

He shook her again, hard enough to make her teeth rattle. "Look at me when I'm speaking to you. I know that you plan on moving back home."

Her shocked eyes darted back to his face, and he grinned.

"You can't hack it here in the city, so you're going to move back home with your old Grandma? You've failed here in New York. No one wanted your art. Your ridiculous attempts at showing in the galleries failed miserably."

The truth of his words stung. She had failed to make it as a real artist. The critics had said her work lacked imagination and soul. *Too realistic and not enough heart*—that was the quote that haunted her. But it was from her heart, and that's what hurt so much. Having her work criticized like that was too much, more than she could stand. How could she paint things that were so personal, so intimately a part of her, but no one else could see it? She could paint a picture with the same precision as a digital camera, but who the hell wanted a painting of something that they could get from a photograph? Tears of humiliation and failure stung the back of her eyes. She blinked them back, refusing to allow this son of a bitch to see her cry.

"You're pathetic. You know that? Do you really think you'll do better than *me*?" His incredulous tone matched the look of disgust twisted into his features. "You're just a waitress." Sam cringed. He said the word *waitress* as if it were something filthy he'd just stepped in. "You're not an artist. You serve people. You're 'the help.'" He laughed cruelly and continued his tirade. "In fact, you should be down on your fucking hands and knees, thanking your lucky stars that I picked you. You could be with me in a penthouse overlooking Central Park, but you choose to stay here." He nodded his head toward her building. He spun her violently and grabbed her with both hands. "We're not over unless I say we're over. I decide. Not you," he screamed. "*Not you!*"

Pain flashed hotly up her arms and into her shoulders as his fingers dug deeper into her. Sam fought to keep the tears at bay. Her face burned with a potent combination of fear, embarrassment, and anger. However, the fear that he might actually hit her was overtaken by raw anger. How dare he treat her this way? She wasn't a piece of meat or something he could just order out of a catalog. He didn't own her, and she didn't owe this rat bastard anything. This selfish bully represented every sleazy art dealer, salesman, and bar patron she had been forced to endure over the last eight years.

No more.

Her existence was hers and no one else's. Her life, her successes, and her failures were all hers. She belonged to nobody but herself.

"You would rather stay in this hovel or go live with some pathetic old woman than be with me?"

Nonie? This bastard had the audacity to call her grandmother pathetic? The moment he dragged Nonie into his venomous tirade, something dormant inside of her sparked to life.

A low rumbling noise seemed to come out of nowhere and surround them. Samantha's eyes tingled, and the rumbling grew louder. The sound vibrated through her chest and radiated throughout the rest of her body. Somewhere in the back of her mind she rationalized that a subway must be going by at a most opportune moment.

Okay. One point for NYC.

"Don't you dare talk about my grandmother that way," she ground out. Her voice sounded so odd, almost like a growl. If she didn't feel her lips moving, she wouldn't even believe that she was the one speaking. "Now, you take your filthy hands off of me."

Roger's eyes grew as big as saucers, and his face went ashen. He snatched his hands back from her arm as if she'd burned him. He shook his head furiously and mumbled something she couldn't quite make out. She watched with smug satisfaction as he half ran, half stumbled down the steps away from her. The rumbling subsided as Roger disappeared around the corner.

"And don't come back," she shouted victoriously in a voice she actually recognized. Sam did a little happy dance as she slipped the key into the door of her soon-to-be former building. Time to throw out the rest of the trash.

Roger didn't stop running until he reached the limo. He threw the door open and dove inside, slamming it shut quickly and locking it behind him. He opened the small refrigerator, grabbed the bottle of single malt Scotch, and proceeded to swig directly from the bottle.

His driver, Rudolph, who didn't even have time to get out and open the door for him, braced himself for the tongue lashing that was sure to come next.

"I'm so sorry, sir. It won't ever happen again, Mr. Van Dousen." He sat perfectly still, braced for impact. However, no temper tantrum came. Rudolph glanced into the rearview reluctantly. "Will your girlfriend be joining us, sir?" He hated to ask anything about this artist chick because it always seemed to send him over the edge.

"Her eyes," he hissed. "Her eyes. You should've seen her eyes." Roger leaned forward and pointed at Rudolph with the bottle of Scotch still firmly in his grip. He rocked back and forth and continued mumbling to himself.

Rudolph cleared his throat to stifle the laugh that began to bubble up. If it came out within earshot of his employer, it would lead directly to the unemployment line.

"Yes sir, Mr. Van Dousen. I'll just give you some privacy for the ride home, sir."

He hit the button for the privacy divider and held back on his laughter until it closed with an audible thump. The Golden Boy had finally lost it.

Chapter 2

Sleep eluded Malcolm consistently, until the early morning sun began to crest outside his bedroom and rise above the rippling ocean. It cast fiery glints along the waves below. He was brimming with anticipation of what lay ahead. He couldn't wait to set eyes on his mate. See her in the flesh. He'd been waiting a lifetime to have her with him, and the day was finally here. He showered quickly and readied himself for the day. Staring out over the crashing waves, he ran various scenarios over and over. Exactly how was he going to tell Samantha who she really was? The right way escaped him. He ran his hands over his face, rubbed his tired eyes, and cursed quietly under his breath. A rap at his bedroom door ripped him from his mental exile. "Come in, Davis," he said with slight exasperation.

Davis entered, carrying a tray of fresh coffee and toast. He was a slightly stooped over British gentleman who in his youth had likely been a rather imposing figure. While time had robbed him of much of his strength he was always impeccably dressed and had a constant twinkle in his eye. Davis was the family butler for years and a member of the Vasullus family. Generation after generation of his family served the Amoveo. They were the only branch of humans that knew of their existence, other than the Caedo. They lived to protect the Amoveo people from harm or discovery.

"Davis, why do you even bother knocking? It's just the two of us here."

"Well, sir, I wanted to be sure you were prepared for visitors this morning. I know it's a big day today, what with Ms. Samantha arriving back and all. I thought you might be feeling a bit nervous and didn't want to give you a fright," he said with a quiet smile. Gently, he placed the tray onto the enormous mahogany nightstand. It looked small in comparison to the looming four-poster bed it stood next to.

"Why on earth would I be nervous? I'm her mate. She is mine. Period," he growled. He stepped into his cavernous walk-in closet and haphazardly threw on a rumpled polo and khaki pants.

"Somehow, I don't think it's quite that simple, sir. She doesn't even know she's an Amoveo. That alone is a bit of a pill to swallow." He poured a fresh cup of coffee and handed it to Malcolm. "Besides, her own grandmother doesn't even know. Now she's a right saucy dish that Nonie." He winked.

Malcolm shot Davis an irritated glare and took a sip of his coffee, but stopped abruptly at the sound of a car crunching its way into the neighboring driveway. He passed the clattering cup and saucer back to Davis, brushed past him, and ran down the sweeping stairway to the bay windows. He stood at the edge of the window taking great care not to let her see him. He didn't want Samantha to see him just yet. Malcolm, his body rigid with expectation, gently pulled back the thick drapery and stared at the little red car in the driveway below.

His heart skipped a beat, and his breath caught in his throat at the sight of his mate. He called up the sharp

eyesight of the eagle. It took much of his limited powers
to do it, but it was well worth it. He saw every beautiful
detail of her face—her large almond-shaped eyes that
reminded him of Ceylon sapphires, regal high cheekbones, a delicate nose, generous pink lips that begged to
be kissed, and her face framed by lustrous blonde hair
that gleamed brightly in the sunlight. He envisioned
burying his nose there and breathing her in. His body
responded urgently, tightening and hardening with an
overwhelming desire he'd never experienced. Quickly,
he stepped away from the window and let the drape fall
down to block out the sun.

——◆◆◆◆——

After the brutal drive along the I-95 corridor from NYC,
Samantha finally pulled her old VW Bug into the long
gravel driveway of her childhood home. The poor car
had barely made the trip back to her grandmother's
house. She stopped for a moment, giving the old girl a
rest before forcing it up the large hill. The enormity of
what she was doing finally hit her. Self-doubt crept in
and crawled up her spine. Was she doing the right thing?
Was she really being brave and starting over, or was she
running home a failure like Roger said? Her stomach
tightened, and anger flared hotly in her chest. No! She
was taking charge of her life, and he could kiss her ass.

A flash of light caught her eye, interrupting her inner
dialogue. Sam looked over at the house that loomed
ominously next door. She forgot how huge the old
Victorian was—it dwarfed Nonie's little Cape. It was as
creepy as it was big. The Drew family had owned it for
generations. Instead of looking stately, it looked aloof

and horribly lonely. The wolf dream wasn't the only dream that had played over and over. There was another one that didn't have the same effect. She shuddered at the memory of the persistent nightmare she'd had since high school. She would wake up sweating, frightened, and just a little bit sad.

Sam shielded her eyes from the glare of the setting August sun as she peered at the old Drew house. She could swear the house looked like it was sitting there waiting for something. Sam shuddered slightly and threw the car into first gear. As the old rust bucket lurched up the gravel drive, she got the overwhelming feeling that someone or something in that house was waiting for her.

Sam climbed out of her car at the top of the drive and gave her stiff body a long, lazy stretch. She grinned, hearing her name carried in the breeze. She looked over and saw Nonie waving from the top of the beach stairs. Although well into her seventies, Nonie still had spunk. Her silver hair was swept gracefully up in a bun with loose pieces flying around her twinkling blue eyes. She scooped Sam up as though she were still the little girl with pigtails and braces. She thought Nonie gave the best hugs. They made her feel completely enveloped in warmth, like she could stay cradled there forever. *Cherished, always cherished.*

"Well, my goodness! Samantha Jane Logan, it's good to have my girl home! How was your trip? Not bad traffic, I hope," Nonie said, slowly releasing her grip on Sam.

"No more than usual. It's so good to be home Nonie. Are you sure you're going to be able to stand having me around again?"

"Well, I'll have to tell all my lovers to back off, but it's worth the sacrifice," she said teasingly. "Come on now, bring your things in, and let's get you settled."

Lovers? Sam knew she'd been teasing, but the idea still made her queasy. It wouldn't be outrageous to think that Nonie got more action than she did. Sam had only had two lovers in her life, and neither one had lived up to her expectations. The first was her college boyfriend of three years, and the second was the only boyfriend since. It had been a brief affair that lasted less than a year. Sex and love were intermingled for her. She had friends that could separate the two, but not her. That pesky thing called her heart always got in the way of the whole friends-with-benefits thing. The sex she'd experienced so far didn't exactly inspire her to seek it out. In the movies or on television, it was portrayed as this electrifying event. Well, it just wasn't like that for her and she doubted it ever would be.

She brought her bags into the house and realized that it was probably better she felt that way. She smiled wryly, looking around her childhood home. If she did meet someone now, she couldn't exactly bring him back to her place. Nonie insisted Sam get herself unpacked and settled while she got lunch together. Sam knew what was for lunch when she had walked in. The whole house was filled with the comforting aroma of Nonie and Pop's conch chowder. Smiling wistfully, she climbed the stairs up to her old room and started getting settled. She put her clothes away and slipped back into her old room easily. Like a pair of comfy old blue jeans. She stood at the bay windows, overlooking the ocean and the beach below. A glint from the Drew house caught her eye, as it had earlier. This time she could see someone in the window upstairs. She cranked the window open and leaned out to get a closer look. Whoever it was stepped back and the drape closed. *Strange*. Who was there? Her curiosity was peaked.

Growing up here all those years, she never saw anyone except the live-in butler, Davis. She swore the guy was older than dirt. She and her best friend, Kerry Smithson, would double-dog-dare each other to go over and step just one foot on their property. Sam smiled at the memory. They usually ended up giggling, screaming, and running back home. The Smithson family owned the house to the left of Nonie's. It had been the family's summerhouse for years. She and Kerry grew up together sharing everything, every summer since either of them could remember. During the rest of the year, they'd stayed in touch with letters and phone calls. Sam had gone to boarding school because it was too desolate in the off-season. Nonie didn't want her growing up alone.

"Sam! Lunch is on," Nonie called.

"Coming, Nonie," Sam shouted as she closed the window. She bounced down the stairs and slid into her chair at the kitchen table, just as she had so many times as a girl. "It smells amazing, Nonie. Now I know I'm home."

"Well, dig in, my dear," she said.

Sam ate the first spoonful and smiled. "Thank you, Nonie." Her throat tightened, and her eyes began to well up. The swell of emotions took her by surprise.

"It's just soup, dear." She covered Sam's hand with her own.

"No." She sniffed. "Thank you for everything, for

raising me, for taking me in now, for the soup, for all of it." She giggled a bit through her tears, feeling foolish for such a display. New Englanders aren't exactly known for free-flowing emotions.

"Now, now. I should be thanking you. If it weren't for you, I'd have no family left. You keep me young. I'm thrilled to have you here with me. Kerry's parents have left for the summer already, off to Paris or something." She waved. "So that would leave me with old Davis next door, and he's even older than me." She chuckled. "Thank goodness you're here. The winter will be much more tolerable this year." She smiled. "Come on, your soup's getting cold. Eat up." She gave Sam's hand a squeeze.

"Wow. Davis is still taking care of that old place? How old is he now? He was like a fossil when I was a kid." Sam smiled over her bowl at Nonie.

"Very funny, missy. He's not that much older than me, smarty pants."

Sam chuckled and dug back into her chowder, savoring every bite. They fell into a slightly awkward silence. Sam had never really explained to Nonie why she was coming home, probably because Nonie hadn't asked. A few weeks ago, she simply called up and said she'd be moving back home.

Time to acknowledge the elephant in the room.

Sam didn't know how to start or where to begin. Nonie's sea blue eyes were inspecting her intently, and it made Sam squirm a bit in her seat.

"So," Nonie began, "are you ever going to tell me why you decided to leave New York?"

Elephant acknowledged.

"Not that I'm complaining. Please don't misunderstand. I'm just… well I'm worried about you, Samantha Jane." She took a sip of her tea but didn't take that intense gaze off of Sam for one second.

Sam pushed what was left of her chowder around the oversized bowl and stared into it as if the right answer would be revealed in the bay leaves. Nonie was a bit of a velvet steamroller, and she always got what she wanted with gentle but persistent measures. To be honest, Sam was surprised it had taken her this long to start the inquisition.

Sam took a deep breath and a large swig from her glass of milk, really wishing that it was a shot of bourbon. "I couldn't hack it." She shrugged. "I got tired of waiting."

"Waiting?" Nonie cocked her head, and her eyes squinted with obvious confusion. "You mean waiting tables?"

"Well, that sure. Since I'm an artist, I suppose there's no way around that one." She laughed softly. "But more than that. Waiting for my art to sell, waiting for Mr. Right." She sat back in the chair that had once seemed so big. "Just waiting. I came to a point where I felt like I was waiting for my life to start, but at the same time life was passing me by." She leaned on the table with her elbows and rested her chin in her hands.

"Is that all? Something must've sparked this revelation." Nonie's eyes narrowed, and that I-know-you're-not-telling-me-everything tone dangled in air.

Sam avoided her gaze and immediately gave more attention to her chowder. "I had a dream," she mumbled.

"I'm sorry, dear? I didn't catch that. What did you say?"

Sam cleared her throat and said it again. "A dream," she said with a bit more volume. She grimaced because she knew it sounded crazy. Hell, it sounded even crazier once she said it out loud. She forced herself to look up at her grandmother. To her relief she was met with a small smile and the same loving eyes she'd seen her entire life. "Sounds kind of nutty, huh?"

Nonie shook her head slightly and placed her teacup in its saucer. "Not nutty at all," she said serenely. "What kind of dream was it?"

Sam hesitated and nibbled on her bottom lip. "I dreamed of being here at the beach." She smiled back at Nonie and took another sip of her milk. "It just made me want to come home. That's all. Besides, I'm in my thirties now. I gave the big city a shot in my twenties, but… new decade… new start."

Nonie made a small sound of understanding but clearly knew Sam wasn't telling her everything. Sam avoided telling Nonie the whole truth about the dream. She wasn't sure why, because normally she told Nonie everything. She wanted to keep that private.

Change the subject, change the subject.

"Nonie," she said with more enthusiasm than necessary. "Is someone living in the Drew house with Davis? I could swear I saw someone in one of the upstairs windows."

"Oh, fine." She sighed. "Change the subject."

Sam smiled and shook her head. Nonie always could always see right through her.

Just call me Ms. Cellophane.

"Seriously, I saw somebody in one of the upstairs windows. It was a little *creeptastic*."

"Maybe it was Davis." Nonie smiled slyly.

"Okay. What's the deal?" Sam leaned in and pushed the now empty bowl aside. "You know that house has always given me the creeps. With only that old caretaker guy, Davis, living in it, the place always had a major haunted house vibe. Lonely and sad looking you know." She shivered and rubbed her arms. "It always gave me the creeps... not to mention nightmares."

"What nightmares?" The stern tone of Nonie's voice caught Sam completely off guard. "Samantha Jane Logan. Answer me."

Sam sputtered a bit before answering. "Well, it's really not a big deal."

"Fine, then tell me," she said more softly.

Oh yeah, velvet steamroller.

Sam rolled her eyes and smiled. "You are like a dog with a bone."

Nonie simply smiled and sat back with her wrinkled hands folded delicately in her lap, patiently waiting to get the explanation she asked for.

"Ever since high school, I've had a recurring dream that I'm lost in that house with someone calling my name." Sam leaned back in her chair, and her gaze wandered to the kitchen window and landed firmly on the old Victorian next door. Her voice wavered and dipped to almost a whisper. "It's a man. His voice is deep and almost hypnotic. I can hear him calling me. He sounds so... desperate. I run from room to room, but I can never find him. It's dark, and I'm alone." Her eyes filled with tears at the vivid memory of it. She sniffled and wiped at her eyes with the back of her hand.

"Seems more sad than scary," Nonie said quietly,

her eyes searching Sam's. She opened her mouth to say more but shut it quickly. She fiddled with her teacup and continued to inspect Sam with worry-filled eyes.

"It's just a silly childhood dream," she said with a wave of her napkin and a swipe at her nose.

"Mmm hmmm," Nonie murmured, not sounding all that convinced. "I do remember you having trouble sleeping. Why didn't you tell me about this when you were younger?"

Change the subject, change the subject.

"Hey, you never answered my question. Who's living in that house with the old guy? Did one of the Drew family members actually move in?"

Nonie remained silent and gave a coy shrug.

"You stinker," she teased. "There's someone else living in that house now isn't there? There's gotta be because the person I saw through the window was way bigger than Davis. Come on, Nonie," she prodded. "You must've met one of the Drews in all the years you've lived here. I never have, and I know Pop never mentioned it."

Nonie leaned in and lowered her voice as though she didn't want to get caught sharing the juicy bit of gossip. "Well, from what I understand, young Malcolm Drew lives there now. He's supposedly the brooding, loner type. Very mysterious," she whispered. "According to Millie at the diner, he runs the family fortune, overseas shipping, or some such thing. Recently moved back here—alone—and now runs the whole business from right next door. He was an only child just like you. I heard his father had died a couple of years ago. I never met the mother, no one here has. Oh, heard rumors of course. But who knows. Maybe you could go over and introduce yourself? Bring him a plate of cookies or something." She winked playfully.

"Nonie! I've been here less than twelve hours, and already you're trying to set me up. With some weirdo shut-in no less. No. No men. My first priority is finding a job."

"I thought your first priority was your art?"

"Well, first I've got to find a job to support my art. As I firmly established in the city, it's not exactly in high demand." She sighed. "I was thinking of asking Millie if they needed any help at the diner."

"I thought you were tired of waiting tables?"

"Millie's place is like my second home. Besides, she usually loses her staff at the end of the season when they go back to school."

"Sounds good," Nonie said with her typical optimism. "Let's go see her at the diner tomorrow and see what's what."

Within a few moments, they fell into a comfortable silence and listened to the soothing sounds of the ocean while they ate.

He'd followed her back from New York. He had his orders to run surveillance on the Logan woman again. They'd observed her off and on over the years. Watching carefully to see if she showed any sign of infection, but so far zip, she was just a woman. He sighed with boredom as he watched her go into the house with her grandmother. Dropping his binoculars on the seat next to him, he quickly took down some notes. Tony hated this assignment because he was convinced there was not going to be any action. He wanted to be in the thick of it and bag an Amoveo for himself, not following some pathetic, freak waitress around. They hadn't killed one for years, not since her parents. That had been a big job, bumping off an Amoveo and his human whore. He cringed at the thought of it. A human woman knowingly mated with one of these animals. It infuriated him. The worst part was that they created some kind of mutant offspring. This woman was a walking atrocity, half human and half animal.

Anger and disgust welled up inside of him. He remembered some of the stories he'd been told. How his ancestors had hunted down and killed these creatures, freaks of nature that practically spat in the face of God. His grandfather had told him about some of the kills he'd made back in the day. They hadn't gotten any good ones in years. What he really loved though was that you got two for the price of one. Kill one Amoveo and their bitch died too. What could be better than that? It had been a great side effect to help them wipe them off the face of the earth. They had gotten very good at hiding from his family—from the Caedo. They were a sneaky bunch of bastards. His grandfather told him—*Don't ever think your job is done. We cannot rest until all of these devils are eliminated from our world.* Tony couldn't let his grandfather down. He wanted to make his mark and do his family proud. Recently, he had taken measures on his own that were *outside the box*. He smiled smugly to himself, admiring his own creative brilliance. He was making his final notes when the cell phone rang loudly next to him. He saw the number and smiled. It was his partner. "Hello?"

"Have you seen her?" the voice asked.

"Yes, she just got home. She's inside with the old lady. Nothing major has happened. I'll call you if—"

"Shut up and listen."

The command was abrupt. Tony hated being told what to do, but waited in silence.

"Her mate has found her. Do not let her out of your sight. He will definitely try to make contact with her soon. If he does, you know what to do."

"Yeah, look I'm not stupid." His comment was met with a click as his partner hung up on him with no warning. "Yeah, good-bye to you too." Tony hurled the phone onto the seat next to him. "Screw you. Think you can tell me what to do? You fucker," he spat. Furious, he pulled away from the side of the road. As he drove away from the house, he kept repeating his new mantra, the one that kept him going. "The enemy of my enemy is my friend."

Chapter 3

SAM CLEARED THE TABLE AND ATTEMPTED TO DO THE dishes, but Nonie wouldn't hear of it. She shooed Sam upstairs to finish getting settled. Normally, she would've fought her on this, but Sam was too tired. She went upstairs, took a long, hot shower, and just enjoyed the water as it flowed over her from head to toe. It washed away any doubts she'd had about coming. She went back into her room and was surprised to see her window open. She could've sworn that she'd closed it. Maybe Nonie opened it?

Maybe you're just tired and forgetful.

As she toweled off her hair, she walked over to the large, open bay window and looked out over the rolling sea. She loved the way the light played on the water, like stars dancing in the ocean.

She looked over at the Drew house and again saw someone standing in the upstairs window. The light was on, and she could quite clearly see it was a man, a very tall man. He filled the entire window—definitely not Davis. She could swear he was staring back at her. Sam couldn't look away. She knew it was rude to just blatantly stare, but he probably couldn't see her anyway.

He waved.

Sam quickly stepped back from the window. *What am I doing? I'm being ridiculous.* She rolled her eyes at her silliness and stepped back to the window, but he was gone. *Great, I've been home for less than a day, and already I've insulted the creepy neighbor.* "Nice move, Sam," she said. "Really smooth."

Sam tossed the damp towel aside and flopped down onto her bed with an audible grunt. The rush and excitement of moving home had worn off and been replaced by exhaustion and a hint of fear. Was she doing the right thing? Was moving back home a new beginning or a huge step backward? She let out a large sigh, and one of Nonie's famous sayings came drifting through her mind. She always said, "Everything will work itself out." Somehow that was always true, but it didn't make the journey any less challenging.

Her eyes drifted closed, and she tried to focus on the familiar and soothing sounds of the seashore. The cool evening breeze blew in through the open window in sync with the rhythmic sound of the waves. She inhaled deeply and relished the sharp, salty air that rushed into her lungs and cleared her head. She had planned to do more unpacking, but was too wiped out.

Sam picked up her head and glanced over at the large pile of unpacked boxes and bags that taunted her from the corner of the room. Just lying down for a few minutes couldn't hurt. Right? Right. Who was she kidding? There would be no more unpacking tonight. Nope. After all, the pile of crap would still be there in the morning. She leaned over and turned out the small jeweled lamp on her nightstand.

Her head once again nestled in the large soft pillow. She stared at the ceiling and absentmindedly played with the silver cross at her neck. It had been her mother's when she was a girl, a First Communion gift. Jane had it put away for Sam after she was born. Nonie, of course, then gave it to Sam on her First Communion. She never took it off.

People often asked her if she missed her parents. That was a difficult question to answer because she was usually misunderstood. They died in a boating accident when she was just six months old. She had no memory of them. It's hard to miss people you never knew. She missed the memories she never got with them, but Nonie and Pop were always there. Every holiday or birthday, Nonie would have a story about her mother, Jane, and one or two about her father, Lucas. She wished she could've known them. Based on the stories she knew, she would've loved them. Sam did love them, just not in a way she could easily explain.

As she drifted off to sleep, her thoughts went to the man in the window. Who was he? Did he live there all alone? Then she smiled sleepily and told herself that tomorrow, after she found a job, she was going to go over there and introduce herself to the neighbor. He can't be all bad, she thought. After all he waved. Then she fell into the welcoming arms of sleep and dreamed.

Sam dreamed of the house next door.

~~~

She was walking along the beach at sunset with the wind whipping her hair up into her face. She heard her name whispered on the wind. It was him.

"Samantha."

His voice was deep and rich, a caress along the nape of her neck. She turned toward the familiar baritone as it curled like mist inside of her. High above her on the bluff loomed the Drew house, and at the top of the beach steps was a man. Her dream lover. Her lips curved into a small smile. She started toward him, drawn to him almost inexplicably. The sun glared brightly behind him and blocked out his face. He cut a hulking, shadowy figure, waiting for her with an outstretched hand.

"I've been waiting for you," he purred.

His silky familiar voice slid inside of her, sending delicious shivers through every inch of her body. She grasped the rough wooden railing and recognition flooded her pounding heart.

It was him. The man who'd been calling to her in the house for all those years was her dream lover. She was sure of it. She swallowed hard and steadily made her way toward him.

Heart racing, fingers trembling, she reached out to take his hand. Eyes squinting against the setting sun, she struggled to see his face.

Without warning, a huge black-backed seagull shrieked and swooped down toward her. Startled, Sam reeled back and felt herself falling. She heard him curse loudly as she flailed wildly, and her body plummeted helplessly toward the beach. She squeezed her eyes shut and braced herself for what was sure to be a painful impact on the beach below. Somewhere in the back of her mind, a slightly hysterical voice reminded her that she was dreaming.

Wakeeupwakeupwakeup.

Suddenly, a vice like grip had a hold of her arms. Her body jerked as though she'd pulled the rip cord on a parachute. Her eyes flew open, and to her surprise the waves splashed far below her dangling bare feet. She was no longer falling, but flying. She was soaring high above the dark blue water, and her bathrobe fluttered open around her legs. She licked her lips, and although it was just a dream, she could actually taste the salt on them. Were you supposed to be able to taste things in a dream?

Breathless, Sam took in the sun-kissed ocean as she soared high above the crashing waves. To say it was beautiful would have been an understatement. If only it were this blue in real life. She had dreamed of flying before, but this was different. She wasn't flying. It was more like she was being flown. Something, or someone, had a hold of her.

A slight pressure on her upper arms increased almost imperceptibly. Her breath stilled, and she closed her eyes. Ohmigod! You're going to be fine. It's only a dream. Steeling herself, she cracked open one eye and glanced quickly at her right arm. The white terry cloth puffed out between yellow, and sharply taloned feet of what could only be a bird. Was it that weird seagull? She swallowed hard and summoned her courage. C'mon Sam. It's just a dream. Right? In a moment of bravery, she looked up to see what held her so effortlessly.

Her mouth went dry at the sight above her. The most enormous bird she had ever seen held her as though she weighed nothing at all. Massive brown and bronze feathered wings pumped loudly in her ears and matched the pounding of her heart. Brilliant yellow eyes peered down at her over a sharply hooked beak. The scream, which had been brewing inside of her, bubbled up and boiled over, shattering the night.

Sam woke up to the shriek of her alarm. The sun streamed into the room, and she squinted against the blinding light. With her breath coming in ragged gasps, she ripped the covers off and launched herself out of bed. "What the hell kind of dream was that?" she blurted a bit too loud. She slapped her hand over her mouth to keep any more outbursts from attracting Nonie's attention. She walked over to the open window and slowly peered outside. The world looked normal. No giant, weird, yellow-eyed birds. Sam took a deep breath and closed her eyes.

"Okay, Sam. Calm down. It was just a dream, a really weird dream." She closed the window and went over to quickly make the bed. Sam rationalized that the dream was merely a result of being overtired from moving in yesterday. That would make perfect sense, she thought, not really convincing herself.

After a hearty breakfast of Nonie's famous blueberry pancakes, they set out for town. It was a late summer day, deliciously warm with a breeze that had cleared every cloud from the sky. She had almost completely forgotten about her bizarre dream. They drove with the windows down because it was a gorgeous day and because the old Bug didn't have any working air-conditioning. They pulled into the diner parking lot, and Sam smiled at the memories, which flooded her mind. The Dugout was a classic, old-fashioned diner, which Nonie and Pop took her to every Sunday after church. It was a popular spot in town with both locals and summer people. Millie Sparks ran it like a kitchen on a Navy ship. There was a lot of colorful language and not much patience for stupidity.

When they walked into the diner, the old bell above

the door announced their entrance. They were immediately greeted by Millie who practically knocked over the busboy on her way to the door. Millie was a short, robust woman with a mischievous grin, and Nonie's best friend for over forty years. Her salt and pepper hair was cut short and stuck out in a thousand directions around a round face with mischievous eyes.

"Well slap me silly, and call me Millie!"

She always did have a way with words, Sam thought with a smile. "Hey, Millie, it's so great to see you," Sam said. Millie grabbed her in a big bear hug, then pulled back and eyed her suspiciously.

"Sammy girl, how are you? You are gettin' too damn skinny! Sit down at my counter, and I'm gonna make you the biggest stack of French toast you've ever seen!"

"Thanks, Millie, but Nonie already filled me with blueberry pancakes." She rubbed her stomach. "If this keeps up, I'll get even fatter."

"Why do you young girls always want to be skinny? Men like a girl with meat on their bones. Ain't that right, Billy?" she said to the loyal busboy who also happened to be her son. It was the same sweet guy she'd almost plowed to the ground a moment ago.

"Yes, ma'am," he said. "Hey, Sam, welcome home."

Billy was a sweetheart. Nonie called him a *gentle soul*. He was pretty much raised in this diner, bussed tables for his mother, cooked, whatever she needed. Sam had known him all her life. "Hi, Billy." She hugged him. "It's great to see you. How's Mary? I heard you had a baby?"

"Yup, little Willie. He's six months old already." Beaming with pride, he instantly pulled a family picture from his back pocket.

Sam looked at the smiling faces, and a twinge of longing hit her. *What is it like to have that?* she thought wistfully. "He's adorable. You've got a beautiful family Billy." Sam handed the photo back.

"Well, quit the yappin', and get back to work, Billy boy." Millie slapped him good-naturedly on the back.

Sam and Nonie took a seat at the counter as Millie poured them some coffee.

"So, your grandmamma tells me you need a job, and as fate would have it, I need a good waitress. These summer kids are gonna split on me in the next couple of weeks, and it'll just be me and Billy. If you take it, it'll be just like old times. You interested?"

"Absolutely, Millie, you're a lifesaver." Sam smiled.

"Well, we aim to please round here. What's say we have you start the last week of this month? Give you a week to get back in the swing of the things before the Labor Day crush. Sound good?"

"I could start tomorrow."

"Well, I don't know about that. Your grandmother just got you back. I'll never hear the end of it if I hog up all your time right away." Millie pursed her lips and scratched her head. "How 'bout the day after tomorrow?"

"Well, OK." Sam sipped her coffee and shrugged. "Day after tomorrow sounds fine, I guess."

"She's right dear," Nonie chimed. "Besides, it will give you a bit of time to concentrate on setting up your art studio." She smiled at Millie over her coffee.

"What art studio? What are you talking about?" Sam sent a confused look to Nonie who was busy sharing a conspiratorial glance with Millie.

"You'll see when we get back to the house. Right now,

we need to head over to the art supply store and stock up. Bye, Millie. See you tonight at your place for bridge."

Nonie put money down for the coffee and walked out to the car, leaving Sam sitting there with her mouth hanging open.

"Well, you gonna just sit here like a wide mouth bass? Don't do that, you're scarin' my customers. Go on. Git. I'll see you the day after tomorrow for work." She flicked her dish towel at Sam.

"B-but," she stammered, feeling bewildered.

"No buts. Go with your grandmother. She's been planning this surprise for you ever since you said you were comin' home."

She stood up, slipped on her aviator sunglasses, and went out to the car. Nonie sat in the passenger seat with a satisfied smile on her face. Sam started the engine and stared at her grandmother. "Okay. Spill it."

"You drive. I'll *spill* as you say."

As they drove over to the art supply store in town, Nonie began to divulge the surprise she'd been carving out. Once Sam told her that she was moving back home, Nonie went to work on setting her up an art studio in the little garage at home. Sam couldn't believe it. She was so used to working in a catch-as-catch-can way. The idea of having an entire studio space for her was like winning the lottery. When they pulled into the parking lot of the art supply store, she shut off the car and grabbed Nonie in the biggest hug she could muster. "Thank you so much." She laughed.

"You're so welcome. Come on, missy, let's get you stocked up. By the way, I'm paying." She raised her hand to stop any reply. "Don't even think of arguing with me. I'm an old woman. If you fight with me about it, it could give me a heart attack. Consider it your thirtieth birthday present."

The crisp air-conditioned air hit her bare arms and legs welcomingly. She closed her eyes and breathed in the distinct aroma of paint with a hint of sharpened pencils. It reminded her a bit of the first day of school. Nonie got a shopping cart, and they went to town. Charcoals, brushes of varying sizes, paints, watercolors, pencils, paper, canvas—the whole kit and caboodle. They paid for their purchases and then spent a good twenty minutes figuring out how to fit it all in Sam's little car. The drive home seemed longer than normal as her excitement grew. She couldn't wait to see what Nonie had done.

They pulled in the driveway, gravel spitting up from the wheels, echoing Sam's impatience at the car's slow climb. Finally, she pulled around to the side of the house and up in front of the little garage. Getting out of the car and taking in Nonie's creation, she was ashamed of herself for not noticing it yesterday. The garage door had been replaced with French doors, and pink and white impatiens created a colorful border along the welcoming little path.

Nonie walked ahead of Sam and opened the doors, leaving her speechless. What had formerly been a dark little one-car garage was now a bright open space. The walls were painted a beautiful eggshell color. The cement floor was replaced with hard wood planks in a warm honey tone, and barren walls were now adorned with built-in shelving and cabinets. There were some easels and various organizational containers just waiting for her to use them. The absolute crowning jewel, however, was the enormous picture window at the back wall. It delivered a breathtaking view of the ocean. On the ledge sat a lovely silver frame with an old black and white photo of Sam with her parents. It had been taken on the very beach she looked down on now. It was Sam's favorite. Overcome with emotion, she picked up the picture. The image blurred through the flood of tears rolling down her face. Nonie came over and wrapped her up in one of her delicious hugs.

"I figured this place had just become a big junk room, and I had to clean it out anyway. So what better way to make use of it than for you to work in?"

Sam sniffled and giggled as she wiped off her face. "How did you get this done in such a short amount of time? This is just too much. Nonie, how am I ever going to repay you for this?"

"Don't be silly." She chuckled. "Actually, I've always wanted a portrait of our home. Perhaps you could see your way clear to whip one up for me?"

"Consider it done." Sam turned and hugged Nonie. "Thank you so much. This is the most amazing gift. I love you, Nonie."

"I love you too, Samantha Jane." She released Sam. "Now, if you can manage to settle in here on your own, I have to get some things done around here before my bridge game tonight at Millie's place."

Nonie gave her hand one last squeeze and headed out of the studio. Sam followed her out and brought in the rest of their purchases. Once it was all inside, she jumped up and down like a little kid, shrieking her delight and good fortune. Out of breath and deliciously exhausted, she turned slowly and surveyed the space, taking in the light from various angles in the room. "Luminous," she said breathlessly. "Absolutely luminous."

From behind her, she heard an oddly familiar voice purr. "I couldn't agree with you more."

Startled, she whipped around to see the most breathtaking man she had ever seen in her entire life—real or imagined. He stood over six feet tall, a body built like a Greek god, chestnut hair, and enormous, gorgeous brown eyes that looked straight through her. He stood there casually with his hands in his pockets, leaning against the doorway. He delivered a sexy smile that said he knew exactly what she was thinking. She realized she stood with her mouth hanging open like a large mouth bass. Sam snapped her mouth shut and desperately attempted to collect herself. "Uh-hi? Have you ever heard of knocking?" She knew how rude she sounded, but couldn't help herself.

"Of course, but you were enjoying yourself so much that I hated the idea of interrupting you." He smiled as he stepped toward her with an outstretched hand. "I'm your neighbor, Malcolm Drew. I just moved into my family's summer home and wanted to come over and introduce myself."

When he took her hand in his, an electric shock went to the very core of her. Surprised, she instinctively took a step back. He loomed over her, and for the first time in her life she felt very small. "Yes, of course my grandmother mentioned something about that to me earlier today." She took her hand back from his possessive grip.

"My family has owned that house for years, but only old Davis has really called it home."

Sam detected an accent of some kind, but couldn't

put her finger on what kind it was. She watched him slowly tour the studio. "It's a shame really, since it's so beautiful here."

He casually walked around her new studio as though he owned the place. He absentmindedly touched the brushes standing up in the various jars on the shelves.

It was starting to piss Sam off. She didn't even know this guy, and he was invading her space big time. "Yeah, well it doesn't feel very beautiful after about eight weeks of digging your car out of snowdrifts and winds that cut through you to the bone." Sam began unpacking one of the bags she brought in. This guy was making her nervous, and she had to do something other than stare at him.

"You grew up here then?" He leaned one hip against her drawing table.

"Yes, for the most part." She avoided his gaze. "I went to boarding school for high school though. Nonie felt it was too desolate here in the winter and that a teenage girl might find trouble with nothing but time on her hands."

"Nonie? Is that your grandmother?"

"Yeah. She and my grandfather raised me after my parents died."

"Are these your parents?"

He picked up the framed black and white photograph from the windowsill and ran one finger along the edge. His hands were visibly strong, and she couldn't help but wonder what it would feel like to have him stroke her with those long beautiful fingers. Her face flushed, and she quickly took the photo from him and placed it gently back on the sill. What was wrong with her? She had just met this poor man and was already imagining herself naked with him. Sheesh.

She cleared her throat and hoped she didn't look as embarrassed as she felt. "Yes. Look, I don't mean to be rude, but I've got a lot of settling in to do here and…"

"Of course," he said. "I'll leave you to it."

Before leaving, he turned to Sam and took her hand in his. His large brown eyes fixed onto hers, and everything seemed to stop. He towered over her, surrounded her, and zeroed in on her. She was right. His hands were strong, and they melded against hers perfectly. She couldn't move. What the hell was wrong with her? She had always fancied herself an independent woman, but at the moment she wanted nothing more than to stay locked in this man's gaze forever.

Lifting her hand to his mouth, he gently brushed her fingers with his firm, warm lips. "It was lovely to meet you, Samantha," he murmured, looking at her more thoroughly than anyone ever had in her entire life.

Their eyes locked, and her stomach did a little somersault. Staring into those spectacular brown eyes, Sam got the oddest sense of déjà vu. If she didn't know better she'd swear she'd met him before. As if he read her mind, he winked, and a crooked grin played at his lips.

"It was lovely to meet you too," she said in a much huskier tone than she intended.

With a smile and a nod he released her hand and seemed to glide out of the studio. Sam folded her arms in an attempt to still her quaking body. She drew in a deep breath to steady herself, and it dawned on her that he'd called her Samantha. Normally that would be fine, but she had never told him her name.

Chapter 4

MALCOLM WALKED INTO HIS HOUSE AND CURSED violently under his breath. He kicked his flip-flops off, sending them into the corner of the front hall.

"Problem, sir?" Davis put the offending footwear in the closet.

"I thought for certain once I saw her in person she'd have some kind of recognition of me as her mate. *Something*. Instead all I got was her irritation at my presence." He sank into the large armchair. Staring into the fireplace, he visualized a roaring fire, and instantly one came to life before him.

"Well, sir, at least your power seems to be strengthening. That's something, then isn't it?"

"I suppose," Malcolm said quietly. "I had gotten a glimpse or two of Sam yesterday through the windows, but when I waved at her, she ducked away like a frightened child. Her reactions are perplexing to say the least." He let out a small laugh. "She obviously has no idea of what kind of power she possesses."

Davis puttered around the couch and rearranged the pillows. "Well sir, there has been no one to show her who she is or the ways of the Amoveo, until now of course."

Malcolm rubbed his tired eyes, and his mind wandered to the dream they shared last night. He had finally made the connection that had eluded them both for so long. Unfortunately, their first true contact in the dream realm had not been what he'd hoped for.

"Did you have any success connecting with her yet?"

Malcolm's eyebrows flew up in surprise, and he turned to look at Davis. The crafty old bird knew exactly what kind of trouble he'd been having but was doing his best to be polite. Davis had been with his family for so many years, and so it shouldn't come as a surprise that he'd seen right through Malcolm's charade.

"Am I that transparent Davis?"

Davis said nothing but just kept straightening out the already neat living room.

Malcolm smiled. "Well, some success yes. At full strength, I can control the entire environment of the dream realm, but last night's encounter proved I'm not there yet."

"How do you mean, sir?"

"A seagull manifested out of nowhere and interrupted us before we could finalize our connection."

"A seagull? That's odd."

Malcolm made a small sound of agreement and stared into the fire. Last night reminded him that he wasn't up to par yet. Just having Sam close had given him so much more of his strength back, but until they were bound by the mating rites he was only running on half strength. Still, the seagull was disturbing more than startling. When it flew at them, it had a look of death in its eyes, and it was directed straight at him.

"Might I make a suggestion? She is a contemporary woman who knows nothing of your ways or traditions. You cannot expect to court her the way you would court a traditional Amoveo female. It seems to me you'll have to court her like a human."

"Don't say it! Don't even think of saying it," he bellowed, putting his hand up to silence him.

"Very well, sir." Davis turned to leave. "Do you require my services anymore this afternoon, sir?"

"No, Davis."

"Good day, sir." He quietly left the room.

Malcolm sat in silence for some time, staring into the fire. After what seemed like an eternity, he walked out the French doors to the deck overlooking the ocean. He wandered around the porch, which wrapped around to the front of his house. The sun slowly set over the marsh, casting a fiery glow over the reeds and pools of water. Malcolm watched the great white egrets as they gracefully walked through the marsh waters. He envied them and the simplicity of their life. He leaned on the porch railing and closed his eyes to better hear the sounds of his new home. However, as much as he tried to, he couldn't block out his frustration.

He kept going over and over the dream in his mind. He replayed that look on her face. It was a look of longing, desire, and then fear. It broke his heart to have her look up at him with absolute terror and scream the way she did. All these years he'd been searching for her, but when she saw his truest form, it horrified her. What if she refused him? What if she refused to accept what she was or what her destiny was? He hated to admit it, but it seemed Davis was right. This was all going to be much more complicated than he thought.

He heard what Davis had said. *Court her like a human.* It's not that he didn't know what to do; after all he'd lived quietly among them his entire life. He saw the ridiculous mating rituals they invested in. To Malcolm it seemed like one big dance of bullshit, pretending to be a modified version of who they really were. Never showing their true self until it was too late to turn back. They kept that side of themselves locked away for so long they were afraid of being rejected for who they really were. As he thought about it, he realized he was actually doing the very same thing.

Sam didn't know that shapeshifters existed, let alone that she had that gift inside of her. If he blurted it out, she'd think he was insane. *Great.* He ran a hand over his face. *It looks like I'm courting her like a human male after all.* He knew he'd have to gain her trust before he could tell her who she really was. As he went back in the house, he reminded himself he owed Davis an apology.

In the amber light of the setting sun, Sam put the finishing touches on her studio. She took one last survey of the space, and after moving a few things around, decided it was exactly how she wanted it. Nonie had a date for a bridge game at Millie's, so she could eat out in her studio guilt-free. She salivated at the thought of the leftover chowder in the fridge. As she ran into the kitchen, Nonie was just putting on her jacket to go out.

"Don't wait up, dear. You know these games can go on into the wee hours."

"How much playing do you really do? I think it's all about the Chardonnay and the gossip," Sam teased as she warmed her chowder in the microwave.

"I'm quite sure I don't know what you're talking about, dear." Nonie walked out the door.

Sam smiled and shook her head. *I hope I have that much fun when I'm her age,* Sam thought. She walked out to the studio with a steaming bowl of chowder and a simmering excitement. What would she paint first? Nonie wanted a portrait of the house, but she needed full sunlight for that. A sunset or a landscape would probably make the most sense, but one image had haunted her all day. That yellow-eyed eagle from her dream had been floating around her brain since she woke up that morning. Mystical was the best description for that bird. Mystical and a little bit scary. Sam liked to put the things that scared her onto canvas. It helped take away the fear. She hit play on her iPod and Amy Petty's song "Sleepwalking to Dreaming" filled the small space. Sam smiled. *How fitting.*

Her gaze danced over her materials, deciding which medium to use, finally settling on charcoal. She set out to sketch the very same eagle she'd seen in her dream. She had it soaring high over the ocean with a large pearly moon looming behind it. She smoothed edges and lines with her fingers, massaging the image to life before her eyes. She intently crafted the curve of the graceful wingspan. With painstaking detail, she carved out the intricate pattern of the feathers. Sam spent a significant amount of time on the piercing eyes, which seemed fixated on her even from the canvas. She was completely entranced, almost possessed by the creation of this portrait.

Finally, after several intense hours, she stopped. Her gaze remained locked on the eyes of the bird. Her breath came in a heavy rush, and her heart began to race. She realized that the eyes weren't quite right. She searched the various bits of chalk and found a bright yellow piece, needing to add this one color. Carefully, she blended the bright yellow hue to the intense eyes. She stepped back to get a fresh perspective at the work before her. "Yes. That is one cool bird," Sam said under her breath.

"I would have to agree," Malcolm murmured from the doorway.

Sam practically jumped out of her skin, letting out an undignified yelp. "Jesus Christ. You scared the shit out of me." She clutched her chest as though she were about to pass out.

"Sorry, I seem to be doing that a lot today." Malcolm couldn't seem to take his eyes off the portrait, and at the moment she was grateful because in all likelihood she looked like shit.

"What are you doing lurking around my studio in the dark, Mr. Drew?" She suddenly felt very self-conscious. She realized her hair was a messy bun, falling out all over the place. Her hands were covered in black charcoal, and it was probably smudged all over her face. *God I must look awful.* She pushed sweaty strands of hair off her face with the back of her black-smudged hands. Sam was wishing she had on something other than old khaki shorts and a charcoal- smudged tank top. She barely knew this guy. Why did she care how she looked? Probably because he was the most attractive man she'd ever met.

"I wasn't lurking, Ms. Logan. I came over to ask you out on a date." His smile was sexy. He was definitely trouble.

"A date? Are you serious? You don't even know me." She narrowed her eyes. "Besides, how do you even know I'm single?" Sam crossed her arms tightly over her breasts. This insanely handsome stranger was knocking her off balance. A dark cloud passed briefly over his face. He'd looked angry for a moment, but it passed as quickly as it had come. Sam shook her head. She must have imagined that. Why would he be angry?

His eyes narrowed, and his voice dropped to almost a whisper. "You are single aren't you?"

Sam straightened her back defensively. The mere memory of Roger was enough to raise her hackles, and the last thing she wanted to do was revisit any of her time with him. "Well, yes... I mean I am now—uh, recently actually." She fumbled and rolled her eyes. "I was dating someone, but it didn't last long." She shrugged.

A small smile curved his perfectly formed lips, and he hooked his thumbs into the pockets of his jeans. "I know."

Sam smiled in spite of herself. "Oh, really?" She shook her head with a soft chuckle and instinctively touched the bit of silver at her neck. She should probably be pissed at his overly confident attitude, but that smile of his completely disarmed her. Her eyes flicked down the length of his body. Perfectly formed... everywhere. A slow burn crept up her belly as she imagined what he looked like out of those clothes. She cleared her throat and forced herself to look him in the eye.

Uh oh. That wasn't any better. Worse in fact. Or better. Shit.

"Davis is something of an informant." He smiled, and those big brown eyes flashed mischievously. "He did let it slip that you just moved here to live with your grandmother—alone. You're alone. I'm alone. So why not check out the nightlife together. Besides, you could show me the hot spots since you grew up around here."

Sam burst out laughing. "Nightlife? Hot spots? Boy, you aren't from around here are you?" Shaking her head, she turned and put her charcoals away. "Other than one or two seafood places on the water and the local movie theater, there's not much *nightlife* around here. The closest thing would be one of the Indian casinos, but I'm not much of a gambler." She turned around to find that he had closed the distance between them. Her breath hitched, and her throat went dry. She looked up into those yellow-gold eyes and froze.

"I'm not much for gambling myself." He delicately brushed a stray lock of hair from her face. His eyes stayed locked on hers, and he tucked the soft strands gently behind her ear. "However, I do like seafood. Are you game?"

Sam had trouble finding her voice because she could swear he was going to lean down and kiss her. This man she barely knew was about to kiss her. What was worse was that she wanted him to. She couldn't look away from him and those mesmerizing eyes. They were so familiar to her. Finally, she found her voice and managed to croak out, "Yeah, sure that would be great."

He leaned in slowly. Sam's eyes widened. However, to her relief and disappointment, he placed a very warm kiss on her forehead.

"I'll pick you up at seven o'clock tomorrow night." Then he walked out as quickly and silently as he'd come in.

Sam absently touched the spot on her forehead

where he kissed her and felt the lingering promise of more to come.

Sam closed up her studio for the night and went to take a very long, very lazy hot shower. She loved the sensation of the water running over her body and the steam enveloping her. As purifying as it was, she couldn't manage to scrub Malcolm out of her mind. She was obsessed like some love struck teenager. She barely knew the guy, and her imagination was running wild with things she wanted to do with him and to him. She kept thinking about those eyes of his, as well as other parts of his body. Sam finally got out of the shower and wandered back to her room. She opened the window and let the warm breeze waft through the room. She closed her eyes and unfastened her robe, loving the feel of the salty breeze over her naked body. She felt alive for the first time in years.

"Music is all I'm missing." She went over to her iPod station and pulled up some Santana. "Perfect." Sam swayed to the Latin guitar while she brushed out her wet hair. She closed her eyes, feeling completely relaxed, and realized it had been far too long since she'd felt this good. Peaceful, tranquil, happy—and turned on. Sam hated to admit it, but Malcolm Drew, who she barely knew, had really flipped her switch.

Suddenly, Sam got the eerie feeling of being watched and knew she was no longer alone in her reveries. The small hairs on the back of her neck stood on end. She froze and clutched her robe closed. She swallowed hard, afraid to open her eyes. Sam cursed silently at her silliness and slowly cracked one eye open. There was no one in her room. The door was still closed. *I'm being ridiculous.* Just as she let out a sigh of relief, she heard a clicking noise behind her. She slowly turned around, and her body froze at the sight before her. Perched on her windowsill was the exact same bird she'd seen in her dream, identical to the one she'd drawn on her canvas. Samantha stood there with wide eyes, uncertain what to do. "Holy crap," she whispered.

The giant bird puffed up, bronze feathers glinting in the light. It shook its head as though displeased with her response.

"Sorry. Nice, birdie," she said through a strained, almost hysterical giggle.

The giant creature didn't move.

It just sat there staring at her, silently watching her with glowing yellow eyes. Sam didn't know what to do so she stared back. Eventually her artist's eye began to study the specimen before her. Her fear soon became replaced by curiosity. It was a mammoth bird of prey, an eagle, she thought, but reminded herself she'd have to look it up later. Its feathers shone with bright streaks in varying hues of browns and bronzes. They glinted brightly in golden flashes with even the slightest movement. She eyed its large taloned feet and sharp, hooked beak. Sam shuddered at the damage they could likely do.

The eyes were the same piercing yellow she remembered from her dream. They didn't move from her face. As she stared into the eyes of her feathered visitor, she got the oddest sense of familiarity. She felt like it was intentionally sitting there so she could study it, like some kind of bizarre introduction. Feeling an unusual bravery, Sam slowly reached out to touch it.

Their odd meeting was abruptly interrupted by the

slamming of the front door. They both jumped at the loud noise. In a blur, the eagle popped up, spread out its enormous wings, and swooped out into the night.

"Sam, I'm home. No need to call the police," Nonie said with a courtesy knock and entered Sam's bedroom.

"What?"

"I know I'm late. I hope I didn't worry you, dear."

"No." She went to the window looking after her unexpected visitor, but it was nowhere in sight.

"Are you all right? Sam?"

"Huh? Oh, yes. Sorry, Nonie." She closed the window.

"Nonie, have you ever had any trouble with birds here at the house?"

"What, you mean like seagulls? Usually just when I'm trying to picnic out at the beach. You know how pesky they can get with food around."

"No. I mean like bigger birds. Eagles maybe?"

"Eagles." She chuckled. "No, honey. The closest thing to that might be an osprey, but they stay away from the houses. Not too fond of people you know. Why do you ask?"

"No reason. I thought I saw something, but it was probably just a big seagull." She waved dismissively.

"Okay, dear, whatever you say. I'm bushed, so I'm going to turn in. Anything big on your agenda for tomorrow?"

"Well actually... I've got a date tomorrow night." Sam sat on the edge of the bed.

"A date! You've only been home for a day, and most of that time has been here at home. What? Old Davis hit you up for some fun?" She sat next to Sam on the bed, giving her long hair a playful tug.

"Close. Malcolm Drew."

"Really," she said hesitantly. "Well, that should be interesting. I've never actually met one of the Drews, so you'll have to get all the dirt and fill me in. Is he handsome?"

"Handsome? I don't think that would cover it. In fact, I'm not sure there's an adequate word to describe him. However, his beauty is tempered by the fact he is clearly arrogant."

"Nothing wrong with a little confidence." Nonie patted Sam's knee. "I think it's great you're giving him a chance. I'm sure he could use a friend, since he's new and all alone. Good night, dear." She placed a kiss on Sam's head.

"Night, Nonie."

After Nonie left, Sam went over and locked the window before crawling into bed. She lay there fiddling with the cross at her neck. Sleep eluded her as she tried to concoct a logical explanation for the giant eagle in her window.

Eventually she drifted off to sleep, but not a dreamless one.

Her dream was filled with the yellow-eyed eagle. It was flying alongside her as she ran on the beach with the waves crashing around her. Again, she was the large gray wolf running down the beach, the wind whipping along her fur-covered body. This time she wasn't afraid of the eagle. She was running with it, as though they were in complete unison. It was a liberating feeling to run with such abandon while the eagle matched her speed.

The two of them connected as though they'd done it a million times before. They stopped once they'd reached the jetty. The massive eagle landed directly in front of her on the rocks. The salty spray from the waves misted over them as their gazes locked, unwavering. They both stood breathless from their race. Sam felt a connection to something she couldn't quite put her finger on. It was a feeling of belonging, of coming home. The spell was abruptly broken by the same large, black-backed seagull. It dive-bombed the two of them, shrieking loudly. Swooping down between them, it herded Sam away from her yellow-eyed companion.

———

Sam was once again torn from her sleep by a shrieking alarm. This time, however, her heart sank with disappointment that the dream was over. She slapped the snooze button on her alarm and threw her arm over her eyes, wishing she could go back and recapture the dream.

Chapter 5

MALCOLM AWOKE THAT MORNING WITH A SMILE ON HIS face for the first time in years. Samantha was slowly warming up to him. After experiencing her wariness of him, he knew that he had to earn her trust. He would have to earn it in both forms if she would ever believe who and what she really was. Last night's dream contact proved to be the most promising one yet. It had been progressing nicely until that blasted seagull interrupted them. His smile faded at the memory of the interloper. The second appearance of the gull in the dream proved that it was not a random manifestation. Someone was intentionally trying to keep them apart, but who would do that and why? There was no Seagull Clan.

Malcolm needed to go for a run and clear his mind. Flight was always better, but he needed to conserve all of his powers for later that evening. He quickly dressed for his run and went down to the beach. He loved running on the beach. It was as close to nature as he could get in his human form. Malcolm kept playing the dream from last night over and over again in his mind. The second appearance from that seagull nagged him. He needed another opinion and the one man he knew could help him, the Prince and leader of their race, Richard Muldavi.

Richard and his wife, Salinda, led their people with regal grace and extraordinary compassion. They found each other over a century ago. Their unity and their age gave them great strength. They desperately needed it to lead their dwindling race into the next generation.

Richard was a member of the Lion Clan, descendent of the fated couple from so long ago. He had been trained to protect their people and worked closely with the Vasullus family leaders to keep them all hidden from the Caedo hunters. Richard led their people with the help of the Council. It consisted of one representative from each of the ten clans and two Vasullus family members. Malcolm's uncle, Brendan Drew, represented the Eagle Clan. Together they all worked to protect their people and monitor any possible Caedo activity. They hadn't lost anyone since the murder of Samantha's parents all those years ago.

Their murderers had never been found and still walked free to hunt and kill again. The human authorities, of course, had assumed it was a faulty fuel pump that had caused the explosion. The Amoveo knew the Caedo family was behind it. They just hadn't found out whom. That unsolved murder haunted all of their people, especially the leaders of their race. The Caedo had become as elusive and invisible to the Amoveos as the Amoveos were to the humans. Malcolm knew that Samantha was unaware her parents were murdered. He was curious, however, that she never recognized any of her own powers.

His mind flooded with beautiful images of her. She seemed completely unaware of her beauty and that made her even more desirable. He remembered how sexy she looked last night, her skin damp from her artistic exertions, the long soft tendrils of hair that framed her

beautifully sculpted face and her determined jaw. Even
with the charcoal smudged in various places, she glowed,
from the inside out. He had felt how self-conscious she
was, and it only endeared her to him further. Desire sim-
mered in his blood as his body tightened from the mere
thought of her. He knew he was lost to her already.

Samantha took her morning coffee out to her studio. She
only had one full day before getting back to work at
the diner. She didn't want to waste a minute. As she
prepared her canvas and materials, her eye was caught
by movement on the beach below. She stepped closer to
the large picture window and looked down to the sandy
shore. Her breath stopped as she got a glorious eyeful
of Malcolm Drew. His incredibly muscled chest glis-
tened with sweat. He slowed to a walk just below her
window. She took a small step back, not wanting to get
caught ogling him, but who could blame her? This guy
was built like something out of her fantasies.

Watching him, she couldn't help but imagine what it
would be like to run her hands up those arms and back
down again. She shook her head, trying to erase the
spicy images from her mind. After all, she had a date
with him tonight, and that reality was enough to leave
her breathless. She was still a little shell shocked that
this beautiful man would want to go out with her. "He
must really be desperate," she said under her breath. She
stopped herself. Negative thinking had been her down-
fall in the past. "Just go with it. Just go with it."

Samantha spent the entire day working on the portrait
for Nonie. It would be a watercolor eventually. She took

her time, penciling every shingle on the little Cape Cod and each blade of tall grass that surrounded it on the dune. Around midday, she stopped and stretched out her sore muscles that were stiff from being perched at the canvas for hours.

With both arms stretched up over her head, she studied the portrait of the eagle from yesterday. She couldn't get away from the sense of familiarity. Those eyes—she knew that she'd seen them somewhere else. She stood lost in the eyes of the eagle. The two yellow orbs focused on her, returning her gaze. Curiously, her mind wandered to Malcolm and that sexy little smile. Sam shook herself from the trance. "Focus, Sam. Focus," she mumbled. She shifted her attention back to the portrait. "What did I get myself into?"

~

Malcolm spent the rest of his day working on family business. Drew Shipping imported and exported various Italian-made products. His parents retired to their villa in Milan, and now Malcolm was overseeing the day-to-day activities. They had previously run the business from Milan and New York. Malcolm's situation with Samantha prompted a move to Rhode Island.

He couldn't get Samantha's portrait of his eagle form out of his head. She'd drawn *him*. All the details were there, but she'd especially captured his eyes. It gave him a glimmer of hope to see this portrait. She had seen his true self. Their connection was growing stronger by the minute.

The shrill of the phone on his desk tore him from his memories.

"Malcolm Drew," he answered with more irritation than he intended.

"Yes, Mr. Drew. It's Barkley," he said. His voice wavered nervously. "I wanted to inform you that we acquired the additional paintings you requested."

Malcolm sat up straight in his chair and smiled broadly. Samantha's paintings were his.

Once he discovered where her artwork was being shown, he went to the gallery to see them for himself. The moment Malcolm stepped foot into that gallery he knew which piece was hers, and he had to have it. As soon as he'd brought *Woman and the Wolf* into his home, he knew he had to have the rest of them. Malcolm immediately put Barkley to work on it, since he handled all of the family's art acquisitions.

"That's outstanding, Barkley. When will they arrive here?"

"They should be at your home tomorrow morning, sir. I am having all of the pieces framed appropriately for your Rhode Island home as you requested."

"Thank you. I'll be sure to inform my parents of what an outstanding job you did for me."

"Good day, sir."

"Good day indeed."

Malcolm hung up the phone and swiveled his chair to look out the window at Samantha's house. He sighed and rubbed his unshaven jaw, so close and yet so far.

He relished the idea of incorporating such a personal part of Sam right here in his home. He wanted to be close to her on every level possible. Having her artwork in his home was crucial. She didn't know it, but part of her Amoveo heritage was directly reflected in her art.

Every piece of her artwork carried her specific energy signature and having it brought into his home would help their connection grow at a faster rate. He needed all the help he could get. The call of seagulls outside interrupted his thoughts, and he was immediately reminded of the interloper. His gut told him that the seagull in the dream plane was much more than a coincidence. As much as he wanted to resolve his mating with Samantha on his own, he knew that he needed help. He knew that his best bet for help was their Prince.

Amoveos had very strong psychic abilities, telepathy among them. Connecting with Sam had thankfully given him most of his strength back. He went out to his balcony to contact his friend and leader. He closed his eyes, concentrating on creating a mental path to Richard.

Richard, I have connected with my life mate, but I'm encountering an interloper in the dream plane. It's a seagull. I need your help, old friend. Can you—

In moments, a tall man with long raven hair and enormous dark eyes materialized next to him. Amoveos could travel at the speed of thought when they were at full strength. He was over two centuries old, one of the strongest among their people, and an exceptionally gifted shifter. As leader of their people, he was ready to lend his help to any who asked. However, their two families were quite close. They were more like family than mere friends.

"How can I help you, my brother?" Richard delivered a small but regal bow.

"Thank you for coming. You didn't even let me finish my sentence. Now that's what I call service," Malcolm said jokingly. He grasped him in a strong, friendly handshake and a pat on the shoulder.

"Only for you, my friend." Richard smiled. Then his face grew serious. "Now, tell me about your mate and this dream interloper."

They went into the study, and Malcolm relayed the events as they'd happened. Richard listened intently to the difficulty he'd been having connecting with Samantha, as well as the disturbing appearances of the seagull.

"You seem to be giving Samantha ample time to connect with you. You've given her much more freedom to choose than is necessary."

"You don't know the half of it. Did I fail to mention that I'm taking her out on a date this evening?" Malcolm ran his hands through his tousled hair.

"A date? Like a human," Richard said with some disgust.

"I don't have much of a choice, Richard."

"It seems to me if you simply explain who she really is and explain the mating ritual and our ways…"

"She'll think I'm crazy."

"She'll think you're crazy," Richard somberly agreed.

"I'm more concerned about this seagull that keeps manifesting during our dream contacts. I know we have no Seagull Clan in our race, but it's clearly an intentional interruption."

"Given her parents' untimely death, I can understand your concern. You're quite certain this is another individual in the dream realm and not a manifestation from her subconscious? She is a powerful psychic, whether or not she knows it," Richard said. "Between her Amoveo blood and the psychic powers from her mother's side, it's quite possible she's sabotaging your meetings herself."

"No. It's definitely not her. I'm gaining her trust. Slowly to be sure, but it's happening. No," he insisted. "Someone else is intruding."

Both men sat in silence for a few moments, contemplating the various possibilities. Neither one of them wanted to admit the most dangerous possibility of all.

"I've heard rumors... that the Caedo have developed psychic abilities over the years," Malcolm began slowly. "To be honest, I dismissed it as paranoid fantasy, but now I'm afraid it's more than that. What if the seagull in the dream plane is a Caedo?"

"I know we don't want to think about this, but is it possible they have found you? Clearly they've left Samantha alone all these years, probably because she's shown no signs of shifting. She's done nothing out of the human norm that would raise any red flags. However, you can be sure they've been watching her," Richard said, his mouth set in a grim line. His voice held a seriousness Malcolm hadn't heard in some time. "If they realize that Samantha has any abilities and that she has an Amoveo mate who has found her, then they'll stop at nothing to kill you both. If you are successful in joining with her, it will only be the second human and Amoveo mating in our history. The Caedo already see us as a threat to human existence. You know how quickly they hunted down and killed her parents. You and Samantha would be seen as an equal threat. They hate us and hate the idea of us mating with humans even more. They feel as though we're trying to breed them out or some such nonsense." He waved.

"It's ridiculous, Richard. Our people have never harmed another, other than to defend ourselves or our clan members. We haven't even had fighting between the clans for over a thousand years. Ironically enough we have the Caedo to thank for that. We have a much more peaceful history than the humans. They have shed far more blood, and yet *we're* the monsters," Malcolm said with frustration.

"True," Richard said quietly. "Malcolm, you do realize how extraordinary this is, don't you? We have been hunted to the brink of extinction. They kill one of us, and it eliminates our mate and any possibility of offspring. If there are more women, or men for that matter, with psychic abilities like Samantha, then they could be mates for our people as well. It could mean saving our race. Your uncle Brendan has been researching this very fact for us. As you can imagine, the Council is very interested in finding out as much as we can. Obviously if we can identify these individuals early, then we can help make their transition that much easier."

Malcolm sat in silence with his head in his hands. He couldn't think about the benefits of his mating for his people or the wider implications it had. All he could focus on was keeping Samantha safe. The idea that the Caedo would attempt to harm her sent a fiery rage through his blood. Even worse, her destiny as his mate was putting her in grave danger. He stood quickly and stalked out to the balcony. It was a feeble attempt to hide his fury from Richard. He grasped the railing as though it might absorb some of his anger. His friend came up behind him and placed a comforting hand on his shoulder.

"I understand your anger, Malcolm," he said with quiet confidence. "When the Caedo came after Salinda, I was almost paralyzed with rage, but we banded together as a people and stopped them. I promise you, we will work together to protect your mate."

Malcolm stood tall, collecting himself, and grasped his friend in the handshake of a warrior. "Thank you, my Prince, and please give my best to my uncle."

"I will go to the members of the council and inform them of your situation. Please contact me right away if there are any more appearances from your seagull interloper." Richard turned to go, but stopped quickly and said, "Oh, and Malcolm. Good luck on your date tonight." Then with a teasing smile, he bowed quickly and vanished in the ocean breeze.

Malcolm shook his head, smiling, but it quickly faded when he saw Samantha. She stood in the doorway of her studio, a look of complete horror on her face.

Malcolm ducked inside, leaving his balcony empty. He knew she'd seen Richard vanish. If she asked about it, he was going to have to tell her something. He'd have to. He couldn't lie to her. She'd been lied to for her entire life, and he was determined not to perpetuate that problem. He was her mate, and he needed her to trust him. He had to earn it, and time was running out.

He went upstairs to get ready for his first real date, preoccupied with what Richard had said. Her mother had been the only human killed by the Caedo, a casualty of their war against his people. Gratefully, they hadn't come after Sam... yet. She showed no outward signs of Amoveo traits, except for the eyes. He would have to be very careful and more alert than ever. If

Samantha was harmed because of him, he would never forgive himself.

———~~~———

Samantha had totally lost track of time out in the studio. When she finally did look at her watch, it was a quarter past six. Seeing how late it had gotten, the inevitable panic set in. She had less than an hour to get ready for her date with Malcolm, let alone find something to wear that didn't make her feel like a whale. Finding the right outfit was all about the state of mind. A bad mood could make a woman feel twenty pounds heavier. Sam pushed sweaty strands of hair off her face as she packed up her tools.

Somehow, this man made her more aware of her appearance than anyone else in her entire life. Not necessarily in a bad way, just *more*. She finished putting away her supplies and closed up her studio. She gave a quick glance over to Malcolm's house. She saw a very tall man with long dark hair standing on the balcony speaking with Malcolm. She shielded her eyes from the brilliant sunlight and watched them for a moment, wondering if they were related. Even at this distance, she could sense a similarity between the two men. Then the next minute, he was gone. Vanished. Poof.

"What the hell." She blinked and rubbed her eyes furiously. She stood there, motionless. *Did I really just see that?* "No. No way. It was just a reflection or something from the ocean."

Samantha closed her eyes and took a deep breath. She steadied herself with her hands, as though smoothing out the air around her. When she opened her eyes, the balcony was empty. No Malcolm. No long-haired guy. Nothing.

"See… nothing. You're just tired," she said, not really convincing herself. "Now, stop talking to yourself, and go get ready for your date with the weird, arrogant, gorgeous neighbor. What the hell am I going to wear?" Sam walked into the house. She gave one last glance over her shoulder to the empty balcony next door. "I'm definitely wearing my cross."

Chapter 6

SAMANTHA STOOD IN HER BATHROBE, STARING AT THE contents of an uncooperative closet. She was in good shape overall. She'd managed to blow-dry her long hair in record time. She loved the summer because just a little sunglow meant less makeup was needed. Now all she had to do was find an outfit. She couldn't very well go naked. Although, being naked with Malcolm had crossed her mind more than once. Considering she never found sex that interesting, she'd been thinking about it an awful lot recently. "Focus, Sam," she muttered into the closet. From the doorway, she heard Nonie's teasing.

"You know, that's the trouble with those closets. You have to watch them every minute, or they sneak away."

"It's not funny, Nonie," Sam said with more than a little frustration. "I don't have anything to wear on this ridiculous date tonight. Ahh. Why did I agree to go?" Sam flopped back onto her bed.

Nonie sifted through the various items and pulled out the black eyelet sundress, pink cardigan, and black flats that Sam had taken out and put back ten times already. "You should always go with your instincts, my dear. They're usually right." Nonie laid the items on the bed next to Samantha.

"Hey! That's the same outfit I kept going to. That's so funny. How did you know?" Samantha was interrupted by the doorbell.

"Saved by the bell," Nonie said under her breath.

"Oh my God! I'm not ready. Nonie, please don't grill him about his family."

"I'll only ask for his social security number and a few references." The doorbell rang again.

"Nonie!"

"Oh stop it! I'm just teasing you. I'll go easy on him. Now hurry up and get dressed." She left to greet Sam's date.

Malcolm squirmed at the front door, feeling a bit foolish. He looked around, fearing one of his Amoveo kin would see him participating in this silly human ritual. He rang the doorbell a second time. Panic hit him, realizing he should've brought her something. Human men usually showed up with flowers, didn't they? He quickly visualized a huge bouquet of assorted roses in vibrant reds, pinks, and yellows. Moments later, they were in his hand, just as the door opened.

Malcolm had to look down a bit to see a lovely older woman standing at the door, her silver hair swept up loosely around a dazzling face with twinkling blue eyes. Although in her seventies, one could see she'd been a beauty in her day, which obviously ran in their family. She smiled at him, but he sensed wariness behind it. She held out her hand and eyed the flowers.

"You must be Malcolm. Lovely to meet you. Please come in. Samantha will be down in a moment." She shook his hand quickly and turned, leaving him no choice but to follow her into the kitchen.

"Thank you. You are Samantha's grandmother," he

said awkwardly, wishing he'd conjured up two bouquets of flowers.

"Yes. I'm Helen Costigan. But you may call me Nonie." She waved. "Everyone does."

"Very nice to meet you, Nonie." He smiled. "Davis has told me a bit about you."

"Really? Well, he's a nice old fellow, but I hope he hasn't been telling tales out of school." She winked.

Malcolm cocked his head with confusion. Just as he was about to ask what she meant, he heard Samantha behind him.

"Hi. I hope you haven't been waiting too long."

Sam's voice floated over him like a warm breeze. For the first time in his life, Malcolm was speechless. She was dressed simply, but was absolutely stunning. Her blonde hair fell loosely around her face and cascaded over her shoulders. The gold in her hair complemented her large blue Amoveo eyes. She wore very little makeup, which he liked, a natural glow. The sight of her knocked the wind out of him. "I'm sorry. What? No." Malcolm felt foolish, stumbling over his words like some ridiculous adolescent. "It gave me the opportunity to meet your grandmother, who I've heard so much about."

Sam smiled, knowing she'd made an impression on him. *Score one point for me.*

Malcolm stilled when he heard her in his mind. Finally, for the first time, he heard his mate in the most intimate form of communication, telepathically. He gave her a big broad smile. This was the most encouraging sign for him yet. Their connection was growing stronger, and she was definitely opening up to him.

"You look fabulous. Here, these are for you." He stuck the flowers out awkwardly, like some pimply teenager.

He cringed at his fumbling attempts at courting.

"They're gorgeous. Thank you." Sam looked at him over the flowers while she breathed in the sweet fragrance. "Nonie, would you mind putting these in water for me." She didn't take her eyes off Malcolm.

"Of course dear, I'll take care of it. Now you two run along and have fun." Nonie escorted them to the door.

Nonie watched them walk out to the car with a growing sense of dread. She knew Samantha was excited about the date and clearly attracted to Malcolm, but she worried all the same. She had already lost her daughter. Samantha was all she had left. No one would take her away. No one.

They approached the black Mercedes waiting in the driveway, and Malcolm stole a sidelong look at Samantha. She was simply radiant. He glanced down at his slightly rumpled linen pants and stuffed his hands in his pockets. He always considered his style "classic casual," but at the moment he felt like a bit of a slob. She looked too damned good for him. He opened the car door for her, and she slid easily in to the buttery beige leather seat just as her velvet thoughts slid into his mind.

Jesus, even his car his gorgeous. I'm a beat-up VW, and he's a Mercedes. What the hell am I doing with this guy?

Malcolm heard her insecure thoughts loud and clear, but was completely perplexed by them. Did she really have no idea how attractive she was? If anything he thought he was the beat-up VW, and she was the slick Mercedes. He wondered how in the world it could be possible that she wasn't confident of her own beauty. Did she not notice the way people turned to look at her? She was magnificent in true Amoveo tradition, both inside and out. "So where to, madam? I'm at your mercy."

His smile turned her insides to jelly. "Well." She played with the cross at her neck. "I thought I'd take you to a traditional Westerly summer haunt. Paddy's. It's a great little place on the beach, right down at the other end of Atlantic Avenue actually. Since its Saturday, there's probably a good cover band playing later on tonight. They usually have an eighties band on the weekend. You know Bon Jovi, Def Leppard, the usual." Sam cringed. He made her so nervous that she was running off at the mouth.

"Sure. I'm up for anything as long as you'll show me the way."

Sam gave Malcolm the simple directions to Paddy's down the road. As they drove along Atlantic Avenue, the sun was beginning to set over the marsh. She looked out her window at an osprey swooping down to its nest. It was perched high, over water dotted with reeds. A few roosts had been placed in the marsh to encourage species growth in the area, and they were all occupied. This one had a large fish in its beak, feeding its young, who in a few weeks would be learning to fly and leaving the nest.

Spectacular.

The whisper was soft. "They are exceptional birds, aren't they," she said.

"Absolutely." Only he hadn't been thinking about the birds. "Many people are intimidated by birds of prey, but I think they're quite interesting, don't you?"

"Mmmhmm," Sam murmured.

"Have you ever seen one up close?" He pulled the car into the restaurant parking lot.

Sam looked at him through narrowed eyes. "Actually, just recently. Why do you ask?"

"Curious, I suppose. I was at the zoo once, the Bronx Zoo, and the birds of prey exhibit was my favorite." He turned off the ignition.

Sam didn't have time to let herself out because Malcolm beat her to the punch, opening her door for her again. *Flowers, opening up doors—very nice.*

Malcolm tried not to grin like an idiot at her approval, but he couldn't help it. Things were going perfectly.

They were seated at a table outside overlooking the ocean. Paddy's was a casual place with various types of patrons. Currently there were lots of families, some just coming in from the beach. Soon it would be pulsing with live music and several liquored-up guests. Sam liked it for the people watching. It was like stepping into a time warp. Everyone who came here for the evening entertainment looked as if they were plucked out of the eighties. The guys with mullets and girls with big hair, wearing lots of heavy metal T-shirts with cutoff jean shorts.

There were the preppy tourists, here and there, stopping in briefly from their family summer homes. Men sporting the shorts with little whales on them. The ladies who looked too perfect, their necks draped with pristine strands of pearls, and flawless bodies covered by Lilly Pulitzer dresses. That crowd ran for the hills before the music got started. Sam never really fit in with either group, but it sure was fun to watch them when their worlds collided.

She and Malcolm talked easily over dinner and well past dessert. The conversation and laughter flowed as easily as the wine. Samantha found herself telling this man, this stranger, her entire life story. She told him about her parents, Nonie and Pop, Kerry, her life in NYC that she walked away from—all of it. At various points, she touched the cross at the hollow of her throat, usually when she spoke about her grandparents.

Never in her life had she ever told anyone so much about herself all at once. She always talked too much when she got nervous, but he didn't seem to mind. In fact, he became quite the chatterbox himself. He told her how he'd grown up an only child, between Italy and New York. His international life explained his unusual accent. He laughed out loud when she told him of the rumor mill about his family. He assured her his parents were alive and well in Milan, enjoying their retirement. He regaled her with stories of Milan, the beauty of the architecture, and the people.

They sat comfortably for a moment in silence. Samantha sipped her wine and looked at him over the rim of her glass. She smiled ever so slightly. He smiled back, holding her gaze. The look in his eye sent warmth through her body. She looked away quickly and touched her little cross.

Malcolm leaned in to inspect the tiny treasure that she gave so much attention to. "This is lovely," he said as he gently caressed the silver between his fingers. "Did your grandmother give it to you?"

"Mmmhmm," Sam murmured. She tried not to think

about her racing heart from having him this close. "It was my mother's and her mother's and so on. Nonie gave it to my mom for her First Communion. After I was born, my mother put it away for me to have."

Malcolm leaned back and released it from his grasp but never took his eyes off hers. It was like a game of chicken, and Sam most definitely lost. She cleared her throat and fiddled with the cross again.

"It's funny. Nonie said Mom used to wear it all the time, but just before she died, she put it away for me. I'm grateful she did. It's all I have of her really."

"I wouldn't say that. She was quite beautiful, and so are you." Malcolm's gaze wandered over her body.

Her cheeks flushed, and her face burned. Her lashes fluttered nervously as she took another sip of her wine.

"This last fellow you dated was a fool to let you go Samantha, but I'm very glad that he did."

Sam scoffed audibly and took a larger sip of her wine. Anger flashed hotly at the memory of just how much Roger hadn't wanted to let her go. Sam knew it was Bad Dating 101 to talk about old boyfriends, but he may as well know now that she wasn't interested in a controlling asshole—no matter how charismatic he was. Roger had been charming at first too.

"Roger didn't have a choice." She lifted her chin defiantly and latched her gaze to his. "I don't make it a habit of being with controlling or abusive men."

His eyes narrowed, and the expression on his face hardened. His left hand curled into a fist as he leaned back in his chair. If Sam didn't know better, she'd swear the air around them thickened. It was as if a huge cloud of humidity landed right on top of their table.

She shifted slightly in her chair as the silence hung between them.

"I would hope not," he said without taking his eyes from hers. "This person should pray I never set eyes on him."

Sam cocked her head and cast him a questioning glance. His intense reaction surprised her, and honestly, flattered her a bit too. Roger was back in New York with his tail between his legs. She was about to reassure Malcolm of this very fact when the music started. It was so loud, continuing any conversation was next to impossible. Malcolm settled the bill, and they went inside to check out the band.

The music thrummed loudly through the small bar and reverberated through her body. Although, having Malcolm standing so close to her might've been causing the throbbing too. She stole a glance up at him as they listened to the music. His profile, much like the rest of him, was perfect. His shaggy hair curled slightly over his collar, and she had to resist the urge to brush it back and rub the silky strands between her fingers. Sam's blood hummed with awareness as their bodies were scant inches apart. Occasionally her arm brushed his, and even that minor contact sent little licks of fire up her spine.

Malcolm tried desperately to keep his desire in check. Her reaction to him was palpable. Small beads of sweat formed on his forehead as he struggled for control over the firestorm building inside of him. He swallowed hard and took a deep, shuddering breath. He had to touch her, claim her. The mere mention of the man she'd been with had just about pushed him over the edge. He was flooded by unfamiliar emotions. He'd never in his life been awkward or unsure around women, but Sam was no ordinary woman.

Just as he was about to take her hand in his, Malcolm was struck by a wave of violent energy. Someone or something evil lurked nearby. The hatred spilled over him in waves, and his desire was replaced by fury.

The ominous flow of hostile energy was directed straight at Samantha.

He quickly scanned the room, searching for the source. The crowd, filled with undulating bodies flailing to the music, writhed wildly around them. His sharp gaze flew around the room frantically.

There.

He spotted a man staring at them from across the room. He stood completely still amid the sweaty, thrashing crowd. At first glance he was rather bland looking, the kind of man who could easily be overlooked and blend into the walls. He was of average height with blond hair and dark beady eyes set in a hard, unsmiling face. His gaze remained locked intensely on Samantha. Malcolm's defenses went up immediately. He put his arm protectively around Samantha's waist. Possessively, he pulled her to him.

Malcolm reached out with his mind to get a reading on this man. Samantha was exceptionally pretty, so he couldn't really blame him for staring. Virtually all of the men in the restaurant had noticed her, although she was completely oblivious to it. This man, however, wasn't just staring at her, he was clocking her every move.

He was tracking her.

Malcolm's eyes narrowed, and he focused all of his energy on him. He reached out to the mind of this stranger and was stunned to hit a mental block. As soon as he touched the unexpected barrier, the man's eyes flew to Malcolm's.

Malcolm's eyes widened in shock, and his gut tightened. This man, whoever he was, obviously had psychic abilities and noticed when Malcolm tried to touch his mind. He glanced at Samantha, but she seemed blissfully unaware of the danger that lurked in the crowd. When he looked back up, the man was gone. He cursed under his breath and pulled her closer to his side. Malcolm wanted to get her the hell out of there. If they hadn't been surrounded by so many humans he would've used whatever strength he had left to materialize them back to the house.

Samantha almost stopped breathing when Malcolm wrapped his arm around her waist. He pulled her against him and took note of the way her body, soft and pliant, molded so easily against his.

"We have to go," he whispered.

She put her hand on his shoulder to ask him what the problem was. Before she could say anything, he took her hand, navigated the crowd, and pulled her out through the patio to the beach. As they emerged from the loud, sweaty throng, Sam pulled back on his hand. "Whoa. Easy there killer. I'm gonna need that arm for later." She removed her hand from Malcolm's grip as he continued scanning the beach.

"I'm sorry. I just got a little overwhelmed by the mob and the noise." He looked past her toward the restaurant.

"It's getting late," he whispered. "I think perhaps I should take you home."

"Right." Sam tried to hide her disappointment. "Nonie's probably waiting up."

She turned to go back to the car, but Malcolm grabbed her arm and pulled her to him. His fear for her safety fueled his passion for her. He needed to keep her safe, to keep her with him. His mouth took possession of hers with a fiery intensity that took them both by surprise. The kiss was hard and hot, his tongue demanding entrance. She opened and welcomed him into the dark, velvety warmth of her mouth. He held her close, and his hands tangled in her long hair. He tilted her head back, deepening the kiss.

Samantha had heard about kisses like this from friends. She had seen it in the movies, but she had *never* experienced it, until now. She reached up and put her arms around his neck. Her body melted against him. She never wanted this kiss to end. She felt like a woman who'd finally gotten water after being stranded in the desert. He tasted like wine and lust, and she was drunk from it.

They stood there in the sand. Lips mating, tongues mingling, Samantha could feel his body responding to her, and it made her want him even more. She was drowning in desire. Desire that was going way too fast. She felt herself spiraling out of control. She pulled herself back, both of them breathing heavily, their mouths inches apart, her lips swollen from his kisses. She looked up and found herself looking into a familiar pair of glowing yellow eyes. She took an involuntary step backward and felt the cold hand of fear crawl up her spine. "Your eyes," she stammered breathlessly.

Malcolm blinked quickly, returning them to normal. "I must admit, I'm surprised that's the body part you're preoccupied with." His smile was sexy. He reached out to pull her back, trying to hold onto the moment they'd just shared.

Samantha stared at him through confused eyes. "I think you're right." She touched her lips, still tingling. "I think you should take me home now." She began to walk quickly to the parking lot.

"As you wish." His body was still pulsing from her touch. He followed her, reluctantly, and gave one last look around to be sure there was no sign of the stranger.

They rode back to the house in a heavy silence. Her bewilderment vibrated around them both and tripped up his spine. He scolded himself. He'd been so caught up in his passion for her, so terrified by the thought of losing her, that he completely forgot to keep his eyes from shifting. His eyes instinctively shifted to their animal form, a symptom of his desire.

She broke the silence as they pulled up the gravel driveway of her home. "Malcolm, who was that man you were talking to on the balcony this afternoon?"

"You mean Davis." He hoped that may satisfy her curiosity, but knew it wouldn't.

"No. You know exactly who I mean," she said with steady resolve. "The tall guy with long dark hair. I saw you speaking with him today on your deck."

The car came to a halt at the top of the driveway.

She looked at him, daring him to deny it.

He saw the determination in her face and looked away. He couldn't lie to her, but he couldn't exactly explain that he was the Prince of the Amoveo either.

"That was an old friend of the family." He got out of the car, hoping she'd be satisfied with that answer.

Sam was starting to get pissed. Her energy waves thumped into him faster and harder. She knew that there was something unusual about the man she'd seen on the deck. He suspected that she'd seen Richard vanish. Guilt seeped into his heart because her instincts were right. But she doubted herself. He wanted her to ask him if he'd vanished into thin air to put him on the spot. If she asked him a direct question, he would not lie. How could he possibly explain who Richard was or what she had seen? Not yet.

Her eyes narrowed, and her back stiffened in defiance as she glared at him from the passenger seat. He knew that the more she ran through it in her mind, the more certain she was that it happened, but she still hadn't come right out and asked him, probably worried she'd seem crazy.

Malcolm opened the door and offered to help her from the car.

Hesitantly, she took his hand. He pulled her effortlessly from her seat. Her breasts gently brushed up against him, a featherlight touch that held a promise of pleasure to come. Their breath mingled on the cool summer evening. Their bodies hummed in unison with anticipation.

"I want you to trust me, Samantha," he said in a low voice laced with desperation and desire.

He brought her delicate hand to his mouth and gently brushed his lips back and forth across her knuckles. He slowly ran his other hand up the graceful curve of her back and began to massage the soft skin at the nape of her lovely neck. Her breathing quickened, and with every breath, her breasts pressed tantalizingly against his chest.

"Please, give me a chance to win your trust," he whispered against her trembling hand.

He brushed small kisses along her palm. Malcolm was on fire. Desire coiled inside of him, and the passion between them grew beyond control. He knew that her head told her to run, but every other fiber of her being begged for his touch. He sensed her resolve slipping away, inch by inch. Her energy wave shifted. The rapid drumming of fear had been replaced by heated pulses of desire.

He knew what he was doing was dangerous. He hid secrets from her that she may never truly believe. Yet despite all the doubts, she was still drawn to him beyond all reason. Her eyes searched his for answers. He wanted to tell her, but the right words escaped him.

"Malcolm." His name came out in a desperate rush through her soft quivering mouth.

He leaned in and this time kissed her gently, slowly seducing her plump lips with his. He took her face delicately in his hands, as though she might break. She opened to him willingly and swept her tongue along his. The slow burn of desire crackled between them. She deepened the kiss and wrapped her warm arms around him. His large frame dwarfed her as she fit easily in his embrace. It was as though they'd been made for one another. His yearning for her clawed at him from the inside out; he needed to touch her everywhere.

He reached out to her mind with his and gently touched the most intimate part of her.

Trust me.

It was as if a bucket of cold water had been tossed over her. Sam's eyes flew open, and she struggled to extricate herself from his embrace. She pushed her small hands against the hard planes of his chest and held him there at arm's-length for a moment. He kept his eyes locked with hers. Her energy waves crashed into him violently. Her shoulders shuddered beneath his hands, and her breath came quickly. She trembled. Tears filled her eyes, unable to register what she just heard.

He held his craving in check and kept his eyes from shifting. He allowed her time to process what had just happened. Looking into her frightened eyes, he reached out and again whispered gently along the edges of her mind. *Trust me.*

Sam's eyes widened further. She shook her head and backed away from him in disbelief. Blindly, she ran into the house, leaving Malcolm alone. One glimmer of hope remained.

He'd been looking into the ice blue eyes of a wolf.

Chapter 7

HE SAT IN THE CAR, WATCHING THEM THROUGH NIGHT vision binoculars. His stomach lurched in response to what he'd seen. Her eyes had shifted; she was one of them, no doubt about that now. He knew what he had to do. It was simple really. She had to die and so did the creature. He pulled away quietly in the dark. He kept the headlights off so he wouldn't attract attention. He knew the creature was distracted with his whore; it wouldn't notice.

Tony smiled, remembering the triumph he'd had earlier this evening. It had tried to read him, and Tony had blocked it—one of the benefits of his partnership. His new friend had taught him how to put up a mental barrier, a means of self-preservation. Over the years, his family had been working to develop their psychic abilities. This way they could fight their enemy more effectively. Tony had done it. He warded off a mental invasion from *it*. Keeping that thing out of his mind took a lot of energy. Doing it also gave him a raging migraine. Tony couldn't maintain the block for long, but he did it. Once he'd been spotted, he immediately focused on keeping him out of his mind. Doing it took so much energy that Tony had to get out of there as soon as he could. He'd almost fainted from the effort, but he'd done it.

He pounded the steering wheel and hooted with

excitement. He couldn't wait to tell his partner about
the latest developments. He drove up to his house, thinking about how they had the audacity to sit there in the
restaurant as though they were normal and had any right
to be there, breathing the same air he did. It infuriated
him. All those people in that restaurant, the clueless mo-
rons. They had no idea about the evil that lurked right
under their noses. He thought about the Logan woman.
She was a nice piece of ass, no one would argue that.
Too bad she was tainted, evil. He thought about how
she'd looked at that animal, and it made him sick. It was
perverted, a human woman and that *thing*. He had to
remind himself that she wasn't really human. Her eyes
had mutated. Tony saw it happen, and it confirmed what
they'd thought all along. Her humanity was being taken
over. She was infected by the animal inside of her, and
now she would have to die.

He got so excited thinking about the various ways he
could do it. It would definitely be easier to kill her and
then let the creature die slowly afterward. He thought
about how much pain and suffering her death would
bring to the creature. He ran different scenarios over in
his mind as a slow smile spread across his face.

Chapter 8

SAMANTHA RAN INTO THE HOUSE AND QUICKLY LOCKED the door behind her. She leaned her forehead against it, trying to catch her breath. Desperately trying to wrap her brain around what had just happened. "What's going on," she said in a frightened whisper.

Nonie called from the kitchen, "Samantha? Is that you dear?"

Sam pulled herself together, knowing that she couldn't tell her grandmother what had just happened. How could she? She didn't even know herself. She wiped her eyes and collected herself as best she could.

Sam entered the kitchen as casually as possible and put on her best game face. "Nonie, I can't believe you're still awake. I hope I didn't wake you." She tried to sound normal.

"Not at all. I just came down to get some tea before bed." She got the mugs from the cabinet. "So how was your date with Malcolm?" She poured a steaming cup and gave it to Sam.

"It was…interesting." She blew on the hot liquid, hoping to cool the drink as well as her blood.

"Interesting. Well, I guess that's not bad. Will you be seeing him again?" Nonie asked over the rim of her mug.

"Of course I will. After all he lives right next door." Sam tried to keep the conversation light and avoided Nonie's gaze.

"That's not what I meant, and you know it."

"I know." Sam sighed. "But the truth is, I don't know. We'll see." She shrugged, trying to be casual about the whole thing, praying Nonie wouldn't notice how nervous she felt. "Besides, I've only been home for a couple of days, and really I was just showing him around. You know, being neighborly. It's no big deal." She tried to convince herself that was true.

"Well, just be careful. Love is a slippery slope, and it's so easy to fall," Nonie said quietly.

"Love? Whoa, whoa wait a minute." Sam held up her hand. "Who said anything about love? I just went out on *one* date with the guy. Nonie, I think you're getting ahead of yourself." Sam stood up with her tea.

"Maybe." Nonie reached out and took Sam's hand. "I just want you to be sure you keep your eyes and your mind wide open, so you can see exactly where you're going." She held Sam's gaze with a rare seriousness.

"Don't worry, Nonie." She leaned in and kissed her on the cheek. "Good night. I have to get some sleep if I'm going to be any good to Millie at the diner tomorrow." Sam stopped before heading up the stairs and turned to look back at her grandmother. "Thanks for the tea. You always know just what I need."

Samantha lay in bed that night, unable to asleep. She kept replaying the day's events in her mind. The disappearing man on the deck, Malcolm's eyes changing, the voice she heard in her head, and of course, the leg weakening kisses. She went to touch the cross at her neck, only to find that it wasn't there.

Her necklace was gone.

Sam shot up in bed and turned on the light. She

frantically searched her bed, ripping the bedding off. She tore apart the bedroom, her bathroom, everywhere. It was amazing she didn't wake up Nonie with the ruckus.

Trying to be rational, she retraced her steps. She grabbed a flashlight from the junk drawer in the kitchen and went out to scour the driveway. She desperately searched the gravel for that precious glint of silver, but nothing. After what felt like hours of searching, she remained empty-handed. Defeated, she went back into the house with broken fingernails and teary eyes.

She knew she'd had it at the restaurant so she must've lost it sometime after that. It was probably when they were on the beach at Paddy's. Even in her current state, she blushed at the memory of kissing Malcolm. Her hand drifted up to the empty spot at her neck. Reluctantly, she resigned herself to the fact that she was not going to find her cross. Not in the pitch black middle of the night. The old saying about a needle in a haystack wafted through her mind. Sam finally went back up to bed and lay crying in the dark for what felt like hours. That cross was all she'd had of her mother. It was her most cherished possession and now it was gone. She wept as though she'd lost her mother all over again and finally cried herself to sleep.

Malcolm called to her in the dream realm.

After the way the evening had ended, he desperately wanted to connect with her again. She'd been so scared, so confused—and it just about killed him. He couldn't leave it like that.

He wandered through swirling pewter mists for what

*seemed like an eternity before he found her. Sam was
on the beach with the waves crashing violently around
her. Her white nightgown was drenched and clung deliciously to the curves of breasts and buttocks; his body
stirred in response. His desire was quickly put aside
when he saw she was crying. She was digging frantically in the sand, her long hair whipping violently in
the wind; wet strands of it clung to her face. The dark
stormy sky was a direct reflection of her grief. This environment she'd created came straight from her soul. He
went to her side and gently touched her shoulder. She
looked up at him with enormous blue eyes that spilled
over with tears.*

*"My necklace, my cross, it's gone. I lost it. I think
when we were on the beach tonight at Paddy's. I must've
lost it there. I can't find it. Please Malcolm. Please help
me," she said between heavy sobs.*

*His heart broke as he knelt down next to her. She
continued to claw at the sand. He saw that the cross
wasn't at her neck as it always was and knew it was lost.*

*"Shhshhhh, I'll find it. I promise I'll find it for you."
He gently pulled her to him. He held her there on the
sand as she wept against his chest, great heaving sobs
that soaked his shirt with tears. He stroked the back of
her head, smoothing her long hair and rocked her soothingly. Her grief and loss tore at his soul, a fiery stab
with every sob. He'd never in his life felt such compassion for anyone, and it knocked him off balance. He'd
always prided himself for his rational behavior, but this
woman drove all reason from him.*

*Malcolm kissed her forehead with excruciating ten-
derness. He trailed soft kisses down her cheek. He tasted*

her salty tears, and he eventually claimed her lips. At first, the kiss was tender and soft. His lips slowly and seductively melded with hers. He swept his tongue softly along her lips, and she opened up, welcoming him into her mouth. He delicately laid her back onto the damp sand as the salt air misted around them, enveloping them. The fire flared inside of him every time their lips met. As their passion grew, the sea raged around them, and the winds howled. He covered her with the length of his body, his mouth branding hers. He held the back of her head, deepening the kiss. He stroked her calf and ran his hand up her leg, slowly bringing the edge of her damp nightgown up with it. He claimed her as his mate with every touch.

Samantha had never felt this kind of craving. It burned her entire body from the inside out. She knew this was only a dream, so she figured what the hell and willingly succumbed to her desires. She kissed him with a new-found abandon, their bodies entangled in the sand. The sea raged as his hand roamed up her leg. She couldn't think. She could only feel. He continued his seductive journey and slowly brushed up her rib cage. He captured her breast greedily. Her nipples tingled and peaked in response.

He trailed kisses down her throat and rained them between the valley of her breasts, eventually taking one rosy peak in his mouth. He suckled as she arched and moaned in response. Samantha ran her fingers in his thick chestnut hair, holding him to her chest, her breath coming in ragged gasps. He rose up, taking her lips once again with his. She couldn't tell where his mouth ended and hers began. She squirmed against him, begging for release from the storm building within her. His leg pressed between her thighs as she rubbed up against him. She moaned her pleasure.

He pulled back to look at her, and even if it was only a dream, she wanted to savor every second. The last thing she wanted was for him to stop. His eyes glowed with passion and a smile of pleasure played at his lips. She loved looking into those brilliant, yellow eyes, glazed with passion. Staring up at him she knew she was lost to him—dream or no dream—forever. She wasn't afraid anymore.

He closed his eyes as she caringly touched the side of his face. As strong as this man was, he had a compassionate side to him that he kept hidden—until now. She traced the strong line of his jaw and ran her thumb along his firm lips. He closed his eyes and leaned into her loving ministrations. Their bodies, still intertwined, heavily hummed with a need they had yet to satisfy. He opened his eyes, and a smile played at his lips.

"Trust me, Samantha. I'll find your necklace. I'll bring it to you. Your happiness is my primary concern." *He placed a kiss on her forehead.* *"But now, mia piccola lupa, it's time to wake up."*

Samantha woke up covered in sweat and twisted up in her sheets. Her body still tingled. Never in her life had she had such an erotic dream. Hell, she'd never experienced anything like that in real life. Rising from the bed, she stretched out her slightly sore muscles and walked slowly over to her dresser. Images of their bodies mingled on the beach still flashed through her mind. The memories alone made her womb clench and her nipples tighten. She blushed at her body's swift reaction. Sam picked up the brush on her dresser and froze when she saw her reflection. The eyes she was looking into weren't her own. They were the ice blue eyes of a wolf, the wolf in her dreams.

Sam stood there, mesmerized by the foreign image. She tried desperately to reconcile what she was looking at. Slowly, she touched her face to be sure she was actually awake. She leaned closer. Sam swallowed hard, leaning both hands on the dresser. She steadied her breathing and squeezed her eyes shut tight for several seconds. When she looked again, they had returned to their usual dark blue.

"What the hell?"

She blinked repeatedly, trying to see if they'd change again, like some kind of crazed genie, but to no avail. She shook her head in disbelief. Out of habit, Sam reached up to touch her cross, only to remember that it had been lost the night before. Tears began to well up again when she heard Malcolm's voice, calm and soothing, in her head.

I'll find it and bring it to you, mia piccola lupa. *I promise.*

Instinctively she reached out and touched his mind with hers.

Please find it, Malcolm.

She closed her eyes as tears of sadness streamed down her cheeks.

The blare of the alarm sliced through the room and

brought her back to some semblance of reality. Sam sniffled and rubbed her teary eyes. She slapped the clock hard and silenced the shrill sound.

"Well, this should be one helluva day," she mumbled to herself as she gathered her clothes. "I hope Millie and her patrons don't mind having a mental patient for a waitress."

When Malcolm awoke, he was grinning. She was finally letting him into her mind and hopefully into her heart. She had reached out and touched her mind to his, consciously using their mental link for the very first time. His smile faded, however, when he remembered how much pain she was in. He must find her necklace. He had to do as she requested; he could do nothing else. Her grief was as crushing to him as a physical blow. His reaction to her pain caught him completely off guard. He'd heard of how strong the connections were between mates, but nothing could've prepared him for the reality. He shook his head and wondered how much stronger it would get once they were actually mated.

He would do anything within his power to find her necklace… it was imperative. It would prove to her that their dream was shared. He would gain her trust, but more than anything, it would make her happy. She was his life mate, and he wanted nothing more than to fulfill her every requirement.

The man from last night also weighed heavy on his mind. He had to find out who he was. He would take great pleasure in hand delivering him to the Council. He came downstairs and was greeted, as usual, by Davis.

"Morning, sir. How was your date with Ms. Samantha?" Davis held out coffee and the morning newspaper.

"I'm afraid the Caedo has found us." He grabbed his car keys and sunglasses.

"Are you sure, sir? It's been so many years since we've had any sign of them. The Council members have even toyed with the idea that they've lost some of their diligence in the last generation or so," Davis said.

"Last night at the restaurant there was a man watching Sam. When I tried to read him, he... blocked me." He looked away, too embarrassed to face Davis, to admit that a human had blocked his efforts.

"Blocked you, sir," Davis asked with some confusion.

"He knew I was trying to read him," he seethed, "and he put up a mental barrier. I couldn't get through it. I looked at Sam to see if she noticed anything, and when I looked back, he was gone." He lowered his gaze, ashamed at this failure.

"Have you told the Prince yet? I'm sure he'll want to tell the Council about this. Yes indeed, sir. They'll absolutely want to know."

"No. I'll call to him again later today. First, I have to go back to that blasted place and find her necklace. She lost it last night, and it means more to her than anything. I don't think I can handle it if I ever see that kind of anguish on her face again."

"Very well, sir. But do be careful. This fellow from last night sounds like he could pose quite a problem for you as well."

"I can handle myself, but Samantha is completely unprepared for dealing with the Caedo. Perhaps you could stop over and check on her today? She's working over at that diner in town but last night she said she'd be back in the early afternoon."

"That sounds like a fine idea, sir. I could drop by with a welcome home basket for her. She'll be just fine." He winked.

"She has to be Davis. There is no other option." Malcolm stalked out the door, his mission clear. He drove down to Paddy's as images of Sam drifted through his mind. She was a captivating woman, and when her eyes shifted to her inner wolf, she was exotic and intoxicating. He was encouraged that she had spoken with him telepathically this morning. He knew she didn't accept what she had done. She probably was passing it off as her imagination instead of an actual conversation. Bringing her the necklace would help prove everything, but most of all it would get her to trust him.

He pulled into Paddy's empty parking lot. The restaurant was closed, but the beach already had a few sunbathers milling about. He went to the very spot where he and Sam had shared their first kiss. He wore sunglasses to keep his eyes hidden. The last thing he needed was some nosy human noticing them and causing a scene. His eyes shifted, and his vision instantly slipped into the binocular vision of an eagle. He slowly and meticulously scanned the area all around where they had been. Even if it took all day and he had to inspect every grain of sand, he wasn't leaving without that necklace.

Chapter 9

SAM GOT TO THE DINER JUST AS MILLIE WAS UNLOCKING the doors for the early morning crowd. Typically, she had one or two regulars who showed up as soon as the sun did. The Dugout was only open for breakfast and lunch. When Millie had first opened the place, Billy was just a baby, and that schedule fit her family best. She lived by the philosophy that there was more to life than work—there was baseball. Millie had been a die-hard Red Sox fan from birth. When Sam moved to New York, Millie's biggest fear was that she'd become a Yankees fan. Live hard, work hard, and play hard—that was Millie's motto.

"Sammy girl! I can't believe you actually got here on time. I thought you were gonna stand me up," Millie hollered as she held the door open.

Sam placed a quick kiss on her plump cheek and grabbed the bright red apron that dangled from her hand playfully. "Why on earth would you think that?" She tied the familiar garment on with practiced ease and made her way behind the luncheonette counter.

"Well, your grandmamma told me that you had a hot date last night with that Drew fella." She winked and snapped Sam's ass with a dish towel.

"Millie," she shrieked and laughed as she dodged the next swat. "You and Nonie are horrible gossips. I knew that's all you did at those bridge games."

The bell above the door jingled cheerfully, and two of Millie's sunrise regulars shuffled in. Edgar and George tipped their caps politely at Sam and flashed partially toothless grins at her.

"Why, isn't that Nonie's girl, Edgar?" George's raspy voice filled the small diner.

"Yes it is," Edgar said with a small pat on his friend's arm. "You don't have to shout you old coot. You'll wake up the whole damn town." He delivered a big wink to Sam over his shoulder.

The fishermen made their way over to their regular booth by the window, and Sam grabbed the freshly brewed pot of coffee.

Millie laughed loudly and pushed through the swinging door into the kitchen. "Billy," she barked loudly at her son. "You gonna get your butt in gear? Edgar and George are here, and they're gonna want the usual."

"Yes, ma'am." Billy poked his sweet face through the doorway. "Hi, Sam. Good to have you back," he said before disappearing back into the clattering kitchen.

"Hi, Billy." Sam chuckled. Smiling, she shook her head at the familiar banter between Billy and Millie that flowed steadily from the kitchen as she poured coffee.

She slipped back into her routine with surprising ease and loved every minute. She never thought she'd really enjoy waitressing again. Ever. But after the incredibly weird events over the past twenty-four hours, she could use a little normal. Yes indeed, the mundane sounded like just the ticket. The loud clanking of the dishes and chatter of the customers reassured her that she wasn't losing her mind—at least not at the moment—and the only conversations she had that morning were audible to everyone. In fact, she started to wonder if maybe she'd dreamt all of it.

The day passed quickly and uneventfully, which was exactly the way Sam wanted it. By the time she actually looked at her watch again it was after two o'clock, and the last of the lunch crowd was leaving. Millie emerged from the kitchen wiping her well-worn hands on an equally worn dish towel. Sam cleaned off the counter as the final patrons headed out the door. She scooped up the tip they left her and added it to the rest of the cash in her pocket.

Sam leaned back against the counter and stretched tired arms over her head. "Nothing like a hard day's work to get the blood flowing." She yawned.

Millie looked at her sideways. "I wore you out already?"

Sam dropped her arms, rested her elbows on the counter behind her, and gave Millie a skeptical look. "Please."

"What? These folks don't give you a run for your money the way the city people do?" Millie made a loud *humph* sound as she walked over to lock the front door. "Now that I've got you back, maybe I should stay open for a dinner shift too." The bell tinkled loudly as she locked it.

"Ha! That'll be the day," Sam scoffed. She turned her back to Millie and continued to tidy up the area behind the counter. "You and I both know that as much as you love this place, there is no way you'd stay open for all three shifts. Aren't you the one who always told me that there was more to life than working?"

"Hell yes," she hooted as she wiped down the rest of the tables. "Now get those coffeepots back to Billy boy so he can get 'em cleaned up for tomorrow morning.

Then you can get your skinny butt back home and spend some time in that art studio. How is it by the way?"

"It's... well, it's a dream come true," she said smiling. "By the way, do you have a schedule for me yet?"

"Well, funny you should ask. I've been wanting to do some freshening up to the place. Y'know, some new paint, new counter, and so on. Well, my handyman called me this morning and told me he had a last minute cancellation and can get to my stuff starting tomorrow. So I'm gonna be closed until Saturday."

"Closed," Sam said with genuine disbelief. "Millie, when was the last time you closed this place?"

Millie paused mid-table wipe and squeezed her eyes shut. "Hmmm. I think it was December 1974."

Sam let out a big laugh. "Good lord, Millie. Why not just wait until the off season?"

"Well, my handyman is real good, and his schedule is always packed. Gotta take him when I can get him." She shuffled some salt and pepper shakers around the counter and put them in their proper place. "Besides I think I deserve a little vacation," she said with a devilish grin. "The Sox have a big game tomorrow, and I can watch it guilt-free."

Sam shook her head and smiled. "So, then you won't need me until Saturday."

"That sounds about right missy."

"Alrighty. I'll get the rest of this stuff cleaned up ASAP." Sam delivered a salute with the coffeepot and headed into the kitchen. She expected to run into Billy, but he was nowhere to be found. She looked around the small, well-used kitchen and marveled at how clean it already was. Millie ran a tight ship, and no one knew that better than her own son. The bell above the front door jingled, and Sam heard Millie talking with someone. Maybe Billy locked himself out? That's weird. She placed the coffeepots in the sink and pushed her way back through the swinging door, ready with a smile and a teasing comment for her old friend. She expected to find Billy, maybe even Edgar or George—but not Roger.

Sam stopped dead in her tracks, and all the blood drained from her face. She swallowed hard and willed herself not to faint. Millie was holding the door open, and Roger stood there talking to Millie as if it was completely normal for him to be there, but he couldn't have looked more out of place. His blue blazer, polo shirt, khakis, and penny loafers weren't exactly standard issue in the little greasy spoon. He had that big phony smile plastered on his face, the same smile that morphed into a leer the moment his eyes flicked over to Sam.

"Here she is," Millie began cheerfully. "One of your city friends has come to call on you…" She trailed off, and her face fell as soon as she saw Sam's reaction. "Sammy girl? You okay?" She glanced back at Roger with a look of uncertainty.

Sam swallowed hard and put her quaking hands into the pockets of her black shorts. "I'm fine," she said in a shaky voice. She cursed herself silently. *Dammit. I shouldn't be afraid of this asshole.*

"Sam and I are old friends, but I probably should've called to let her know I was coming," he said with a wave of his well-manicured hand. "However, I couldn't resist surprising her."

"Yeah… Well, she looks surprised all right," Millie said slowly. "And not the good kind of surprised." She turned to face Roger and crossed her plump arms over her ample breasts. "Maybe you shoulda called. Hmm?"

"It's fine Millie." She took a few steps to her left and settled in behind the lunch counter. If he wanted to talk to her, he would have to do it with some kind of barrier between them. *There's no way he's laying one more hand on me.* In that moment she wished that this man could read her mind. Her thoughts went to Malcolm, and her heart squeezed in her chest. *If Malcolm were here he'd put you in your place. Something tells me he doesn't abide bullies.*

"Uh-huh," Millie huffed, not quite convinced. "Well… I'll give you some privacy. Sammy, I have to run next door to the drugstore. I'll be right back." She walked to the kitchen door and turned to Roger who still stood by the door. "I may look like a nice old lady, but if you get out of line… I'll kick your ass sideways." She gave a curt nod to Sam and disappeared into the kitchen.

Sam smirked and dried her hands with the dish towel. She loved that someone else stood up to this arrogant asshole. Her moment of joy was quickly squashed when she turned to find Roger had seated himself at the counter directly in front of her. His eyes were locked on her breasts, and he licked his lips. In that moment she wished she had on a parka instead of a white T-shirt.

Sam cleared her throat, and his gaze flicked up to hers.

"Miss me?" he hissed.

Sam crossed her arms and glared at him through narrowed eyes. "What are you doing here, Roger?"

"I told you before," he said smugly. "I want you."

She shook her head and looked at him as if he'd lost his mind. "But I don't want you."

"Don't be ridiculous." Roger rolled his eyes and sighed loudly. "How many men would drive all the way from New York City to pick you up in their limo? Come on now."

"Pick me up," she said in the most incredulous tone she could muster. "What don't you understand? Roger, I made it crystal clear that I want nothing to do with you." A slow smile curved at her lips, remembering the way he practically ran away from her. "And based on your speedy departure from the stoop the other day, I thought you got the message loud and clear."

Anger clouded his features, and his nostrils flared. "I-I'd had too much to drink, and I wasn't feeling well," he stammered. "I couldn't remember exactly what happened."

Neither could she, and that was the scary part. That afternoon on the stoop, she'd done something to frighten him. At that time she didn't know what that odd tingling sensation meant. She hadn't thought much of it. She'd chalked it up to adrenaline and fear. But last night she'd felt it again and then again this morning. The difference was that this morning she saw the reason why her eyes felt that way. Her eyes had turned into the eyes of the wolf from her dreams. Is that what he saw that frightened him? She shuddered slightly. Whatever—she'd do it again now if it would make him go away and never come back.

"Here's a recap," she said tightly. "I broke up with you. I want nothing to do with you." She leaned both hands on the counter and got right in his smug face. "Go away." She wished like hell that she could make her eyes do that tingly thing on purpose. "How's that? Clear enough for you? I-don't-want-to-see-you-ever-again!"

Sam tried desperately to control herself, but she couldn't
stop her voice or her body from shaking.

Quick as a snake he snatched both of her wrists. His
fingers bit into her flesh, and he pulled her so that she
was practically lying on the counter top. The hard edge
cut into her belly, and Sam lost her breath. He held
firmly in his grasp, nuzzled her cheek, and placed a kiss
on her ear. "Don't say that," he rasped.

Sam cringed and squeezed her eyes shut. Just as she
was about to scream bloody murder, a deep, familiar
voice rumbled through the room.

"Take your hands off her."

Malcolm.

Sam's eyes flew open, and relief flooded her heart. He
towered behind Roger and glowered at him with the most
menacing look Samantha had ever seen. Was he always
that big? He reminded Sam of some kind of avenging
angel, larger than life, and really, really pissed off.

Malcolm reached down, growled, and grabbed a visibly surprised Roger by the shoulder. He spun him around
to face him. Roger's arms flailed like a spindly rag doll,
and an odd gurgling noise came out of his throat. Sam
stumbled back and stared openmouthed as Malcolm
hoisted him off the ground by the lapels of his jacket.
Roger whimpered slightly and struggled uselessly against
Malcolm. Shock was soon replaced with impotent fury.

"Put me down," he sputtered. "I'll have you arrested
for assault."

Malcolm cast him a doubtful look. He shoved him
down onto the stool that he'd been seated on so smugly
just a few minutes before. "You will do nothing of the
sort," he said in a low and deadly voice. With one hand

still placed firmly on Roger's shoulder, he looked up at Samantha. "Are you all right?" His silky voice slid inside her and instantly put her at ease. All the knots in her stomach loosened immediately. Sam finally let out the breath she'd been holding and simply nodded, unable to form any coherent response.

"Could you do me a favor? Go outside, and tell his driver that he'll be departing in just a few minutes—alone."

Roger opened his mouth to protest, but one look from Malcolm silenced him. He snapped his mouth shut, and a contrite look washed over his face. Malcolm reached into the pocket of his worn jeans and handed her a business card. Sam took it and walked around the counter next to the two men.

Her gaze skimmed Malcolm's long body. Broad shoulders, muscled arms that were barely contained by a light blue T-shirt, and his jeans hung low on his narrow hips. She couldn't help but notice his ass. It was a great ass. Her face flushed with embarrassment. The last thing in the world she should be doing right this minute is checking out his fine backside, but quite frankly, she couldn't help herself. She tore her gaze from his butt and forced herself to look at his face.

Not much better. Those eyes of his could melt the polar icecaps.

Crap.

A small smiled curved his delicious looking lips. Jeez, it's like the guy could read her mind.

Wait.

He actually could.

Double crap.

His lips curved into a lopsided grin as if he knew exactly what was on her dirty little mind. "Give him that card. My cousin Dante owns a security firm. If he's worried about losing his job, you can assure him that he'll have one with Dante as of this afternoon. I'm sure the pay will be better." He glared down at Roger, and his voice dropped to almost a whisper. "I can promise that the employer will be much better."

Sam took the card from him and headed out the door. The bell jingled as she left the diner. She glanced back through the glass door. Malcolm's massive body blocked most of Roger from view. All she could see were his skinny legs and penny loafer-clad feet hanging limply in complete submission. The bells hadn't jingled before Malcolm came in. How the hell did he get in there without a sound?

Malcolm wanted nothing more than to shift into his eagle form and scare the shit out of this smug bastard. He'd heard Samantha's thoughts loud and clear the moment that she'd laid eyes on Roger. He'd been combing the beach for hours in search of her necklace, but so far he'd come up empty. Amid his frustration, her voice slid into his mind and clawed at his heart. Her fear flooded him and sent his heart hammering in his chest. The second she'd made the mental link with him he was able to hone in on her location.

He'd materialized in the diner with very little effort and knew that it was because her strength was bolstering his. It had been an incredibly risky thing to do. One of the beach patrons may have seen him vanish, and that would've broken the cardinal rule of the Amoveo—never to reveal themselves to humans. Ever. Hell, for all he knew the diner could've been bustling with customers. All that mattered in that moment was getting to Sam and making sure she was safe. Seeing Roger handling his mate in such an aggressive, intimate, and uninvited way sent a sizzling rage through his body. It had taken significant restraint to not crush him like the little bug that he was.

Malcolm pinned Roger with a withering stare. His eyes were round with fear, and his lips quivered. Malcolm searched Roger's mind and found it clouded with fear and anger that was largely fueled by his own impotence. Malcolm dropped his hand but continued to tower over him. Roger squirmed onto the seat and smoothed the lapels of his sport coat with quaking hands. He made a small whimpering noise as he struggled to maintain some kind of dignity.

Roger's gaze flicked past Malcolm to Samantha.

"Don't." Malcolm's eyes narrowed, and he poked one strong finger into Roger's chest. "Don't even think about it."

Roger's eyes flicked back up to Malcolm's fierce gaze. "I j-j-just," he stammered breathlessly. "I only wanted—"

"I know exactly what you wanted," he seethed through clenched teeth. Malcolm stood up and crossed his arms over his broad chest but continued to hold Roger prisoner with his glare.

Roger sat up on the stool a little taller in an attempt to regain self-respect. Too late.

"Roger, isn't it?" Malcolm asked tightly. Roger nodded weakly. "Yes, well, Roger, it seems quite obvious that Samantha wants absolutely nothing to do with you. Whatever relationship you had, or perceived that you had with her, is over." He leaned in almost imperceptibly and dropped his voice low. "Let's make something crystal clear. You are never to see, or speak, to Samantha again unless she contacts you first, which I highly doubt she will." He straightened to his full height but kept his sharp gaze fixed on Roger. "Is that understood?"

Roger opened his mouth to protest but thought better of it and snapped it shut instead. "That's better," Malcolm said quietly. "Now, I don't know how you were raised, but where I come from men don't bully women into being with them. Samantha has made it quite clear to you on several occasions that she has absolutely no interest in continuing whatever relationship you had."

"What are you? Her big brother?" Roger leaned forward in a moment of bravery and narrowed his eyes at Malcolm. "Here to save her virtue or something?"

Malcolm smirked and stood his ground. "I'm most definitely not her brother."

Roger stilled, and a slow, knowing smile spread across his face. He laughed. "Well, she's pretty much a dead fish in the sack. I hope you enjoy sloppy seconds."

With lightning fast speed, Malcolm grabbed Roger by the throat and held him against the counter. Roger's eyes bugged out in shock, and his face grew crimson as Malcolm's massive hand threatened to crush his neck like a twig. His mouth opened and closed rapidly, like a fish out of water. Roger clawed at his throat and struggled in vain to free himself from Malcolm's grip. But the more Roger struggled, the tighter his grip became.

Malcolm fought to keep the beast within him at bay.

Intellectually he knew that she hadn't been celibate. He wasn't naïve. She was a thirty-year-old woman, and he was sure she'd had lovers—not that the idea thrilled him—but the very notion that Roger would insinuate lewd things about his mate sent his blood boiling. His body strained against the shift, and the muscles in his back bulged in protest. The image of this human touching his mate—in any way—filled him with a deep primal rage. His eyes shifted into his eagle form and glowed brightly down at Roger, who then let out an odd gurgling sound and pissed in his pants.

Malcolm's mouth curved into a small smile. Mission accomplished. His eyes shifted back to their human state, and he shoved Roger back, releasing him from his grip.

Roger whimpered and glanced down at the mess he'd made. Gasping and clutching his throat, he slipped on the puddle of urine he'd left on the floor, scrambled frantically, and cut a wide path around Malcolm and out the door. He scurried past a stunned Samantha and dove into the back of his limo. Malcolm watched the long black car peel out of the parking lot and down the street as Samantha pushed open the door and joined him inside the now quiet diner.

Sam closed the door behind her but all the while kept her questioning gaze on Malcolm. She placed her hands on her hips and cocked her head at him curiously. "I suppose I should thank you." She looked down at the puddle on the floor behind Malcolm and grimaced. "Is that what I think it is?"

Malcolm straightened his back and nodded. "No one should ever touch you without your permission," he said with more bite than he'd intended. His sharp gaze held hers. "No one will ever treat you in such a way again," he whispered. "Ever."

Sam nodded slowly and closed the distance between them. She eyed him skeptically. "Well, I have to admit your timing was impeccable."

Malcolm glanced down at her wrists, and anger flared through him. Faint red marks marred her beautiful flesh from where that son of a bitch had grabbed her. His entire body went rigid at the memory of it. He reached out and took her wrists gently in his hands. He brushed his thumbs lightly over the fading red streaks on her fair skin. She quivered beneath his fingers, and her heartbeat increased the moment his flesh touched hers. The rapid thrumming of her pulse fell instantly in time with his. He pulled her closer and placed a soft kiss on each wrist. Her skin, warm and silky, felt like heaven beneath his lips. A small sound of pleasure escaped her lips as her soft breasts pressed up against their now intertwined hands.

He opened his eyes slowly and found her large indigo eyes looking up at him expectantly. Long strands of her blonde hair framed her spectacular face. He allowed himself this moment to take in every curve. He kissed her temple and whispered softly into her ear. "You should be cherished."

"Malcolm," she breathed his name softly.

The desire in her voice combined with the touch of her body sent him into overdrive. He wanted to memorize every bit of her, but those full lips, parted slightly, were far too tempting to leave alone. He crushed her mouth with his and felt like a man who'd just gotten water after a drought.

Relief.

Desire.

Passion.

Home.

All these thoughts swamped his heart and his body. He swept his tongue along hers and white, hot lust ravaged him. He couldn't get close enough. He needed her, needed to protect her, to love her.

Her yearning matched his as she pulled her hands from his grasp and wrapped her arms around his back. He growled low in his throat as their bodies pressed tightly against one another. Malcolm grabbed her curvy bottom and pressed her up against the evidence of his desire. Her fingers dug deliciously into the muscles of his back, making him moan softly into her mouth. Her lips melded perfectly with his. He reveled in the sweet touch of her tongue and her taste. Salty and sweet. Small but strong. He'd heard the way she stood up to Roger, and it made him proud. His mate was not a woman to be trifled with. Darkness crept into his mind at the memory of it, and he scolded himself silently. After the encounter she'd just had, he was ravaging her in the middle of the diner like some kind of horny teenager. Nice. Very sensitive.

He held her close and softened their kiss. Suckling her bottom lip, he pulled away gently. He held her there, wrapped tightly in his arms. She opened those big blue eyes and looked up at him through heavy lids. Her lips were swollen and red from his kisses. He'd never seen anyone more beautiful in his life.

"So," she said between heavy breaths, "I should probably tell you that I don't usually make out with people as a thank you."

Malcolm laughed softly and kissed the tip of her nose. "I should hope not."

Pots clanked loudly in the kitchen. Sam slipped quickly out of his arms, like a child about to be caught by her parents, and wiped her mouth with the back of her hand. Cold quickly replaced the warmth.

"Sammy, you okay out there?" A short robust woman burst through the swinging kitchen door with a large frying pan in her hand. Her eyebrows shot up, she placed her meaty hands on her ample hips, and looked Malcolm up and down. "Well, I guess you are." She let out a low cat call whistle and wiggled her eyebrows at Sam.

Malcolm raised one eyebrow and gave Samantha a sly smile.

Sam let out a slightly embarrassed giggle and tucked the loose strands of hair behind her ear. "Millie," she said with a warning tone. "This is Malcolm Drew, and he was just leaving." She moved in next to Malcolm and elbowed him gently in the ribs.

Millie put down the frying pan, reached over the counter, and gave him a hearty handshake. "Nice to meet you, young man." She looked around the diner and cast a glance outside. "Where's that other fella?" she asked with a grimace. "The city boy?"

Malcolm glanced at Sam. "Oh, he had to run."

"Good," she huffed. "I didn't like the look of him."

"Neither did I." Malcolm glimpsed at the clock on the wall. "Speaking of which, I have to be going myself. It was very nice meeting you Millie."

Millie winked. "You too, handsome. I hope we'll be seeing more of you around here. I don't think Sammy girl has looked this happy since she got that red bicycle for Christmas."

"Millie," Sam growled and shot her a look of warning, but Millie just laughed loudly and made herself comfortable behind the counter.

Smiling, Malcolm took Samantha's soft hand in his, and without taking his eyes off hers, he kissed it gently. "Good day." Her deep blue eyes widened as their flesh met, and her energy waves pumped wildly over him. "It's always a pleasure to see you, Ms. Logan."

Her eyes widened slightly and flicked over to Millie when he emphasized the word *pleasure*, but he couldn't help himself. Sam licked her lips and took a deep breath as her hand slipped slowly from his. "Good day."

He gave a quick nod to Millie and headed out the door as the bells jingled happily behind him. He cast one last glance at Samantha and reached out to her with his mind.

I have a necklace to find.

Her eyes widened, and her hand fluttered to her throat.

As the door clicked shut he heard Millie bark, "What the hell is that mess on the floor?"

Chuckling quietly, he went back to Paddy's to keep his promise.

Chapter 10

SAM GOT INTO HER CAR AND GRABBED HER CELL PHONE from the charger. It blinked up at her rapidly. She had three voice mails and several missed calls from Gunther. She popped on her headset and listened to the messages as she drove home. All three were from Gunther, and each one got slightly more hysterical. All he ever said was, "Kitten. Call me back. *Now!*"

Sam shook her head and hit the call button. What on earth was the little sprite up to?

He picked it up on the first ring.

"Holy shit! Where in the hell have you been?" he shrieked. "I've been calling you all damn day, woman!"

"I've been working, Gunther." She laughed. "What on earth is so important that it had you blowing up my phone all morning?"

"I sold the rest of your paintings," he squealed.

Sam winced at the high-pitched shriek and shook her head. He sold her paintings? No way. She must've heard that wrong.

"Hello? Did you hear me? I-*sold-your-paintings*." He punctuated each word as if she were deaf.

Sam pulled her car over into the gas station at Dunn's Corners. The house was only a mile away, but if she did finally sell her work it would be best not to get killed in a car accident upon finding out. That would be a buzz kill. Her heart beat rapidly in her chest from the rush of

adrenaline. She tore out the headset and picked up the
phone. She wanted to be sure she heard this correctly.

"Okay," she breathed. "Did you say that you sold
my paintings?"

"You bet your sweet ass I did," he said rapidly. When
he got excited it was speed-talking all the way.

"What? When?" She smiled with disbelief and leaned
back against the worn headrest. "And Gunther, slow
down. Tell me exactly what happened."

"Yesterday." He giggled and then took a deep breath.
"Okay. I'll slow down, but I've been like *dying* to tell
you this ever since they picked up all the pieces this
morning." He took another cleansing breath. "Okay. So
yesterday, I'm sitting here having my morning latte, and
this guy waltzes in here, like right after we open. Which,
quite frankly, was a tad annoying. But, you can tell, lots
of money. Great suit. Armani. Anyway, turns out he's a
buyer, y'know, not your average bear. Well, he came in
here yesterday and—get this—asked specifically for any
pieces that were done by Samantha Logan."

"Wait." Dread crept up her belly and squashed any
excitement she felt.

Roger.

She swallowed hard. What if this buyer was one of
Roger's cronies? She squeezed her eyes shut and rubbed
her temple with her free hand. "This guy asked for my
work specifically?"

"Hey," he whined. "Are you going to let me tell you
the story or what?"

"Yes." She closed her eyes and prayed for patience.
Gunther's stories could go on for days. "I'm sorry.
Go on."

"Thank you," he sang. "*So*, he asked for any work done by you. Naturally, I was only too happy to accommodate him. Well, he didn't even *look* at them. When I brought him over to the stack against the back wall, he didn't even ask me to open them up. He just handed me his credit card and told me he'd be back first thing in the morning to pick them all up. He didn't haggle or even ask the prices." He shrieked. "Can you believe it?"

"No," she said quietly. "It sounds too good to be true."

"Yeah, well, I know what you mean." He stopped himself and quickly added, "Don't get me wrong. I love your work, but let's be honest babe. Your stuff hasn't exactly been flying off the walls."

"I know. It's okay Gunther." Sam let out a loud sigh and laughed softly. "What was the name on the credit card?"

"Ummm. Hold on a sec. I have to get the slip."

Sam held her breath as Gunther hummed tunelessly while he searched for the paper.

"Here it is. Ugh. I swear, when Milton comes in here and watches the counter for me everything gets all topsy-turvy." He huffed and then added quickly, "It's a good thing he's so damn cute." He giggled. "Barkley Jameson. Ring any bells?"

"No it doesn't."

"Hey! I can't believe you're not excited about this. Come on girl! You just sold all ten of your paintings in one fell swoop and cleared a bundle of cash." He hooted loudly but then quickly shifted into his business voice. "Minus my commission of course."

Sam leaned her elbow on the open window of the car

and looked out the window at the passing traffic. "Did he actually come and pick them all up?"

"Yup. First thing this morning. In fact I had to open up at eight just to accommodate this guy," he snorted. "But hey, he paid a bundle, so I wasn't gonna complain sister. He showed up with two big hulking brutes and a large black van. They packed up all of your pieces and hauled them away." He dropped his voice to a whisper. "I have to admit. I am pretty curious."

"Me too, Gunther." Sam could hear the door of the gallery being shoved open loudly and smiled. "Sounds like you've got a customer."

He scoffed loudly. "Honey please. After that mama-jamma sale, I closed for the day. It's just Milton. So listen, should I send the check to you at your place in Rhode Island?"

"Yeah, that would be great."

"Okay. And listen. Cheer up woman! You are officially a success. Bye baby."

"Bye."

The line clicked off quietly, and Sam tossed the cell phone into her bag on the passenger seat. She gripped the steering wheel tightly and leaned her forehead on her fingers before blowing out a strong breath and starting up the car. Gunther was right. She should be excited. In fact, she should be bloody ecstatic, but she couldn't stop the feeling of dread that nagged at her. What if Roger was the one who bought her paintings? She shook her head and made a small sound of defiance. So what if he did? It shouldn't matter. Right? After all, money is money.

However, no matter how many times she told herself it shouldn't matter—it did. It mattered a lot. The truth was that she hated the idea of her mother's image, or any of the deeply personal images she painted, hanging in Roger's home. Her skin crawled at the very thought of it. No amount of money was worth that. Maybe she'd call Gunther and see if he could get them back and give the guy a refund. She scoffed out loud and rolled her eyes. Right, after everything Gunther had done, she was going to deny him this sale? Not likely.

She threw the car into first gear and pulled out of the gas station. As she drove the last bit of the way back home she went through the laundry list of oddities that had become her life.

Moved back into childhood bedroom at the age of thirty. Check.

Crazy stalker ex-boyfriend. Check.

Miraculously sold all artwork in one fell swoop. Check.

Hot neighbor who can kiss like the devil and use telepathy. Check.

Sam smiled.

Butterflies in stomach when looking at hot neighbor. Double check.

When Sam finally dragged herself into the house, she didn't have the energy to go right out to her studio. She was mentally and physically drained. Working on the portrait would probably help take her mind off everything, but she couldn't bring herself to do it yet. Instead, she made herself a cup of coffee and took it out to the deck. Nonie was already out there, as she was most afternoons, reading the local paper and sipping her tea. They exchanged a familiar greeting with a kiss on the cheek. Sam settled into her chair and blew on her coffee.

Her thoughts immediately went to Malcolm. She replayed the unusual events that occurred over the past several hours. She had seen his eyes change into eagle eyes, and this morning her own eyes had turned into the eyes of a wolf. They were the same ones as the wolf in her dreams. How was this all possible? She felt like she was losing her mind. *Maybe he slipped something into my drink.* She half expected to hear Malcolm's scoffing voice in her head.

"Ridiculous," she said.

"I'm sorry, dear. What's ridiculous?"

She sent Nonie a startled look and blushed for blurting that out. "Oh. Nothing. I was just… it's nothing really." Sam looked back out at the ocean, hoping Nonie wouldn't see right through her. Somehow Nonie always had the uncanny ability to know exactly what was going on with Sam.

"I lost my necklace last night." Sam was unable to look at Nonie, afraid she'd be scolded like a child. She wouldn't blame her. That necklace was an irreplaceable heirloom. When Nonie didn't immediately respond, Sam forced herself to look at her. She was met by a sweet, sympathetic look in her blue eyes.

"I'm sure it will turn up. I wouldn't worry on it too much. These things have a way of working themselves out." Nonie turned her attention back to the paper.

"Wow. You're much calmer about it than I expected. I was up half the night, tearing apart my room and searching the driveway in my nightgown with a flashlight. In fact, I am going to go out and look again before I head out to the studio." Sam rose from her chair. "You're really not upset with me for losing it?"

"I'm not upset because I don't think it's lost," Nonie said with a small smile. "It's just... misplaced. Believe me. You'll have your necklace back."

"I hope you're right, Nonie, and somehow you always are."

They were interrupted by the chirp of Sam's cell phone. She went inside and dug through her purse, which she fondly referred to as *the black hole*. It had the ability to swallow up her cell phone or anything else she was searching for. Finally, she found it, at the bottom of course. She smiled when she saw Kerry's name in the caller ID.

"Hey there, Hollywood." Sam walked back out to the deck.

"Back at ya, Picasso. So listen, want to grab a bite to eat and catch up today?"

"Oh, Kerry, I would love to," Sam said with genuine disappointment. "But I'm not in the city. I'm at Nonie's."

With that acknowledgement, Nonie waved her greetings.

"Nonie says *hi* by the way."

"Hi, back. Hey, are you out on the deck?" Kerry asked.

"Of course, with the afternoon coffee and paper as usual. Why?"

"Do me a favor. Look over at my parents' house, will ya?"

"Sure. What am I looking for?" Sam asked. She looked over at the Smithson's house and saw Kerry standing there on her cell phone and waving. Sam shrieked her delight, and jumping up and down, gave an excited wave back. "Oh my God! You have *no* idea how glad I am that you're here." The beginnings of tears stung her eyes and threatened to spill over. "How did you know I was here?"

"Well, Nonie of course. She called me a few weeks ago right after you called her. It was a conspiratorial surprise, and avoiding your calls has been killing me. Get your sweet ass in a bathing suit, and get over here stat!"

Sam had a grin that went from ear to ear. She hung up and instantly came up behind Nonie's chair. She wrapped her up in a huge hug of gratitude. "Thank you, Nonie. Once again, you know exactly what to do."

"It's true," she said with a small sigh. "Having such insight is a blessing… most of the time." She gently patted Sam's arms. "Now run along and have fun!"

Sam gave her a quick kiss and ran upstairs to change. She realized that they really hadn't spoken directly in a while. Kerry had been overseas on a shoot so there had been a lot of voice mail and text messages, but it didn't matter how much time passed between conversations. Whether it was a month, a day, or a year, they could always pick up right where they left off. It was always like no time had passed. They were still the giggling little girls from all those years ago.

Sam and Kerry were complete opposites in every way. Still they managed to be as close as sisters, which worked out nicely since they were both only children. Neither of them made friends very easily. Sam felt disconnected from most people. Kerry had a major phobia about touching people. When they were little, she called it *the spookies*, but now she admitted to having a germ phobia. Sam was the only person Kerry would hug or touch at all.

Sam changed quickly, donned her aviators, and

grabbed a towel. It was much quicker to go down and cut across the beach to Kerry's place. The driveways were so long out to the road it was practically necessary to drive over. She couldn't cut across between the houses because it was just dunes and sea grass with all kinds of creepy critters who called it home. Not only would she break her neck, but she'd probably get eaten alive by a variety of insects.

Sam climbed the beach stairs to Kerry's place and found her friend waiting with a big smile and a huge glass that likely contained a margarita.

She marveled at how strikingly beautiful Kerry was. Her long jet black hair gleamed thick and shiny. Somehow, it never frizzed, no matter what the humidity was. Sam, on the other hand, ended up looking like a Chia Pet at the smallest hint of humidity. Kerry's large eyes were chocolate brown with flecks of gold in certain lights. She had high cheekbones and full lips that many women paid thousands to try and attain. Her creamy white skin was unmarred by the sun, and the woman didn't have a wrinkle in sight. Kerry's bright red swimsuit showed off her long curvy body. Bam baby. Once you met her in person, it was blindingly clear how she had become the hottest plus-size model since Emme. She and Sam couldn't have been more different physically if they tried.

"So... am I still huggable? Or do I give you the spookies like the rest of the world?"

"Shut up and hug me," Kerry teased.

The two friends hugged each other and giggled like schoolgirls. Sam broke the embrace first, knowing a short hug was all Kerry could take. She stepped back to get a good look at her. "You know, it should be illegal to look as good as you do. You make us regular girls look bad," Sam said teasingly with a shake of her head.

"Oh please. I'm an amazon who dwarfs most men on the planet. Besides, you're one to talk with that amazing tan. I would kill for color like that! I look like a damned ghost. Not exactly a sexy look. Here." She handed Sam the frosty beverage.

Sam glanced down and smiled. Yup. Margaritas.

They laid their towels out on the lounge chairs, with Sam maneuvering for the best angle of the morning sun, and Kerry under the umbrella to avoid it. Within seconds, Kerry began the inevitable best friend inquisition.

"Okay. So let's go. Spill it." She slid on her supersize sunglasses as she settled into her chair. "What's going on, and why have you moved out of the coolest city in the world to live… here?"

"Don't hold back, babe. What do you really think about it?" Sam smiled as she got comfortable and welcomed the warm summer sun.

"I'm not judging. I'm just perplexed. I mean really! How many times did we stay up until all hours of the night talking about the ways you wanted to get out of here? You can't blame me for being a little bit surprised."

"I know, I know. To be honest, I can't believe I did it either." Sam gave a small groan.

"Okay, so what prompted this move? Money?"

"No. I mean, I wasn't rolling in it, but I wasn't starving either. I… jeez, you're going to think I'm nuts." Frustrated, Sam sighed.

"No I won't." She shook her head. "I'm the one who can't stand touching other people, remember? I promise

I won't laugh or think you're crazy." She held up her hand as if she was swearing in a court of law.

Sam took a deep breath and squeezed her eyes shut. After a dramatic pause, she finally spit it out. "It was a dream."

"A dream? "Kerry emitted a stifled laughter. "Ooookay."

"Hey, you said you wouldn't laugh spookie girl." Sam unleashed a giggle of her own.

"Right." Kerry cleared her throat and regained her composure. "You're right. I'm sorry. Go ahead."

"If you're going to laugh about the dream, then you're going to get absolutely hysterical when I tell you about the other dreams… and Malcolm."

"Malcolm? Yummy, who's that? Now we're getting somewhere. I was hoping a guy would be involved. You've been single for far too long! Now this is getting good." She clapped her hands excitedly. "Okay, I'm all ears. I won't interrupt, and I *swear* I won't laugh. Cross my heart." She made the sign across her heart.

Sam knew that if she could tell anyone in the entire world about what had been happening over the last couple of days, it was Kerry. She thought that if she told the story out loud it wouldn't sound crazy, but she also knew that she wasn't ready to tell her everything.

She took a deep breath.

"Okay. Remember those dreams I used to have when we were kids?"

"You mean the one with your mom and the wolf, or the one where some guy is calling you?" Kerry licked the salt off the edge of her glass.

"The wolf ones. Well, the night of my thirtieth

birthday I dreamed about the wolf again. Except this time, I *was* the wolf."

Kerry narrowed her eyes. "Huh? You mean you were actually a wolf?"

Sam nodded and swirled the ice in her glass. "Yup. A giant gray wolf."

"What on earth were you doing?"

"I was running. Here at the beach. I ran with complete and total abandon. I was free, completely unencumbered… and it felt delicious. When I woke up the next morning, I had a longing for Nonie and the beach house. In that moment, I had total clarity. I was sick and tired of waiting."

"Waiting? Waiting for what?" Kerry asked.

"Everything." Sam shrugged. "Lately, it felt like my life was on hold somehow. So, I decided the only way to jumpstart things was to make a drastic change. I figured the dream was a sign."

"That's all very fascinating, but I want to hear about the date." She wiggled her eyebrows. "Who's Malcolm?"

Sam laughed and sat back in her lounge chair. "How did I know that you'd want to get right to the good stuff?"

"Because you're my best friend, and you know I'm a dirty girl at heart."

Sam laughed loudly at her friend's remark and took a sip of her drink. Looking out over the familiar shoreline her thoughts wandered to Malcolm. "He's… special."

She told her about Malcolm and their date and of course about the mind-bending make out sessions. She also told her about the practically pornographic dreams.

However, she held back on the truly bizarre things. She left out the part about the eyes, the eagle that visited her room, the vanishing guy, and of course, about hearing his voice in her head. If she told her any of that, Kerry might put her in a psych ward. She wouldn't blame her. She was starting to think she should check herself in.

She knew it sounded crazy, but she also knew it was real. Malcolm confirmed that this afternoon with his parting message. When his voice slid into her mind, she'd just about fainted right there on the diner floor. Thank God Millie had been there and anchored her to reality.

Kerry sat in rapt attention. By the end she was sitting up cross-legged on the lounge, her sunglasses on her head, and her mouth hanging open. "Wow. I can't remember the last time I got that hot over a guy." Kerry whistled and shook her head in amazement. She went over to the bar on the other side of the deck to collect the pitcher of margaritas. "He sounds a lot better than that other guy you were dating. What was his name," she called over her shoulder. "Van Douche?"

Sam giggled and sipped the last bit of her margarita. "Van Dousen, but I think your version suits him better." She wiped at the condensation on her glass with her thumb and avoided looking at Kerry. Her voice dropped low. "He's become a bit of a problem."

Kerry sashayed over with the pitcher and refilled Sam's glass. "What does that mean," she asked, her voice laced with concern. She put the jug down on the table and made herself comfortable on the edge of Sam's chaise.

"Well, apparently he hadn't gotten the memo that I broke up with him." She took another sip and relished the sweet and salty bite that a good margarita always had. "He even showed up at the diner today."

"Hello? Stalk much?"

"Tell me about it." Sam scoffed and rolled her eyes. "You know, showing up uninvited at my apartment in the city was one thing. But following me all the way out here, to another state, is another level of creepy."

"So what happened?" Kerry took a big sip of her drink and cast Sam a look of concern.

"Well, clearly he's deluded. The man is not used to hearing the word no about anything. Told me he wants me and that's that." Sam squeezed her eyes shut and took another sip. Anger bubbled up at the memory of the way he grabbed her. "He got kind of rough. Grabbed me and practically dragged me over the counter." Sam let out a shaky breath and opened her eyes. "I'm not sure what would've happened if Malcolm hadn't shown up."

Kerry leaned closer, and her voice dropped to a whisper. "No way! The hottie showed up and rescued you?" She let out a loud hoot and slapped her own leg. "I love it!" She nudged Sam's arm with her glass. "What did he do? Please tell me he beat the shit out of that little worm."

Sam gave a small smile and shook her head. "He didn't have to. He's twice Roger's size and lifted the guy off the ground like he weighed nothing at all. And given the fact that Roger—quite literally—pissed in his pants, I don't think I'll see him again."

Kerry laughed. "Ohmigod," she squealed. "He didn't actually pee his pants?"

"Yup." Sam nodded and giggled. "He left a big old puddle right there on Millie's floor."

The two of them laughed until they were breathless and crying.

Kerry wiped away the tears with the back of her hand and moved to her own chair. "Well, this Malcolm guy sounds like a keeper. If he has any tall chivalrous friends who like a woman with meat on her bones, be sure to send 'em my way."

"Come on, you are constantly surrounded by hot guys. You mean to tell me none of them do it for you?"

"Please." She rolled her eyes. "The men in my industry are slimy pigs and often dumb as stumps. They either want to get into my pants and say they bedded a model, or they want to get into my wallet." She slipped her sunglasses back on and waved away the notion. "No thanks. Besides... I'd have to be able to tolerate touching someone in order to have sex."

That definitely surprised Sam. She wasn't aware her friend had been as lonely as she had.

"I think it's pretty wild that this guy lives in the creepy house from our childhood. Did he tell you anything about his family? I mean, there's always been such a cloak of secrecy around them and that house."

The overflowing tray of fruit, cheese, and crackers looked delicious. As kids, they'd shared secrets over Diet Coke and M&M's, but that evolved to margaritas with a fruit and cheese platter as they'd gotten older. Sam picked at the assorted goodies Kerry had laid out on the table. She selected a small bunch of green grapes and sat back in her chair.

"He told me some. His parents are still alive and kicking and living the good life over in Milan. He runs his family's shipping business from the house. It's just him and Davis, the butler."

"Oh my God! That guy is still alive? He was like

a fossil when we were kids. Christ, he must be positively ancient now." Kerry popped a cube of cheese in her mouth.

"I guess." She shrugged "I mean, I haven't met him yet. Just from across the way y'know." Sam sipped her drink. The ice cold liquid was a welcome sensation as it coated her dry throat. She closed her eyes and willed the margarita to dampen the heat that flared through her body. All she'd done was talk about him, and it got her all hot and bothered. She was in big trouble.

"So when do I get to meet your hunky hero?" Kerry wiggled her eyebrows.

"Um... I don't know," Sam began with some trepidation.

"I'm sorry. I don't mean to be pushy. It's just that you are clearly nuts for this guy, and I figure I get best friend approval rights."

"Of course you do," she said quickly. "It's just that I barely know him."

"Really, you could've fooled me. The way you talk about him, you'd think you were soul mates or something."

"Please. He is not my soul mate. You know I don't believe in that crap. He's just a hot neighbor who kisses like the devil." She sighed as the color rose in her cheeks.

"Holy crap, are you blushing?" Kerry grinned. "You are. You're blushing. God, the guy isn't even here, and you're getting horny. Shit, does he have a brother?" She put the cool glass to her forehead.

"Stop it." Sam smiled. "And, he's an only child. Like us."

"Oh well." She sighed. "Looks like dumb models and gold diggers for me."

And with that, they both broke into hysterical giggles. They spent the rest of the afternoon bouncing between various conversations. They shared beautiful fits of laughter and occasionally the comfortable silences that can only happen between true friends. As the sun made its leisurely descent, Sam knew it was time to head home for dinner with Nonie. She looked over at her friend and smiled. "This has been one of the nicest afternoons I've had in a very long time. I needed some girl time more than anything. Thanks."

"Well, don't think that this is it. I'm here for two more weeks, and I fully expect to be hanging out on a regular basis. I definitely want to meet the hottie."

"That's perfect, but I have to get the rest of my schedule from Millie."

"Sounds good. Is Billy still waiting tables for his Mom?"

Sam shook her head. "He's the cook, so he's running things more often than she is now. He's primed to take the place over. She and Nonie would have bridge games five days a week if they could."

"Bridge is a game for four isn't it? Who else do they play with?"

"Well, Millie's husband, Pete, and… come to think of it, I don't have any idea who Nonie's partner is." Sam frowned. She felt terribly guilty that she didn't know that tidbit and made a mental note to find out.

"Really, well maybe you aren't the only one with a new love." Kerry smiled slyly.

They started gathering up the remnants of their afternoon nosh while both giggled at the idea of Nonie and a boyfriend. They were rudely interrupted by the slamming of the front door and footsteps tromping up the wooden staircase in the front hall. The unexpected noise had Sam jump about a foot in the air with a shriek.

"Jesus Christ, what or who was that," she said, her hand to her chest.

"Well, hello to you too," Kerry shouted into the house. "Sorry about that. It's my cousin, AJ. Remember him? He stayed with us that summer before we started college? His dad is my mom's brother."

"Oh right!" Sam grimaced. "Wasn't he the one with the Dungeons and Dragons obsession?"

"Yeah." She rolled her eyes. "Actually he's gotten to be kind of cute. I was considering setting you up with him before I heard about your new obsession." She winked.

"Very funny." She followed Kerry into the house with their dishes. "Why is he staying here?"

"He's a marine biologist and has a temporary gig as some kind of fish consultant over at the Mystic Aquarium this summer." She shrugged. "My parents told him he could crash here before they knew I was coming to visit you. It's fine really," she said with a wave. "He works a lot, and I don't even know he's here most of the time."

"Fish consultant?" Sam put the dishes into the sink.

"Actually, I'm here to gather some data on their beluga whale population," said a voice behind them.

They turned around to see her cousin standing in the kitchen doorway. He had a big grin on his face that gave him giant dimples. Kerry was right. He was much cuter than he'd been in high school. Then again who wasn't? He was tanned with dark brown eyes and sun-bleached hair. He definitely had a surfer dude look. Not the weenie Sam remembered.

"Hey there, Cousin." Kerry waved and quickly gestured to Sam. "You remember my best friend, Sam Logan?"

"Of course I do," he said with a big dimpled smile. "How could I forget the most beautiful girl at the beach? Hey, Sam." He shook her hand and gently kissed her on the cheek.

"Yeah, yeah," Sam said teasingly. "I remember you, AJ, but I don't remember you being such a charmer. Sorry about the *fish consultant* thing. It was Kerry's fault." She nudged her friend with her elbow.

"Traitor." Kerry feigned annoyance through narrowed eyes.

"Don't worry about it." He laughed. "A lot of people have no idea what I really do. My mother still tells people I swim with the dolphins."

"How long are you here for?"

"Well, I should have most of my data gathered in the next week or so, and then I can take it back to our facility in Miami. I'm comparing the mating habits of belugas in captivity with those in the wild. The aquarium in Mystic has the best population of belugas on the east coast. My aunt and uncle were kind enough to take pity on me and let me stay here."

"Well, you're definitely a quiet guest. My grandmother thought the house has been empty all summer."

"You know how it is." He sighed and leaned one shoulder against the kitchen doorway. "I don't want to get kicked out. Especially now that the diva here has moved back in," he said, nodding toward Kerry.

"Keep it up, and you'll be *sleeping with the fishes*, wise ass." Kerry threw an olive at him.

AJ laughed good-naturedly as he dodged the mini-missile.

"Say, Sam. Would you like to get dinner with me one night this week?"

Sam suddenly became very aware that she was wearing only her one-piece black bathing suit as his gaze wandered over her body. It made her unexpectedly uncomfortable. "Dinner? Well I…"

"She's already got a man, AJ. Sorry. You're a day late and a dollar short," Kerry said. "Hey, maybe we can all go out for dinner. Not a double date because you're my cousin and that would be gross. Not to mention illegal, but still could be fun."

"Sure." He delivered that big dimply smile again. "That sounds like fun. I haven't done much socializing since I've been here, and a night out with human beings sounds great."

"Then it's settled," Kerry said before Sam could protest. "So what's today? Tuesday? How about this Saturday night? We could all go over to Mohegan Sun and grab some dinner at that great Asian place. Do a little gambling. Sam, why don't you and Malcolm pick up me and my cousin here at around seven?"

"Okay." Sam smiled. "I'll talk to Malcolm later and see if he's up for it."

AJ's phone beeped loudly, and he quickly looked to see the caller. "I've got to take this. It's a work call. Bye, Sam. See you Saturday."

They heard him greeting his caller as he made his way back upstairs.

"Jeez, I forgot how pushy you can be," Sam said in a loud whisper as she got her stuff and began to head out the back toward the beach.

Kerry responded by sticking out her tongue and giving Sam a good old-fashioned raspberry.

"Oh, and mature too. Nice."

"I've got a meeting in NYC tomorrow, so I'll be gone for the day, but do you want to go shopping on Thursday? Think Millie can live without you for a day?"

"Actually, I've got the next couple of days off from the diner so Thursday sounds great. What's the meeting in the city about?"

"I'm doing a cover shoot for *Vogue*. Can you believe it? A plus-size model on the cover *and* a full spread inside." Kerry smiled and shook her head as she wrapped up the leftover nosh. "Let's just hope the entire interview doesn't focus on my weight. How are we ever going to change the way people think—or the industry, for that matter—if every interview I do is about my size?"

"You're gorgeous. That's why you're as successful as you are. Face it girl. You sparkle at any size." Sam winked and blew her a kiss. "I'll call you later."

"Shopping and lunch in Watch Hill on Thursday!"

"Sold! I'll see you then."

Sam waved and made her way down the steps to the beach.

Chapter 11

MALCOLM HAD BEEN COMBING THE BEACH ALL DAY after the incident at the diner. He had to take a cab back because he couldn't risk materializing in front of anyone. He got dropped off about a block away. Once he returned to Paddy's he scanned the minds of the various patrons and was relieved to find that his abrupt departure earlier had gone unnoticed. He breathed a sigh of relief and resumed his search for her necklace.

Earlier in the day, he had asked the restaurant manager if they'd found anything, but to no avail. He continued his search outside and went over and over the paths they'd taken. He persistently scanned the sandy shore for any glint of that precious silver. He sensed that the beach and restaurant patrons were a bit unnerved by him and his resolve. He could feel their apprehension from every angle. Malcolm, as with all Amoveo, was a gifted telepath. He had learned over the years to block out the thoughts of others unless he specifically wanted to hear them. What couldn't be blocked were the strong emotions of the humans around him.

Over time, all Amoveo grew accustomed to the emotional onslaught; it was something that came with age and maturity. However, it was still an annoyance much of the time. He tried his best to filter out the emotions around him so he could focus on Sam's residual energy. If he couldn't see it, then perhaps he could feel it.

After hours of looking, the sun finally began to set, and he was still empty-handed. In one last ditch effort, he stood on the spot where they'd shared their first kiss. He closed his eyes and stretched his arms out around him with his palms facing the sandy beach. He concentrated on Sam. Her eyes, her smile, the fresh smell of her skin, the spicy taste of her lips. He took in a large breath, desperately trying to pick up her signature.

Then it hit him.

Samantha.

His eyes flew open. He tore off his sunglasses and looked down to his left. His vision zoomed in, and there it was. Directly below his left hand he saw the smallest glint of silver flashing at him. Triumphantly, he plucked his treasure from its sandy bed. He'd probably been over that spot a hundred times that day and hadn't found it. A huge smile cracked his face. He straightened up with the prize dangling from his fingers and heard a little girl to his right.

"Hey, mister. You found buried treasure. Are you a pirate?"

He absentmindedly looked over at the pigtailed little girl without shifting his eyes back. He was promptly greeted with a shrill scream as she ran back to her family. Abruptly brought out of his trance, he shifted his eyes back to normal and made his way back to his car. While walking to the parking lot, he could hear the little girl screaming about the man with animal eyes. As he suspected, the parents brushed her comments aside as nonsense, dismissing her as a child with an overactive imagination. *If only they knew.*

Most humans were blind to the existence of anything beyond their own version of normal. Samantha had been one of them, at least until recently. That was all about to change. Tonight he would bring Samantha her necklace. He would reveal the hidden world around her and inside of her. He just prayed she would be able to accept him. Their lives depended on it.

---~~~---

Sam walked into the house and was greeted by the pleasant sound of Nonie's laughter from the kitchen. Surprisingly, it was mixed with a male laugh, which threw her for a loop. She tiptoed from the back door and made her way toward the kitchen. She peered around the corner, looked into the kitchen, and was completely stunned by the scene before her. Nonie sat at the little kitchen table holding hands with none other than old Davis from next door. He looked up and caught Sam's eye.

"Samantha Jane, stop peering around doorways like a spy, and come in to say hello," Nonie said without even turning around.

Sam shrank inside with embarrassment. She got busted by her grandmother. Nice. She stepped into the kitchen, and Davis stood up to greet her, his hand extended and his smile charming.

"Hello, Ms. Samantha. It's so very nice to finally meet you. I've heard so much about you from Helen and of course from Malcolm as well." He winked with all the charm you'd expect from an English gentleman. He shook her hand gently and gave her a genuine smile. "Please sit down, and join us for some tea."

"Well, I don't want to interrupt."

"Don't be ridiculous, dear. Davis has been dying to get to know you. Look, he even brought you a *Welcome*

Home gift," Nonie said, gesturing to the enormous white wicker basket on the table. It was beautifully decorated and spilled over with biscuits, teas, lotions, cookies, and various other items. It would probably take hours to go through it and discover all the goodies buried within.

"Please, Ms. Samantha, do join us." Davis pulled out the empty chair for her.

"All right." Sam sat in the chair between Nonie and Davis. She looked back and forth between them and realized that she had interrupted her grandmother's date. It was a very odd sensation. She didn't quite know what to make of it. Pop had been gone for a few years, and she didn't want Nonie to be lonely, but she also wasn't sure if she was ready to see her with another man.

"Now tell us about your visit with Kerry," Nonie said before a sip of tea. "How's she doing?"

"She's great. She's been jet-setting all over the place and is glad to be getting a break. Thanks for telling her I'd be here, Nonie. I really needed a visit with her." Sam sipped the tea Davis had poured for her. "Oh, by the way, she's not staying there alone. Her cousin, AJ, is staying with her. Do you remember him? Apparently, he's a marine biologist working over at the Mystic Aquarium and is staying here while he works."

"AJ? I don't think I recall him. Is he a cousin from her mother's side or her father's side?" Nonie asked.

"Her mother's, I think. Why?"

"Oh no reason." She smiled. "Just curious I suppose." Nonie glanced at Davis over the edge of her teacup.

"Davis. Is Malcolm home? Kerry and AJ want to go out on Saturday night, and we thought Malcolm might like to come."

"He's been out most of the day, Miss. In fact, I should be getting back so that I'm there when he arrives." Davis lifted his creaky body from his seat. "You know, I don't think that boy would eat unless I made sure he did so. He's been very...preoccupied lately." He winked at Sam, and she felt her face redden. "It was lovely to meet you, Ms. Samantha." He took her hand and placed a chivalrous kiss on top of it. "Please don't hesitate to call on me if you require anything." On his way out, he leaned down and gave Nonie a sweet kiss on her cheek and a pat on her shoulder. "Good night, and take care of my girl." He shuffled his way out the door.

Sam sat in steely silence, staring at Nonie through squinted eyes. Nonie didn't flinch and sat quietly sipping her tea as though nothing odd had happened. Sam crossed her arms. "Okay, *Helen,* so how long have you been canoodling with old Davis?"

"I don't *canoodle*, missy. And if you want me to answer any of your questions, you will continue to call me Nonie, thank you very much." She sat back in her chair, crossing her arms, looking back at Samantha.

"Okay, Nonie." Sam raised her hands in defeat. "I'm sorry, but seriously, when did you and Davis start seeing each other? You know the hand-holding, the giggling."

"Let's just say Davis and I have common interests. After all, I needed a bridge partner, didn't I," she said with feigned innocence.

"Okay, a partner for your bridge game is one thing, but you two have clearly crossed the bridge."

"Very funny, smarty pants." Nonie gently swatted Sam's arm.

"Look, Nonie." Sam sighed. "I want you to be happy.

I really do. It's just going to take some getting used to that's all."

"I know. Believe me, dear, I never thought I'd have a relationship with anyone again. Your grandfather was the love of my life, and I always thought anyone else would pale in comparison."

"Davis doesn't?" Her question came out much more surprised than she meant it to.

"Oh no, he does." She chuckled. "But you see I'm not looking for a great love. I already had that. I had it for over fifty years with Pop. Davis and I are good friends. We had a common interest, and it evolved." She shrugged one thin shoulder. "What do you kids call it? Friends with benefits?"

Sam grimaced and held up her hand to stop Nonie from going into further detail. "Okay! I get it. He's a companion. Please don't tell me anymore." Sam squeezed her eyes shut and shuddered. "Ew."

Nonie laughed and took Sam's hands in hers. "All right now. All I'm trying to say is that I had my great love. He had his." Her wise eyes smiled back at Sam. "He was married, but she was taken from him so young. He's been lonely for more years than I can imagine. Davis is a friend, a good friend. Once you have your great love, nothing and no one can compare. Pop was the love of my life. Nothing will ever change that. Believe me my dear, someday you'll know exactly what I'm talking about."

Sam smiled and squeezed Nonie's hands. "Hey, you know what? I just realized something. We're both dating the neighbors in the creepy house."

"Speaking of which... Have you spoken with

Malcolm since your date last night?" Nonie got up to clear away their teacups.

"Well, yes actually," she said slowly.

Sam thought about the incident at the diner that day. She didn't want to tell Nonie about Roger's uninvited visit and erratic behavior. She knew that it would only upset her and make her worry. Besides after his run in with Malcolm she figured Roger was now permanently in the past and no longer an issue. But she knew that Millie would be spilling the beans about meeting Malcolm so she'd have to acknowledge it.

"He stopped by the diner... to say hello." Before Nonie could ask anything more about it Sam quickly added, "Nonie, if you don't mind, I'm going to finish unpacking and turn in. You know how lying in the sun for hours can take it out of you."

"All right, dear," she said hesitantly, "if you're sure."

"I am," she said with a weak smile. "Night, Nonie."

Sam placed a quick kiss on her cheek and went upstairs to shower and change for bed. She closed her eyes as she pulled herself up the steps trying to reconcile the latest piece of shocking news. "Nonie and Davis," she said a few times under her breath, as though the more she said it, the more she'd get used to it.

"Well, I'd know better than anybody that stranger things have happened," Sam mumbled as she went into her bedroom to change. She hated to admit it, but she couldn't wait to fall asleep and dream of Malcolm.

―∿―

Malcolm arrived home victorious with the necklace in his hand, and Davis was nowhere to be found. That made him nervous. Davis was always here. He had asked him to watch over Samantha; perhaps he was next door. Was she all right? Had something happened? Just as his stomach began to churn, he heard Davis come through the side door. He let out the breath he didn't even realize he'd been holding. "What is this woman doing to me?" he said under his breath.

"She's saving your life, that's what she's doing," Davis said loudly from the kitchen. "Not just your physical well-being, but your emotional life as well, sir. If you don't mind my saying so."

Malcolm shook his head and smiled. The guy still had the sharpest hearing of any human he knew. He knew that all Vasullus family members were special, but not all of them had this old bird's acute hearing. Still smiling, Malcolm walked into the large kitchen and held up the fruit of his labors. The little silver necklace glinted brightly in the cavernous gourmet kitchen. "I don't mind at all, Davis, because you're absolutely correct."

"You've found it, sir! Wonderful! Ms. Samantha will be so pleased." Davis began to putter around the kitchen, gathering together the ingredients for dinner.

"Speaking of Sam, did you see her?"

"Oh yes, sir. I got to meet her this evening. She's even prettier up close. Quite a beauty, that one. She had been out all afternoon with a friend. I didn't mind though." He winked. "It gave me time to be with Ms. Helen. She's a saucy old girl."

"Helen? Do you mean her grandmother?"

"Yes, sir."

"I didn't realize you two were friends," Malcolm said with some embarrassment. He'd cared for Malcolm's family's needs forever, and yet Malcolm realized he didn't know much about Davis at all. Davis had a girlfriend. Malcolm smirked. *The old dog.*

"Oh yes, sir. Good friends." He grinned mischievously. "She's my bridge partner too."

"Wait. Did you say Samantha was with a friend all day? What friend?" Could Roger have come back with Samantha's blessing? Malcolm battled something that resembled jealousy. He'd never been jealous in his life.

"Ms. Kerry Smithson." Davis put the pasta into the huge pot of boiling water on the enormous stainless steel stovetop.

Malcolm let his breath out, along with the tension that had so quickly bunched up in his shoulders. He scolded himself silently. How could he think for even one second that she'd be with Roger? He shook his head at his foolishness and rubbed the small bit of silver between his fingers.

"Her family has the house on the other side of Helen's. Have for generations, sir. As long as your family has had this house, I believe." Davis pinched salt into the pot.

"I see." Malcolm absentmindedly stared at the silver treasure in his hand. "No sign of that fellow I mentioned to you earlier? The Caedo?"

"No, sir. But I do think you should notify the Council about that. Perhaps Sir Richard or your uncle Brendan should come here to provide you both with some extra protection? At least until the mating ceremony has been completed," he added quickly.

"I know," Malcolm said quietly. "I was just so preoccupied with finding this necklace for her. Quite frankly,

I couldn't do anything else until I found it." Malcolm shook his head with a small smile. "You know, Davis, no one tells you how hard it is."

"How hard what is, sir?"

"This whole life mate thing. It may well do me in." He furrowed his brow.

"Ah yes." Davis smiled sadly. "Love of your life. We only get one of those. Even human beings, sir." He sprinkled basil and oregano into the sauce bubbling up in a neighboring pot. "Sadie was mine. I miss her every day," he said in a shaky voice. "She was taken from me so quickly, but I loved her a lifetime's worth." A pained expression came over him, and tears threatened behind his eyes. Malcolm knew that Davis didn't want to break down in front of him. The old boy cleared his throat and focused more intensely on the sauce.

"I'm sorry." Malcolm placed a strong hand on Davis's shoulder. He'd always felt a kinship with Davis, but now he truly could empathize. The idea of losing Samantha the way Davis had lost Sadie terrified him. He knew that if something happened to her, he wouldn't want to go on without her, and death would likely be a welcome relief.

"Not to worry, sir." Davis sniffled and cleared his throat in an attempt to dispel the sudden onset of emotion. "Will you be having your dinner in your office this evening?"

"No. I'll come in for it later. I've got to speak with Richard and Brendan about the man from the other night." Malcolm turned to go to his office. "Davis?"

"Yes, sir?"

"I almost forgot to ask. Did Samantha's paintings arrive?"

A large grin cracked Davis's wrinkled face, and he clapped his hands. "Yes, of course. I'm sorry sir. I forgot to tell you. Barkley had them hung throughout the house in the locations that you requested."

Malcolm smiled and took a deep breath. "Thank you, for everything. You know I don't think I've ever said that to you before."

"No worries, sir. You are more than welcome." Davis bowed slightly with a smile. Davis was only about five foot ten and looked like he'd been shrinking for the past couple of years. He stood in that kitchen with a sauce-stained apron over a crisp white shirt, his signature bow tie and pressed pants, and still managed to look like the most regal gentleman Malcolm had ever met.

Smiling, Malcolm walked into the living room. Sure enough, set perfectly centered above the large fireplace was Samantha's painting *Woman and the Wolf.* He suspected it was something of a self-portrait, although she probably didn't realize it yet. He closed his eyes and focused on the painting. A slow smile spread across his face as her energy signature slipped over him. He opened his mind and concentrated on finding the other paintings. Each sent out a tentacle of energy that was distinctly Samantha. He sucked a deep breath and took it all in. Her sweet warmth and quiet strength rippled over him like the summer ocean. He felt his own strength increase, and his eyes shifted abruptly.

"Perfect," he breathed. He knew that when she came into his home, she'd instantly feel at ease. Having her paintings here would give her the emotional equivalent of a blood transfusion.

Malcolm made his way back to his office with the

necklace clutched tightly in his hand. In the office, he gently placed the jewelry on top of his desk. He laid it out delicately so that the chain would stay free of tangles and snags. His smile faded as he thought about the man from last night. The confrontation with Roger was nothing compared to what could happen if this Caedo got to her. Malcolm knew deep down that the man watching them at Paddy's had been Caedo; there could be no other explanation. He'd reeked of hatred, bigotry, and rage. Malcolm hated to admit it, but he needed help. He wanted Samantha's transition into their world to be as trauma-free as possible. He couldn't possibly do that and devote his attention to seeking out the Caedo. No. He definitely needed help. His pride would have to take a backseat to her safety.

He stood in the center of the room, closed his eyes, and reached out to Richard and his uncle Brendan at the same time. He focused on creating a mental link with both men and did it with much better speed than he had in a long time.

Richard and Brendan, I need to speak with you both. I am certain that the Caedo have found us once again, and I believe we are being hunted.

Within moments, both Richard and Brendan materialized on either side of him. He immediately turned and embraced his uncle. Anyone could tell that the two men were related, although they looked more like brothers. Brendan was over one hundred years old. As with all Amoveo, the aging process slowed significantly once he'd found his mate. His uncle was also just over six feet tall with chestnut hair, although he kept his longer and tied back in a low ponytail at the base of his neck.

The most obvious physical difference between the two men was their eyes. Brendan's were almost black. He was his mother's brother and a member of the Kodiak Bear Clan.

It was unknown which clan a child would favor until adolescence. In addition to the challenges of human physical changes, Amoveos also undergo their first shift to their animal form at the onset of puberty. Malcolm knew his father was very proud that his son favored the Eagle Clan and would often give Brendan a hard time about it. Brendan and his mate, Sophia, of the Fox Clan, had twins. His daughter, Mariana, favored the Bear, while her twin, Dante, was of the Fox Clan.

"Hello, Nephew. I see Davis is still feeding you well. Good God, you are a big fellow." Brendan released Malcolm from a good old bear hug.

"Good to see you, Uncle Brendan. And you as well Richard." Malcolm turned to shake his friend's hand. "Thank you both for coming so quickly. Let's go into the living room."

Malcolm gestured toward the doorway and allowed the Prince to lead the way.

The three men entered the room, and Brendan stopped short. His gaze was fixed on the painting above the fireplace. "Is that hers?" he asked quietly.

Malcolm puffed up with pride. "Yes." He smiled and stood next to his uncle and admired his mate's work. "It's quite good isn't it?"

Brendan nodded slowly. "Her father, Lucas Logan, was quite a talented artist as well. Wasn't he?" He delivered a sideways glance to Malcolm and crossed his arms over his chest. "It's interesting. Her artistic abilities don't seem to be diluted at all. It will be interesting to see if her Amoveo talents are as strong or if they're diluted also."

"Diluted?" Malcolm's body tensed, and he eyed his uncle.

"Well, she is a hybrid Malcolm. We've never had one before. We don't know what she'll be capable of," Richard interrupted and sat in the large leather chair next to the fireplace.

Malcolm's eyes narrowed. "I see," he said quietly. He instantly felt defensive. She was his mate. Hybrid or not, she was Amoveo. He felt some anxiety coming from Richard, but Brendan was a blank slate. Nothing.

Brendan slapped his shoulder and let out a short laugh. "Easy nephew, remember we're all here for the same reason."

Malcolm searched Brendan's face and found the same smiling eyes he'd seen all his life. Some of the tension left his body, and he ran his hand through his hair with some embarrassment. "I know," he breathed. "Please Uncle, sit down."

Richard's sharp eyes stayed fixed on the two men, and he cleared his throat. They seated themselves on the brown leather sofa across from him. "I filled Brendan and the Council in on the earlier issue you had with the dream interloper. As you can imagine, we are all concerned for you and your mate," Richard said solemnly. His sharp gaze flicked between Brendan and Malcolm. "You are a very unusual coupling. The truth is that your mating could hold the key to our race not only surviving, but thriving in the future. It is in everyone's best interest that you are protected. Brendan and a few of the others have been researching to see if we can find other humans like Samantha and her mother."

"What happened last night?" Brendan interrupted.

"As I'm sure Richard delighted in telling you," he began tensely. "I took Samantha out on a date." He put his hand up to stifle any comments. "Yes, before you say anything, like a human."

"I didn't say a word." Brendan smiled, his hands up in a position of surrender.

Malcolm shot him a look of warning. "At any rate, we were listening to the music, and I suddenly felt this hatred. It rolled throughout the entire crowd in waves. I saw a man. He was definitely tracking Sam. I reached out to read him, and he blocked me," Malcolm said with strangled frustration. He quickly waved his hand, and a fire burst to life in the fireplace next to Richard. He needed to put his anger somewhere, and the fireplace was as good a place as any.

"He blocked you?" Richard leaned forward in his chair. "He's a telepath," he said with disbelief.

"Apparently," Malcolm murmured and stared into the fire.

"Well, we have heard rumors that the Caedo have been actively trying to develop certain psychic abilities. I must say the ability to block a telepathic probe is a good one," Brendan said quietly.

Richard stood and paced restlessly in front of the fire, clearly concerned with this latest development. "Good for them, bad for us." His apprehension flowed through the room and over both men. Malcolm and Brendan exchanged a look. There wasn't much that rattled the Prince. "One of our major advantages was being able to ferret out what their plans were by searching their minds. But if they've learned to block that, then we really are flying blind."

Brendan turned his attention to Malcolm. "You've got to take her away from here, Malcolm. You should bring her to one of our safe houses. They've found you both and will surely make a move on you sooner than later." He laid a hand on Malcolm's shoulder and gave it a squeeze.

"Absolutely not," Malcolm said. His golden eyes glittered with determination. "Her grandmother is everything to her. I can't possibly take her away now. Besides she still doesn't know... well... anything, really. I'm just beginning to gain her trust, and I can't very well take her away from everything she knows."

Silence hung between the men. Malcolm's mind wandered to Roger and the way he'd tried to force himself and his very presence on Sam. He would never make her do anything against her will. His gaze flicked back to Brendan. "No," he said adamantly, "we've got to find another option."

Richard stood still, silently staring into the fire, his hands clasped behind his back. He glanced back over his shoulder at the two warriors behind him. "I agree with Brendan," he said firmly.

Malcolm's heart sank. Richard was the leader of their people, an ancient one, and everyone followed his instructions without question. That was how they'd managed to stay safe for so many years.

"However, Malcolm is in very difficult and uncharted waters here. It is not a usual mating situation at all. Samantha is going to have a lot to accept in the coming days, and I agree that moving her now would cause more harm than good."

Relief and gratitude washed over Malcolm. "Thank you, Richard."

"My Prince, with all due respect, I disagree," Brendan added quickly.

Richard held up his right hand and glanced sharply at Brendan, silencing him with a look from his now shifted golden, lion eyes. Richard was the Prince, and his orders were to be followed without question, especially in times of battle. Malcolm was surprised that Brendan would even think of contradicting Richard at a time like this.

Brendan bowed his head. "As you wish," he said tightly.

Malcolm stood up and nodded with respect to Richard. "My gratitude."

Richard gave a quick nod and turned to Malcolm's uncle. "Brendan. I want you to go back and convene the Council immediately. Inform them of the latest news. We will gather three warriors to help protect them. Your son Dante, William of the Falcon Clan, and Steven of the Coyote Clan." He turned stoically to Malcolm. "These three will be watchful eyes for you. They will guard you and your mate until the mating rite is complete. Once she has full understanding of the situation, you can take her to one of our safe houses until we can find the source of this threat."

Malcolm nodded his acceptance and thanks.

"Brendan, please do as I ask. I will join you there shortly."

Brendan accepted the order with a curt nod. He then turned and looked somberly at Malcolm. "Good-bye, Nephew. You know I wish only the best for you." With that, he uttered the ancient words and vanished into the air.

Malcolm and Richard walked outside to the deck in a shroud of silence.

Richard stood stone still and crossed his arms over his broad chest. He stared out over the seemingly endless ocean before them.

Malcolm could sense the apprehension coming from his mentor. It floated over him with the spray of the salty sea air. "I can feel your concern for us, Richard." Malcolm stood quietly next to him, his hands behind his back, like a soldier with his commander. "I have to admit, I feel much better knowing that three of our finest warriors will be here to watch my back and watch over my mate. Especially my cousin Dante, he is fiercely protective. I am eternally grateful for all of your help."

Richard didn't respond immediately, merely kept watching the moon dance on the water.

Malcolm sensed he was choosing his words with great care.

"I am concerned for you and Samantha on many levels. Your mating is definitely an oddity among our people and one that may be difficult for some to understand. Are you ready for what may follow?"

Malcolm cocked his head and narrowed his eyes questioningly. "I'm not exactly sure what you mean by that."

"Never mind." Richard waved it off. "Let's deal with the threat at hand. I will contact you as soon as we've updated the Council. I'm sure your brothers in arms will contact you once they arrive." He offered a strained smile. "Just remember, these three men aren't mated yet."

"That is worrisome given that they are already well into their twenties." Malcolm furrowed his brow. He, more than anyone, could empathize with their situation because it was exactly where he had been until not too long ago. He shuddered slightly at the memory of the emptiness he'd felt before finding Samantha.

"True, and unfortunately that seems to be a growing problem with our young people," Richard said absently. Then he turned to Malcolm with a mischievous smile. "The upside is that it makes them even more ferocious warriors."

Malcolm nodded in agreement and extended his hand to Richard. "I look forward to receiving news of their arrival." He shook Richard's hand firmly and solemnly held his gaze. "Thank you, Richard, for everything."

"Be well, my friend." Richard vanished into the late summer breeze.

Malcolm turned his attention to Samantha's window next door. Her light was out, and he knew now was the time. He reached out and touched her mind with his. He could feel her distress, and it was killing him. He would bring her the necklace and open her up to a world she had only dreamed of. He knew that she needed more time, but that was a luxury they didn't have. He went to the office to get her cross. He prayed silently to himself that she would accept him and the fate that lay before them both.

He'd watched her all day on the deck of her friend's house. She was so vulnerable just lying there out in the open. He'd had a clear shot and contemplated taking it, but that would've been way too easy. Besides that, his partner would've been really pissed. The more he watched her, the more he understood the creature's attraction to her. She was gorgeous with all that golden hair, her full breasts, and womanly rounded hips. Maybe he'd take her and show her what a real man could do before he killed her. She was half animal, but mostly a woman. He knew it was wrong to want her since she was tainted, but no one would have to know.

Her friend was beautiful too, a model. The kind of girl that made fun of guys like Tony and thought they were too good for him. He hated girls like that. They'd made fun of him his whole life. Maybe he'd kill her too, just for fun. The stupid bitch deserved it.

He started to get hard thinking about killing both, and he reached down to stroke himself. His fantasy was interrupted by the shrill of his cell phone. "Yeah," he barked, failing to hide his annoyance at being interrupted.

"Are you watching her?"

"No, I'm baking a fuckin' cake. Yes, of course I'm watching her."

"If I were you, I'd watch the tone you take with me. It may appear that we're on equal ground. But I assure you it only appears that way," said the icy cold voice at the other end of the phone.

"Sorry." Tony felt like a scolded child. "I've just been feeling a little frustrated. Y'know. Not being able to take them out and all."

"You'll soon get what you want. We are running out of time. Her abilities are beginning to develop so we've got to move quickly. If they have a chance to perform the mating ritual, she will be much stronger, and he will be practically unstoppable."

"Relax! Her eyes shifted, that's all."

"No, you moron. That's not all," his partner hissed over the line. "She's begun to communicate with him telepathically, and their connections in the dream realm are getting stronger. You will finish them soon. Wait for my call, and I'll give you the details. In the meantime—"

"Don't let the bitch out of my sight. Yeah, yeah I know." Tony snapped the phone shut. He picked up his binoculars and peered up at her bedroom window. He watched her while she brushed out her wet hair. She was wearing nothing but a bathrobe. As soon as she shut out the light, he would pack it in for the night. His partner had one major advantage that Tony did not, the ability to walk the dream realm. The nights were out of his hands, and that only pissed him off more.

Chapter 12

SAMANTHA LAY IN HER BED, ENVELOPED IN DARKNESS, but sleep eluded her. She touched the empty spot at the base of her throat, wishing she had her necklace, wishing Malcolm was there with her. She turned onto her side and stared out at the moon and stars, which lit up the night sky. Samantha hadn't seen Malcolm or heard from him since he'd walked out of the diner. She remembered the way she'd heard him in her head and the breathtaking way her body responded from that intimate connection.

I'm going nuts.

She threw her arms across her eyes. She was terrified because she needed to see him. There was an aching emptiness in her chest that Sam knew only Malcolm could fill. She lay there wishing he would come to her and bring the necklace as he'd promised. She was thoroughly confused by the events over the past few days, dreaming of him, hearing him in her mind. The irrational attachment she felt was more disturbing to her than anything else. She craved that feeling she had when she was with him. Connected. Alive. For the first time in her life she felt alive. It was as if he'd awakened her, and she'd been sleepwalking until the day she'd met him.

Christ, she actually *craved* him. Like a fat kid craves cake. Her sanity was slipping away by the second. She had always prided herself on her ability to be rational, never getting caught up in romantic notions like so many of her friends had. *Well, so much for that.*

Samantha.

She heard Malcolm whisper along the edges of her mind. His voice was deep and hypnotic, a seductive caress that tickled her inside and out. She sucked in an unsteady breath.

Get out of my head. This is crazy. Yet even as she sent that message to him, her body betrayed her. Her nipples peaked and tightened; her womb clenched as heat pooled low in her belly. She sucked in a quick breath and squeezed her eyes shut. Sam tried desperately to fight the tears that pricked the back of her eyes. She had absolutely no control over her body's reaction to him.

She heard a scratching sound and opened her eyes. Through the fluttering ivory panels at her window, she saw the hulking bird who had visited her the other day.

Sam lay there completely still and kept her wide eyes fixed on her feathered visitor. She was unsure whether to scream or pinch herself to see if she was awake. They stared at one another, neither moving. Sam fought the overwhelming urge to cry out for her grandmother, like a child.

The bird finally cocked its head to one side and made a small squawk, as though it was saying hello. Sam jumped slightly. She opened her mouth to say "shoo" or something, but her eye was immediately caught by a glinting at the animal's beak. Her breath caught in her throat. Mustering up her courage, she sat up slowly and pushed aside the cotton sheets. Her bare feet touched the cool wood floors, confirming that she was indeed awake. The late summer breeze hit her arms as the sheer curtains fluttered around the magnificent bird.

Bird? No, that didn't even seem like an appropriate word to describe it. A bird was a sparrow or a crow, something ordinary. This creature was far from ordinary. It was majestic. Raptor. Wasn't that what birds of prey were called? Sam swallowed hard, and her gaze flicked down to the massive talons that were wrapped around her windowsill. Yes, that was much more fitting.

She stood carefully, not feeling completely steady on her feet. Squinting, she looked closely at what it had in its beak. Sam froze. Disbelief flooded her, and she licked her lips nervously. Dangling from this eagle's beak was her silver cross.

Sam reached out and hesitantly approached the magnificent creature before her. "Shhhh. It's okay," she whispered, inching slowly toward the bird. She repeated this mantra in hushed tones as she moved closer, wondering if she was saying it for the bird or herself. After what seemed like an eternity, she finally had her trembling hand under its beak. The bird promptly dropped the delicate silver strand into her quivering palm. It looked at Sam with those piercing yellow eyes that had become oddly familiar. She stared back at the bird and closed her fingers around her reclaimed heirloom. The silver felt cool against her hot skin.

Sam didn't know what to do next. *Do I say thank you?*

Then she heard Malcolm answer her in her mind.

You're welcome.

Sam's head snapped up, and she looked at the bird in her window. "Malcolm," she said in a small, shaking voice.

Unblinking, he just sat there looking at Samantha. She stared back at him with a mixture of fear and wonder. He looked into her dark blue eyes, and her lips trembled. She swallowed hard.

I told you I'd bring you your necklace, and I always keep my promises.

With that thought, the gigantic bird spread his golden wings and shimmered as if she was looking at it underwater. The air around them thickened, and the entire room crackled with something akin to static electricity, causing every hair on Samantha's body to stand on end.

Within seconds, Malcolm stood before her in his human form.

Sam stared at him, her mouth wide open, something that resembled a silent scream. She backed away. Her legs hit the mattress, and she abruptly sat down, bouncing on the edge of the bed. She slowly shook her head with disbelief. Her brain couldn't quite grasp what she had just witnessed.

The eagle was gone and replaced by Malcolm. He towered above her, all six feet, four inches of him. He was a solid wall of muscle. His face was sharp edges. His eyes glowed—the eyes of the eagle—like two yellow embers, and seemed to bore right through her. "No way." She still shook her head. "This is not possible. What the hell are you?" she whispered.

He blinked, and his eyes shifted back to their human state. His features softened, and he slowly knelt down in front of her. His large hands swallowed hers in tender warmth, the cross clutched tightly in her fist. Initially, she stiffened at his touch, but he did not retreat. He held her gaze and continued to kneel before her, waiting for her to relax and absorb all that she had seen. They stayed there for several moments as she searched his eyes for some kind of answer. Slowly, he pried her fingers open and revealed the silver treasure.

Silently, Malcolm took the necklace and reached around her neck. She closed her eyes and breathed in his distinctly male scent. Sam held her breath as he hooked the small clasp at the back of her neck.

His breath was warm and moist on her skin. She shivered slightly. Sam could barely breathe, let alone move, as he returned the necklace to its rightful home. He leaned back on his bare feet and carefully adjusted the small cross at the hollow of her throat. She tried desperately to steady her breathing before she spoke. She opened her mouth to begin the inevitable line of questioning, but Malcolm placed a finger over her lips. Then achingly, he brushed his thumb along her bottom lip. This small movement sent little licks of fire skittering up her belly.

He never took his eyes from hers, and she searched them desperately for answers. Samantha reached up and placed her hand over his. She closed her eyes and leaned into his touch.

This was real.

His warm flesh pressed against hers, his hard belly brushed ever so gently against her knees as he knelt before her. She kissed his palm and opened her eyes slowly. He was absolutely beautiful. His eyes shifted and glowed bright yellow. She sensed that he wanted to tell her more, to explain everything, but all she could think about was the taste of him. She licked her lips quickly, and her gaze flicked down to his firm lips.

Then one word thundered into her mind. He practically growled it.

Mate.

He cupped her face with both hands and took possession of her mouth. A rush of desire flooded her body, and her lips responded eagerly to his. As his lips seared hers and their tongues danced, he whispered that word over and over again.

Mate.

She was his. Malcolm gathered her hair in his hands and angled her head back so he could delve deeper into the silken darkness of her mouth. She wrapped her arms around his neck and lay back on the bed, pulling him down with her, wrapping her leg around his as he settled between her thighs. He covered her body effortlessly with his, his desire hot and heavy, begging to be released from the confines of his jeans. Pressed against her feminine core, he could feel her damp and needy. Sam thought she might come apart.

She reached up under his white T-shirt and raked her nails over his back. She relished the way his muscles rippled just beneath the skin. She was hungry for him, needed to feel him as close to her as possible. She pulled the shirt over his head. The sight of his beautifully muscled chest over her caused her to draw in a sharp breath. She tossed the shirt hastily aside. He rained kisses down her neck and into the valley between her breasts, all the while tangling his hands in the length of her hair. She was shocked at the intensity of her own desire. It was building up inside her, cresting somewhere between pleasure and pain. She clung to him, her breath coming in ragged gasps. She wondered if it was possible to be addicted to another person. She held his head to her breast as he nuzzled and pushed away the thin cotton of her nightgown.

Their hands roamed freely over each other, fingers exploring, lips discovering. He took the rosy peak of her nipple in his mouth and suckled. He lavished attention on her breasts, and small cries of pleasure escaped her lips. Her need increased as his mind connected with hers, and his voice slid into her head. *I may go mad with wanting you.*

She knew he was doing all he could to maintain control, and the sounds of her pleasure were probably driving him to the brink.

He plundered her mouth, one hand cradling her head, and the other sliding down her rib cage into the dip of her waist. He reached beneath her and grabbed her bottom, pressing her harder against him.

He whispered softly, "I need to feel your skin beneath mine." He grabbed the top of her nightgown, and with very little effort, tore the offending fabric from Samantha's body.

He looked down, feasting on the sight of her. Her eyes tingled, and she knew that they'd shifted into wolf's eyes. His glowed brightly back at her and were glazed with desire. In that moment she knew that she could trust him. This man, this incredibly unusual man, would never do anything to harm her.

―❦―

Her lips were pink and swollen from his kisses, her hair tousled around her head like a golden halo. He brushed his knuckles lightly across her breast, down her rib cage, and ran his fingers across the quivering muscles of her flat belly. His gaze wandered back up to see the ice blue eyes of the wolf.

He leaned in and greedily devoured her lips with his, enjoying the feeling of her silky soft skin against his. She gratefully returned his kiss with eagerness, holding his face in her hands. Malcolm ventured down, sliding his fingers under the edge of her satin panties. He found her wet and ready for him. She pushed and bucked against his hand. She moaned her pleasure along their now fused lips. He struggled for restraint as he plunged two fingers into her and was greeted with another surge of wetness. He wanted nothing more than to bury himself deep inside her, but he couldn't claim her as his mate until she knew everything.

She writhed against him, holding his head in her hands, eagerly exploring his mouth with hers. She was completely lost. Sam felt the exquisite pleasure building up and taking her over the edge. The orgasm tore through her body mercilessly. Cries of pleasure muffled against Malcolm's mouth as wave after wave rippled through her body and carried her into oblivion.

Breathless, Samantha lay there for several minutes, curled up in the crook of Malcolm's arm, trying to calm her breathing. She wanted to say something smart or witty, but all she could muster was, "Wow."

Malcolm smiled and kissed the top of her head. He pulled her closer and covered them both with the comforter from the foot of the bed.

She looked at him in the moonlight and saw that he still had his eagle eyes. She stroked his forehead ever so lightly with her fingertips.

Malcolm closed his eyes at the almost unbearable tenderness she showed him. He knew that he was lost to her. Mating ceremony or no mating ceremony, he was hooked.

Sam dropped her hand and chuckled softly. She lifted the covers and had a look. "So how is it that you managed to keep your pants on, and I'm basically naked?"

"You have pants on." He smiled slyly.

"I don't think this scrap of underwear actually counts as pants." She held the covers over her naked breasts.

"I was trying to be a gentleman." He was completely serious.

"Really? Well, if tonight was you being a gentleman, I don't know if I'll survive your version of a cad." She smacked his chest. She sat up, looking around for her nightgown. Spotting it, she slid from the bed, snatched up what was left of it, and put it on as fast as she could.

He watched her, puzzled by her sudden modesty.

She pulled the ripped neckline tightly across her chest and folded her hands over her breasts. She looked silently out over the crashing waves below for several minutes.

Although his instinct was to go to her, he gave her the space she needed.

Sam turned around and sat on the windowsill, staring at him through narrowed eyes. "So do you want to tell me what you are? Or do I have to guess?"

"What do you think I am?" He didn't take his gaze off her for a moment.

"Well, you're not a vampire. Although I may have a hickey or two, you didn't suck my blood."

"Correct. Not a vampire." He sat on the edge of the bed.

"Alien?" She raised an eyebrow.

"No." He smiled. "Our people have been here as long as humans have. We are an indigenous people. Just like humans."

"Nope. Not just like humans. We don't turn into birds, or have our eyes change into weird colors," Samantha said in a tone that sounded slightly hysterical.

"You do." He folded his arms across his bare chest.

"I do not turn into a bird." She laughed nervously. He knew she tried to keep her voice down. The last they needed was Nonie waking up and finding him in her room. "And we're not talking about me. We're talking about you. So, if you're not a vampire or an alien, what the hell are you?"

He could tell she was struggling to maintain her composure. Her determined little chin tilted up at him defiantly. She was feeling pretty defensive, and he couldn't blame her. This was not exactly something normal for her. He knew that he just had to tell her. Rip off the Band-Aid so to speak.

"I am Amoveo." He sat up just a bit taller. "We are an ancient race of shapeshifters. There are ten clans among our race. I am of the Eagle Clan, a golden eagle, as you've seen."

"Uh-huh," she muttered with skepticism.

"Shall I continue?"

"Oh, I am all ears. Please go on." Sam waved her hand. "This should be good."

"All Amoveo are shifters. We can communicate telepathically. We have the power of visualization. Once we are mated, we age much slower than humans and live considerably longer. The older we get, the more powerful we become."

"Anything else?"

"Yes. We can travel at the speed of thought."

"Ah ha." Sam pointed at him. "That guy did just vanish from your balcony the other day! I knew it! I didn't just blink and miss his exit."

"Yes. That was Richard, our Prince."

"Well, at least I didn't imagine it." She rubbed her temples and sat back down. "A Prince, huh? Okay so this whole Amoveo thing sounds good. You guys seem to have it made. You've got pretty good powers. You don't really age. Not a bad deal."

"Unfortunately we are not without our own set of problems. We've lived in secret for centuries because we are being hunted."

"Hunted? By who?"

"The Caedo." A shadow passed over his stone-like features.

"The Caedo? Who are they?" Sam's brows knitted in concern.

"They are one of only two groups of humans that know about us. They've made it their family's mission to annihilate our race."

"Why? Did you eat their babies or something?"

"Don't be ridiculous." He stood swiftly and threw his shirt back on. "We are peaceful. The Caedo, like so many *humans* throughout history, fear what is different and what they don't understand."

"Okay, so they killed a few of you over the years."

"You don't understand, Samantha." He loomed over her.

His frustration mixed in the air with her fear and uncertainty and created a volatile force in the room. Sam

grew pale, wavered slightly, and braced herself against
the wall with one hand. He scolded himself silently. He
wouldn't make this any easier on her by getting frustrated. He took a deep breath and focused on sending
her a sense of calm. A flicker of confusion came over
her face, and she relaxed slightly as he soothed her, the
color returning to her cheeks.

Better.

"All Amoveos are born into this world with one predestined soul mate, and we can only have children with
our mate. When they kill one of us, they kill off potential
offspring." He looked away from her. "For all of our
strengths, we are actually a rather fragile race."

"Okay. So how do you find this 'mate'?" She made
air quotes with her fingers.

"From the time we are born, we are taught to look for
our mate in the dream realm. Once we connect there,
we can connect in the physical realm and complete the
mating ceremony. If we do not find our mate by our
thirtieth birthday, we begin to lose our abilities, and we
eventually die."

"That sucks," Sam said. "Actually, I know a lot of
human women who feel that way about being single
in their thirties." She chuckled wryly. "So where's
your mate?"

"Right here." He took her delicate hand in his.

"What!" She snatched her hand back from him and
quickly walked around to the other side of the bed.
"You said you had to mate with another Amoveo." Sam
pointed at him accusingly.

"True."

"Well. *I* am not Amoveo. I'm just your good

old-fashioned, run-of-the-mill human," Sam said, not really believing it. Until recently, she never would've doubted it.

"Well actually, you're both."

"I beg your pardon?" A look of dread came over her, and she wrapped her arms tightly across her chest.

"You are a hybrid, the only one that we know of. Your mother was human, but your father was an Amoveo. Lucas Logan was of the Wolf Clan."

"So you're telling me my father was a dog?"

"No," he said, exasperated. "Lucas was a member of the Gray Wolf Clan bloodline. And so are you."

"You're crazy," she scoffed. "I am not a wolf."

"Really? Had any good dreams lately?" He didn't take his gaze from her shocked face.

"Oh my God. It's you. You're the one who's been calling me. The voice in the house." Tears glittered in her eyes as all the pieces came together. "The wolf dreams. All of it," she whispered.

"You are the only one of your kind." Malcolm slowly approached her around the bed. He kept his voice steady as he continued. "Your parents' mating was the first known pairing between a human and an Amoveo. From what we know, your mother possessed some psychic abilities. That's the only way she could possibly have paired with an Amoveo."

"This is insane." Tears swam in her deep blue eyes. He knew that her mind scrambled to make sense of his words.

"Humans and Amoveos are from the same origins. We're just two different branches on the same family tree. It was only a matter of time before our two races evolved enough to mix." He kept talking quietly, all the while moving closer, and closing the distance between them. "Think about it, Samantha. The dream you had before you decided to come home—that was the first time I connected with you. I finally found you and called you here to me." He reached out and wrapped her delicate body in his arms. He held her to his chest and kissed the top of her head. She didn't embrace him but kept her arms folded over her breasts. He was just happy she didn't flinch and that she allowed him to hold her.

Her confusion wounded him deep in his soul. Now, more than ever, he felt the connection to her, and it terrified him. The idea that she would reject him alarmed him beyond all reason.

"We've walked in the dream realm together several times now. That was how I knew your necklace was lost. Remember?" He stroked her long silky hair and rocked her gently.

Sam leaned her forehead on Malcolm's chest and let the tears fall silently. Finally, she pushed at him, and reluctantly he released her from his hold. She sniffled and wiped the tears away with the back of her hands, trying to pull herself together. "Okay. So all of the crazy dreams I've had in my life and the weird things that have been happening since I got home… You're telling me this has all been part of some elaborate matchmaking scheme by the universe?" Her confusion was now replaced by anger. "All of these things that have started happening to me since I met you… this is your fault."

"Your abilities have obviously been dormant, and now that we've connected they'll continue to come out. I suppose you could blame me." He shrugged.

"That's fine if it will make you feel better. I'll help you, Samantha. I can show you how to control your gifts."

"Well, that's just great." She shoved his chest, but he didn't move. She may as well have been shoving at a brick wall. "So what? Now I'm going to sprout fur and get fangs? No thanks! You can keep your *gifts*. I want no part of this."

Malcolm stood there watching Sam's reaction, amused. She was even more beautiful when she got angry. Her eyes flashed at him, and her chin set in determined defiance. Malcolm could see that he would never be bored with his mate. She was one feisty woman.

"Don't be ridiculous. You are Amoveo. You are my mate, Samantha. I am yours. This cannot be questioned or changed. It simply *is*." He reached out and brushed the hair from her forehead.

———

Much to Sam's dismay, her body's reaction betrayed her, and Malcolm knew it. He leaned toward her, and she stiffened, helpless to the power he seemed to have over her. He tipped her chin up with his fingers and brushed his lips softly over hers. It was a featherlight touch that she felt all the way down to her toes. It took every ounce of resolve she had not to kiss him back. Her eyes tingled, shifted to their wolf state, and remained locked on his in a look of utter defiance. Malcolm flashed that arrogant grin, which reduced her insides to jelly.

He took a few steps back, tilted his head back, spread his arms wide, and whispered, "Verto." Instantly, the air in the room thickened and crackled. Malcolm shimmered and shifted into the huge Golden Eagle. With a shriek, he flapped his massive wings and swooped out the window into the night.

Sam looked out after him. He was silhouetted against the enormous moon looming high above the white-capped ocean. She closed her eyes as the breeze brushed her hair back. Instinctively, she touched her necklace. It was once again thankfully at the base of her throat, but the comfort she sought eluded her. When Sam opened her eyes, Malcolm was nowhere in sight.

She pulled the window closed and lay down in the welcoming cloud of her bed. She silently prayed that sleep would claim her. His scent still clung to the pillow. She breathed it in. It was familiar and unsettling at the same time. She replayed the information he'd told her in her head. The last thing she heard before drifting into a fitful sleep was Malcolm. He whispered along the edges of her mind.

Sleep well, mia piccola lupa.

Chapter 13

THE NEXT MORNING, SAM WOKE UP EXHAUSTED. HER sleep had been dreamless and fitful. She couldn't stop thinking about everything Malcolm had revealed to her the night before. As the sun began to rise, she knew lying in bed tossing and turning was getting her nowhere. She decided the best way to clear her muddied brain was to go for a run.

She looked in the mirror and couldn't believe how puffy her eyes were. *Well, at least they're my eyes.* Sam threw her hair into a ponytail and got into her running clothes. She was shocked that none of their *conversation* from last night had awakened Nonie. If it had, she was kind enough not to bang on the walls. Sam's cheeks reddened at the very thought of it.

She tiptoed downstairs to the kitchen and chugged a quick glass of orange juice before she headed out. Sam did her warm up and listened to all of the sounds around her, the gulls shrieking, the ocean, and even the gravel crunching under her Nikes. She wanted to focus on normal sounds, not the insane story he'd told her and shown her. Yet no matter how hard she tried, she couldn't stop thinking about it.

"What a crock. Amoveo. Shapeshifters. Right." She shook her head as she walked down to the beach.

It is not a crock and deep down you know who and what you really are. The sooner you accept that, Samantha, the better off we'll both be.

She stopped dead in her tracks as Malcolm's voice invaded her head. Now she was really getting pissed. Who did this guy think he was? Can't a girl have any privacy?

Get out of my head and leave me alone. Her fists curled up tightly at her side. She wasn't even sure if she was doing it right.

You're being silly, Samantha. His usual smug confidence seeped through.

She could picture the smirk on his face and had the sudden urge to smack it off. The man was completely infuriating. *Fine. You can call me whatever you want. Just leave me alone. I'm going for a run, and I'd like to do that without you in my head.*

You should not be out alone. It's not safe.

Oh please. I think you scared Roger off for good. Look, spare me the caveman routine, bird boy. Sam rolled her eyes and continued to make her way onto the beach.

I will go with you then.

No you won't. Good-bye. I'm hanging up now. Or... whatever. She stood with hands set on her hips. She listened for a reply, but was met with silence. She gave a sharp nod, feeling rather pleased for getting her way. "Jeez, what an ego." She began her jog along the shore.

Sam loved running on the beach early in the morning. Usually there weren't too many people around, especially on a weekday morning. Today the sand along the edge of the ocean was packed nice and tight. It was perfect for running and much easier on the knees than pavement. She kept thinking about all of the things she'd experienced. She hated to admit it, but his story was getting harder and harder to deny. Her dreams were pretty solid proof.

She had several about being a wolf, running on this very beach. How would he know that? She dreamed of being with that eagle, with Malcolm. It was true that nothing was known about her father. He had no family they knew of, and her parents' courtship had been extremely brief. They'd only known each other a few weeks before they were married. Could her mother have been psychic? Was Nonie? She did know about stuff before it actually happened. She always had an uncanny sense of what was needed. As Sam approached the halfway mark of her run, she realized that Nonie might know much more than she'd let on.

Samantha's run seemed longer than normal, and she was beginning to feel nauseous. After what felt like forever, she reached her halfway mark at the jetty. Gratefully, she turned to head back to the house, hoping the second half would go by more quickly, and her stomach would settle down. As she jogged by the beach club, she heard someone calling her name. She looked over and saw Millie, perched in her beach chair underneath an enormous plaid umbrella.

"Hey, Sammy girl." She waved.

Sam didn't really want to stop and lose her momentum, but for Millie she could make an exception. Millie was surrounded by various sand toys, a cooler, and a few chairs. There was an adorable little boy playing at her feet. He couldn't have been more than a year old. He was bald as a cue ball with big brown eyes in a spectacularly chubby face. His entire body was covered in sand. He was deeply engaged in eating a shovel.

"Come on now. Don't eat that. You'll be poopin' sand castles all week long." Millie hoisted the boy and tried in vain to free him of his sandy snack.

"Hey, Millie." Sam tried to catch her breath. "Is this your grandson? He's adorable."

"This is my little man. They're all stayin' at my place right now. Y'know, while they finish some renovations on their apartment." She plopped him back down on the blanket and brushed him off a bit. "Well, this little bugger gets up so damn early. This morning I just had to get us all outta there. Too nice to be hanging around inside, and Lord knows we spend enough time in the diner."

"So you really did it? You closed the diner?" Sam said in disbelief. She leaned on her knees, still trying to calm her breathing.

"Hell yes." She winked.

"Is Billy here too?" Sam looked around.

"Yeah. He's up at the cabana getting a bottle out of the fridge for our boy here." She glanced to the large white building behind them.

"So your grandmamma tells me she met your new man too." Millie smiled briefly. "I liked him lots better than that city fella. I hope you're not seeing him anymore."

"No ma'am."

"Well, I like that big handsome devil." She wiggled her eyebrows. "Your grandmamma told me that y'all are going out again."

"Oh really? Well, no secrets around here, huh?" She raised her eyebrows and thought desperately for another topic to talk about. "I guess you already knew about Nonie's new man though."

"You mean Davis?" She laughed. "He's a fine fella.

Good card player too. You know, she wanted to tell you about it, but I think she felt funny. Y'know, she didn't want you to think she was replacing Jack, your pop."

"I know. It's just going to take some getting used to." She squatted down and brushed some sand off the baby's arms.

"Where in the name of Davy Crockett is Billy?" Millie looked behind her. "He's takin' a dog's age up there getting that bottle."

"Well, tell him I said *hi*." Sam stood and felt another wave of nausea.

"You okay, Sammy girl? You look a little green around the gills."

"Yeah, I haven't gone for a run for a few weeks. I guess I pushed it too hard today."

Millie shook her head. "I told you. You young girls are so worried about being skinny. Not good for ya." She winked.

Sam laughed softly. "I'll keep that in mind. Well, I've got to get back. I'm working on a portrait for Nonie, and I really want to get it finished today. Bye, little guy," Sam said to the sandy little cherub. She was rewarded with a big drool-filled smile and giggles.

Malcolm had gone out to his balcony and watched Samantha as she began her run. He was very concerned about the Caedo from the other night. Guilt reared its ugly head. She thought the danger he referred to was Roger, and he did nothing to make her think otherwise. Malcolm scoffed audibly. As if that runt was any match for him. He realized that he'd made a mistake to keep the information about the Caedo from her. However, if she knew how dangerous her situation was, she'd never willingly give herself to him. It would make the world of his people even more terrifying. He wanted to respect her wishes, but her safety was more important than anything else.

He visualized his eagle form and shifted. He flew high above the ocean and followed her. He stayed far enough away to avoid being spotted, but was still able to keep her within his sight. He enjoyed watching her jog as her long blonde ponytail swayed hypnotically.

He felt very satisfied with himself for getting his way. The flight was invigorating and made him appreciate her even more. Before he'd found her, his powers were all but gone, and now they were back full force. He'd missed flights like this one very much. He kept pace with her all the way along the shore to the jetty. He moved in closer when he saw she was no longer alone on the beach. Suddenly, he was hit by the same wave of hostility that he'd felt at the restaurant the other night. It slammed into him, throwing his flight off balance.

He scanned the beach below, searching the minds of the few people in the area. There was an old man fishing who was thinking of his late wife. The young mother playing with her two children in the waves, thinking about the errands she had to do that day. He scanned the rest, but none of them were the source of this hatred. Someone down there hated Sam. He flew over and landed on the roof of the beach club adjacent to the jetty. It was a better vantage point, and he could see Sam and everything around her.

Malcolm watched Samantha as she spoke with the woman from the diner and the child. He could feel the fondness that flowed between them all. However, as reassuring as that was, he could still feel the wave of evil hatred. He sensed it was coming from somewhere nearby, and it was directed right at Samantha. It was the same energy signature from the restaurant the other night. He wanted to swoop down there, grab her by the arms, and take her back home. However, a sight like that would not go unnoticed by the few humans on the beach. He had told her about the Caedo, but had not told her she was a target. If she knew that, then she may never want to be a part of his world. Although their mating was predestined, he still wanted her to be with him willingly. He would never force her to be with him. He would rather die than cause her unhappiness.

Finally, to his relief, Samantha left Millie and began to make her way back to the house. He flew to a higher altitude so he could avoid her sights, but still keep her in his, all the while, keeping his eyes peeled for the man from the other night. Malcolm knew he was down there somewhere, and it was maddening that he couldn't find him.

Malcolm watched Samantha as she approached a woman he'd never seen before. He could tell by Samantha's comfort level that this was the friend that she had spoken of so fondly. In stealth flight, he soared over and landed silently on Kerry's house. The hatred he felt continued to permeate the air around them. He grew edgier by the second because he couldn't pinpoint the source. He scanned the mind of her friend and was surprised when he couldn't get a solid read on her. She wasn't blocking him, at least not consciously. He knew she wasn't a threat to Sam, but there was something about her that he couldn't quite put his finger on. That bothered him immensely.

She's no threat to you or your mate, Malcolm. I will keep watch over her and make sure that's true, said a steady voice.

It was his cousin Dante, of the Fox Clan. Malcolm heard the strength and resolve of a warrior. He felt better knowing that his Amoveo brothers had arrived. He scanned the sea grass in the dunes below. He spotted Dante hidden beneath the deck of the Smithson house. He was an unusually large red fox with a white face and auburn on the edges of his ears, brown socks on his paws, and dark rings around his bushy tail.

Thank you, Dante. Are the others here as well? Malcolm could see most of the surrounding beach from his vantage point on the roof.

I am here as promised.

William's ice-cold voice resonated in Malcolm's mind. He looked over to see him perched on the eaves of Samantha's home. William was a Gyrfalcon and a formidable warrior, known for his intelligence and calculated thought. Malcolm would hate to fight him in battle and was grateful he'd been chosen to help protect Sam. He was a gigantic specimen with bright white feathers, spotted with brown. His large ebony eyes did not move from Samantha.

Me too, added Steven. *We couldn't let you have all the fun with this Caedo hunter by yourself, now could we? Besides, I'm actually more interested in watching Malcolm try to tame his woman. From what I hear, she's kind of feisty. You know, the Wolf is known for having a bit of a temper, and they hate being told what to do.*

Malcolm could hear the smile in Steven's voice. It didn't take long for Malcolm to find him. He was hidden further down the beach, also in the tall grasses of the dune. The beige coloring of his fur allowed him to blend easily with his surroundings. He lay unnaturally still, and his emerald green eyes were completely focused on Samantha.

Just wait until you find your mates. We'll see who's laughing then, Malcolm countered.

You know, boys. I think Malcolm's gotten a bit cranky. Looks like Samantha's really got you twisted up, doesn't it? Steven teased.

Malcolm could swear he saw a smile on the coyote's face.

William interjected with his usual seriousness. *I don't think this is a situation to make light of. You should complete the mating ceremony and be done with it. The hunter is nearby somewhere. I can feel it, but I cannot seem to pinpoint his location.*

I have been having the same issue all morning.

Man, these women sure can yap, Steven said.

Not much different from our females, William added.

She is one of our females. You can all go inside and make yourselves at home. I will handle it from here, Malcolm said sharply.

Someone's touchy, Dante teased.

Malcolm could hear them chuckling as they vanished into the air.

Sam had picked up her pace significantly after chatting with Millie. She focused on her breathing, hoping it would settle her sour stomach. She thought about how great Millie was and how lucky they all were to have each other. Sam wished she'd had a bigger family. Holidays had been wonderful, but it was always just Sam, Nonie, and Pop. Growing up, she'd hoped that someday she'd find the man of her dreams, get married, and have a huge house full of children. Could she have that with Malcolm? He was literally the man of her dreams. However, the rules had changed. He wasn't even human, and apparently neither was she.

The run helped burn off some of the wine and cheese from yesterday, but it hadn't done much for clearing her head. Sam approached Kerry's house and slowed to a walk to cool down a bit. She wiped away the sweat as it dripped down her forehead and lifted her face to the sun. The cool breeze was a welcome relief. Once again, she heard her name in the wind.

"Sam!"

She shaded her eyes from the sun. She saw Kerry standing on her deck with a cup of coffee. Her long dark hair was blowing loosely in the wind. She waved and sashayed down the steps to meet her.

Sam shook her head. "No one should look this good at this hour of the morning. I know you just rolled out of bed."

"What gave it away? Was it my fabulous ensemble?" Kerry motioned to the yoga pants and tank top. "God. How do you have energy to go running? I'd rather stick a hot poker in my eye." She sipped her coffee.

"Clears the head… at least it's supposed to," she said with a wry smile. "We still on for lunch and shopping tomorrow?"

"Absolutely." Kerry smiled. "But more importantly,

are we still on for our night out this weekend to meet
your new man?"

Sam felt guilty because she'd forgotten all about that.
With a pained expression, she said, "I'm sorry. I haven't
had a chance to ask Malcolm yet."

"Hey! You found your necklace!"

"Malcolm found it for me actually. He brought… gave
it back to me last night." She touched the necklace and
felt her cheeks grow hot at the memory.

"You're blushing again." Kerry wiggled her eyebrows at Sam, and they both broke into giggles. "He
must be some guy."

"Oh, he's something all right," Sam said quietly.

Movement on the roof of Kerry's house caught
Samantha's eye. Anger flared hotly through her body
at the sight above her. It was a gigantic golden eagle
perched on the roof, watching everything.

Malcolm.

He was sitting up there blatantly spying on her. Sam
was so angry she could scream. However, she couldn't
exactly explain to her friend that her boyfriend was a
bird and that she herself was a wolf, or part wolf.

Samantha had tried to keep her cool while she said
her good-byes to Kerry, but now she was going to let
it all hang out. She was absolutely steamed. She gave
Kerry a quick kiss and headed home.

She held it together as she climbed the steps to her
own house. Sam's entire body was tensed into one big
knot, and her fists were balled up at her side. How could
he think that this was okay? After everything he knew
about what had happened with Roger, why would he do
something like this?

Samantha saw Malcolm swoop off the rooftop. She expected him to grab her and carry her off like some caveman, just like he had in her dream. To her relief, he flew down and landed behind her studio, out of sight. Sam reached the top of the steps, rounded the corner, and ran face first into Malcolm's chest. She stumbled backward, and he grabbed her by the arms, pulling her close.

"Let go of me." Sam shoved at him.

He released her immediately.

Sam stumbled back and promptly landed on her butt. *Good-bye dignity.*

She stood, brushed herself off, and delivered her most withering look. "Just who the hell do you think you are?"

"I am your mate, and I have every right to make sure you are safe." Casually, he put his hands in the pockets of his jeans and leaned one hip against the studio doors. His white linen shirt was as rumpled as his hair, and he flashed that devastating smile.

"Your mate, huh?" She stood defiantly with her hands on her hips and flashing eyes. "Well, where I come from men don't go around bonking women on the head like giant Neanderthals. What about free will? I have something to say about this whole mate thing, don't I?"

"Of course you do, Samantha. I would never force myself on you." He reached out for her hand.

"Really." She crossed her arms, refusing his touch. "Well, if you want me to try and wrap my brain around this whole thing, you might start by respecting my wishes. I had my fill with controlling assholes when I dated Roger."

Malcolm's eyes softened, and his voice dropped low.

"I am not trying to control you, Samantha. I would never treat you the way that he did."

Guilt tugged at her heart as she looked into his apologetic face. Comparing him to Roger was a low blow. She knew he was nothing like that, but he still didn't have the right to spy on her.

She tilted her chin up at him and let out a sound of frustration. "Well, I asked for privacy, and you completely ignored that."

"Well actually, you asked me to get out of your head. Which I did," he pointed out.

"Nice. You're a smartass as well." Her temper began to cool. This time when he reached for her hand, she let him take it. She looked down at their fingers linked together and loved the trails of fire he left behind, even with the tiniest and most tender strokes. No, he was nothing like Roger. Roger had never been caring. He'd only wanted to possess her.

She looked into Malcolm's eyes and squeezed his hand. "I need you to give me some space, Malcolm. You've laid an enormous amount of information in my lap, and it's going to take some getting used to. The last thing I need is to think I'm being watched twenty-four hours a day."

"Of course." He stroked her velvety soft palm with his thumb. "I'm sorry I've upset you. I will try not to let that happen again." He pulled her to him and placed a gentle kiss on top of her head.

Samantha allowed herself to melt into him, but stopped. Why was he so worried about her safety all the time? She pulled back and looked him dead in the face. She narrowed her eyes in suspicion. "And by the way, what on earth would make you think I'm not safe? Is there something *else* I should know that you haven't told me?"

Malcolm wanted to tell Samantha about the hunter, but he didn't want to upset her more than he already had. He still needed time. They had to complete the mating rite so that they could be in full possession of their abilities. If she did end up in a battle, she'd need all of her Amoveo powers. However, he hoped that they would be able to exterminate the hunter without Samantha ever knowing about it.

"Well, after your visit from Roger you can't blame me for being concerned." It wasn't really a lie… just an omission of the truth. Looking into those fired up eyes of hers, he felt like a shithead for being even the least bit evasive. His gaze softened, and he stroked her cheek with his thumb. "Your safety is my primary concern, *mia piccola lupa*. I will do my best to respect your wishes."

"What is that, Italian? Because I have to admit…" She smiled. "It's pretty hot." Again, she rested her head on his chest.

"Yes. It means *my little wolf*." He played with her ponytail and relished the silky feel of the gold strands between his fingers.

She rolled her eyes, popped up on her toes, and gave him a quick kiss on the cheek. She held him at arm's length and patted his chest. "Easy there. I still don't buy the fact that I am going to turn into a wolf."

"You still doubt this? Even after everything you've seen, everything you've felt?" he said with a featherlight stroke down her arm.

They stood there in silence for a moment, eyes locked, hers searching his for answers.

"Come with me." Malcolm took her hand. Reluctantly, she followed him into her studio. He flipped on the light and walked over to the canvas in the corner. He lifted the drape and revealed the portrait of him that Sam had made. "You've known the truth… you put it here. You saw who I really was before I told you. Your talent is one of your Amoveo gifts. We have many gifted artisans among our people, and I am proud to say you are one of them." He didn't take his gaze from Samantha.

She moved slowly toward Malcolm and the image of his eagle form. It was surreal to have them there, side by side. As the sun streamed in the studio through the large picture window, it cast a golden light across Malcolm's face. His eyes, although not shifted, still gleamed yellow. Looking at both sides of him, she knew deep down that everything he'd told her was true.

It terrified her.

"So what now?" she asked quietly, not taking her gaze off the portrait.

"You need to learn how to control your gifts, for your safety, as well as the people around you."

"Why, am I a werewolf or something? Am I going to try and eat Nonie?" She lowered herself onto the stool. Her shoulders sagged in defeat.

He walked over and knelt down in front of her, taking her hands in his. "Of course not." He laughed softly. "You will still be yourself. You will be your truest self."

She avoided his gaze.

Please look at me, Samantha, he whispered in her mind.

Samantha complied, compelled by his voice. She

stared at him, her gaze silently searching his. She wondered if she would ever get used to hearing him in her mind. It was the most intimate sensation she'd ever felt. Hesitantly, she touched his face. His skin was warm and smooth along his high, strong forehead. She brushed the back of her fingers down his cheek and along his jaw, which was rough with an early morning beard.

He closed his eyes and allowed her this moment to explore. It was all true. This man was most definitely an unusual man. Hell, he wasn't even entirely a man. He was so much more. She ran her thumb along his firm lower lip. Then, tentatively she reached out to his mind with hers. The instant they connected her body was swamped with an overwhelming sense of relief. His eyes flew open, shifted, and glowed brightly back at her.

She was home.

I trust you, Malcolm.

He took her face in his hands and tenderly kissed the corners of her mouth. She knew that giving him her trust was the last step before she could give him her heart. She covered his hands with hers and leaned her forehead against his.

"Just don't lie to me. Okay?" Her voice was weary. "Apparently, my very existence has been based on half-truths. I don't know how many more surprises I can take."

"Of course." He kept his eyes closed and prayed he'd be able to keep that promise.

Sam placed a kiss on Malcolm's forehead and stood up. His hands fell away from her with reluctance.

"Where are you going?"

She could feel his eyes on her as she moved to the doorway.

"Inside to take a shower, and then I'm going to speak with Nonie." Sam raised a hand to silence him. "Look. I know you're part of some secret race and everything, but…"

"We," he corrected.

"Okay, fine," she said, exasperated. "*We're* part of some secret race, but Nonie is my family. She's my *only* family. I have to find out what she knows. And if she doesn't know, then I have to tell her."

"I really don't think that's wise, Samantha."

"Shit, you're bossy," she mumbled under her breath. She turned to confront him, and the small smirk on his face let her know he'd heard that remark. He cocked one eyebrow.

"Well, Malcolm," she said defiantly. "This really isn't up to you." She turned and walked out the studio door without giving him a chance to respond. As she stepped outside, she was shocked to have Malcolm materialize before her out of thin air.

"What are you doing?" She quickly looked to see if anyone else was around. "What if Nonie saw you do that? Or Kerry?" She grabbed his hand and pulled him back into the studio. "You forgot to mention this little gift to me."

"It's our preferred method of traveling. Right now, Samantha, you are my primary concern," he said with that same irritating calm. "And I don't think that now is the time to be telling your grandmother anything."

"Really, well I do." She crossed her arms.

"Samantha. Are you going to fight me on everything?" He sighed. "Please. Just wait until you've gone through your first shift and learned to control it. Nonie may need some convincing, and if you can't show her and let her see with her own eyes…"

"She'll haul me off to the loony bin." Frustrated, Sam went to the portrait of her parents on the windowsill. She picked it up and touched the images, their faces frozen in time behind the cool glass. "I have his eyes," she said in an almost inaudible voice.

Malcolm wrapped his strong arms around her waist. He pulled her close, and she noted how hard his entire body felt. Her mind flashed back to that dream she'd had the night before she came home. There was no doubt that Malcolm had been the man who had been calling her all these years. She was home. She had never felt delicate before, but in his arms, she felt positively tiny.

Oddly enough, she also felt safe.

She placed her hand over his as he spoke softly in her ear.

"Yes you do, and he gave you so much more. Come to my home this evening, and I will show you how to enter our world. It is a world that you have only dreamed of."

Sam placed the frame back on the windowsill and turned to him. She took his hands in hers and looked up into his incredibly handsome face. She knew deep down in her knotted up belly that she was falling in love with him. Staring into his shifted, glowing eyes, she knew she'd be linked to him and his foreign world forever.

Chapter 14

HE'D WATCHED THE LOGAN WOMAN RUNNING DOWN the beach this morning. He was able to keep her in his sights almost the entire duration of her jog. His partner had informed him late last night that it was nearly time to finish them. Tony knew why he wanted to kill them both, but he was definitely stumped by his partner's reasons. When Tony was approached a few months ago, he'd been more than a little surprised and definitely skeptical. He got over that quickly and figured whatever the reason was it worked in his favor. He shouldn't look a gift horse in the mouth.

He couldn't track her the whole time because the creature was flying overhead. He was watching her too. Tony knew the creature would sense him, but he'd been able to block him enough to hide his position. That damn thing flying around meant he had to stay in the shadows. He'd been spotted at the restaurant, and he couldn't risk being seen again. It would spoil everything. He wasn't afraid of it. Oh no. He couldn't wait to stand in front of it, look it in the eye, and drive a bullet through its black heart. In fact, he came up with a hundred different ways to kill it. He spent hours trying to formulate the most tor-turous ways to do it, but it had to be at the right time. He also had to be sure there were no other creatures around. Taking down one was hard enough, the last thing he needed was a swarm of them.

Tony sat in his room for hours, cleaning the various weapons in his arsenal. He had them all carefully laid out on his bed. He had a twelve-gauge shotgun, a long-range rifle with a sight scope, and two twelve-inch serrated daggers. His personal favorite was an enormous black crossbow with stainless steel arrows. It was perfect for puncturing the wings of the creature. He picked up the bow and carefully inspected every angle. He checked the sights to be sure the alignment was as it should be.

This was a graceful weapon. Exactly the kind of weapon one of God's chosen would wield. Tony knew that's what he was. He was a chosen one. He was sent to save the earth and save the humans from annihilation. He knew that one arrow in the wing wouldn't kill it, but would render it flightless. Best thing of all, it would make it suffer. A smile spread across his face at the very thought of it.

He rubbed the polishing cloth along the cold steel of the arrows. He loved the way that they glinted in the sunlight from his window. Satisfied with that, he moved on to the black-handled daggers. He meticulously rubbed the steel to a mirror finish. Tony worked on the blade, slowly at first. However, the more he thought about killing the creature, the more furiously he polished. Soon beads of sweat formed on his brow, which was knitted in fierce concentration. After several minutes, he admired his handiwork and saw his own reflection.

"The end is almost here." He spit on the knife and feverishly rubbed it with the cloth, striving for perfection.

Chapter 15

SAMANTHA FINALLY AGREED TO HOLD OFF SPEAKING with Nonie. She also consented to see him at his home later that evening. He'd promised a wonderful meal and a lesson in shapeshifting. In exchange, he'd leave her alone for the rest of the day so she could work on her painting for Nonie. After the past twenty-four hours, all Sam wanted to do was immerse herself in something normal and tangible. Nothing kept her more rooted in reality than her art. She felt like her entire life was spinning out of her control, and that frightened her more than anything. The watercolor of *The Bluffs* kept her anchored; without it she might go spiraling into the void.

Sam spent the rest of the day in her studio, not even coming out for lunch. The music was set at a deafening level. It drowned out everything, except her thoughts. She had finished sketching the portrait earlier and had moved on to the actual watercolors. As she added various colors with her brush, she would lean back periodically to view her progress—the comfortable worn gray of each shingle, windows like eyes that gave the impression of smiling out from the canvas.

The dewy sea grass in varied hues of greens and browns wrapped up the little house in a hug from Mother Earth. The azure sea came into sight just behind the modest Cape, all of it capped with a cloudless blue sky.

Sam stepped back to look at her nearly finished work. Her smile faded. The dark ocean behind the house held a sense of foreboding. It was as though a cold, sticky hand went right up the back of her spine. Sam jumped and brushed at her neck. It felt like she'd walked through cobwebs. "Ecch. Enough." She started to clean up. "I need a shower and a very strong drink."

—∞—

Malcolm left Samantha to the privacy of her studio and went home to see his waiting guests. He was comfortable leaving Sam to work because he could still feel her. If she ran into trouble, he would know and could be by her side in a blink. He knew his friends were going to give him a hard time and braced for it before he even got inside. The moment he walked through the door of the deck, he heard the smattering of applause and the occasional *bravo* coming from Dante and Steven. Both men were seated in the living room on the sofa barely trying to hide the smiles on their faces.

Apparently, they saw how upset Samantha was with him and found it amusing. William, however, was seated stone still in the far corner of the room. He did not look pleased. All three men, in true Amoveo tradition, were tall and well built. Each of them possessed the typical large Amoveo eyes. Dante and Steven were dressed comfortably in jeans and polo shirts. William, however, was as buttoned up as always. He wore a dark suit, crisp white shirt, and blood red tie. His shoes shone with a mirror-like finish, and Malcolm could see his reflection in them from where he stood. His long white hair, streaked with brown, was slicked back and tied tightly at his nape. Those sharp dark eyes sliced through the room and didn't move from Malcolm's face.

"I don't think there is anything to joke about," William said in a cold, steely voice. He sat motionless in the large upholstered chair.

"I have to agree with you, William." Malcolm shot a reprimanding look to his cousin, Dante, and his friend, Steven.

"Sorry." Steven held up his hands in defeat. "It's just that our boy, Malcolm here, has always had a reputation for being able to handle the ladies, and it seems this one has him all twisted up." A big grin cracked his face, and he ran a hand through his long sandy blond hair.

"My apologies, Cousin," said Dante. "But you have to admit it. You don't know if you're coming or going." He chuckled. Looking at Malcolm's unsmiling face, his amber eyes grew serious. He cleared his throat as he stood. "We are here to help you, Cousin, and we offer ourselves in protection of you and your mate." He gave a small bow before he seated himself again next to Steven.

"Thank you, Dante. Thank you all for coming." He nodded. "I take it that the Council filled you in about what we're up against?" Malcolm seated himself in the chair next to the fireplace.

"Sounds like the usual." Steven grabbed a handful of peanuts from the crystal dish on the coffee table in front of him. "A Caedo hunter wants to bump off a couple of our own. We're here to stop him and hopefully get rid of him in the process."

"There is nothing usual or normal about this situation, gentlemen. Malcolm's pairing with Samantha is unorthodox to say the least, and it has caused ripples of uneasiness through our race," William responded coldly.

"Uneasiness in *our* race? I don't understand," Dante said with confusion, gesturing to the three of them. "None of us have connected with our mates yet, and this could be the answer to our very survival. Think about it. It's more than likely that our mates are more highly evolved humans like Sam's mother," Dante said with more passion than expected.

William, however, seemed unfazed by Dante's response and continued. "Samantha's existence and now her pairing with Malcolm has reignited the Caedo's mission," William said with steely reserve. "None of us have been hunted by them since Samantha's parents were lost almost thirty years ago. Now that the peace has been disrupted…" He paused as though he was searching for the perfect words. "Well, it's unsettling for all of our people." William reached down to rub a miniscule scuff mark from his inky black shoes.

"I hadn't seen that side of it," Malcolm said with some embarrassment.

"Well, with a spitfire like that, I can see how you might be distracted." Steven nodded toward Sam's house.

"How much more time will you need before the mating ceremony can be performed? Once the two of you are officially mated, your strength will be greater than you've ever known," Dante said with a brooding look.

Malcolm was somewhat taken back by Dante's reaction. He watched him carefully. Dante seemed restless. He rose from the couch and looked out over the ocean.

"My hope is that after tonight, we will be able to perform the ceremony within a day or two. I know Richard has said he will come on a moment's notice to officiate the public ceremony."

"Very well." William rose from his chair and straightened his jacket. He glanced to the painting above the fireplace and stilled. "That is hers." He said it as a statement—not a question.

Malcolm smiled and rose from his chair. "Yes. I purchased all of her paintings from that gallery in the city." He crossed over and adjusted the portrait slightly by the corner of the gilded frame. "I thought that it would make her feel more at ease to have her work here in my home." His smile faded when he saw the stoic look on William's face. Malcolm frowned slightly. "Is there a problem?"

William didn't answer but kept his gaze fixed on the picture.

"William, I asked you a question," he said in a low menacing tone.

William's dark eyes flicked back to Malcolm. "Not for me."

Steven and Dante exchanged a confused look over this unexpected confrontation. Both men moved cautiously toward them as the tension in the room increased by the second.

"What exactly does that mean?"

William sighed and brushed a piece of lint from his lapel. "I don't envy your position. The last time a mixed couple was openly mated it didn't end very well. Did it?"

Malcolm's eyes shifted harshly and every fiber of his body tensed. "Is that a threat?"

"No," he said with his eyes firmly locked on

Malcolm's. "It's a fact. You are my friend, and I am concerned for your well-being. I would hate to see you and Samantha meet the same fate as her parents." William rolled his eyes and let out a sound of exasperation. "Your mate is right. You are a bit overbearing." He glanced at Dante and Steven. "She referred to him as bossy, didn't she?" His voice lilted in a teasing tone.

Malcolm cracked a small smile and chuckled softly. Dante and Steven joined in, and the tension eased slowly from the room. William was nothing if not direct. Malcolm shook his head and ran his hand through his hair. He felt foolish for getting so defensive and overprotective. Damn, this woman may be the death of him… or his dignity. He was ready to beat the crap out of anyone who even implied anything negative about her.

"Samantha will be here with me this evening, and I would be eternally grateful if you men would watch the perimeter of my home so we can be together undisturbed. Samantha has much to learn and very little time to learn it."

Malcolm stood and made eye contact with each of the men in his presence. He extended his right arm out, his palm facing down. All three of them approached and formed a circle. Each man placed his right hand into the center. They grasped hands, their eyes shifted, and they uttered the ancient language, "*Iunctus*." Each proclaimed their unity against the enemy, willing to lay down their lives to ensure the future of their race.

––––– ∽ –––––

At the end of the day, Samantha indulged in a nice long bubble bath. She broke out all the stops, including candles and music. She needed any opportunity to clear her head before the evening ahead of her with Malcolm. After her bath, she took her time getting ready. Just as she turned off the hair dryer, she heard a knock at the door.

Nonie came in and sat silently on the bed. She smoothed out the white covers nervously. "Where are you headed all dressed up?" Nonie gave a sidelong look at Samantha.

"I'm wearing a cotton sundress. That's hardly gussied up, Nonie." Sam avoided the question.

"Come on now. You know what I mean." She stared directly at her, her hands folded in her lap. "You're going out with Malcolm again." She stated it as a fact, not a question.

Sam leaned against the weathered oak dresser, fiddling with the hairbrush in her hands. She wanted to tell Nonie what had been going on, but knew that it wasn't the time. Not yet. "Yes." Sam looked at her hands. "Is there a problem or some reason I shouldn't be with him?" She looked back up at Nonie, searching her eyes for answers.

Nonie simply smiled as she stood and crossed over to Samantha. "Well now. The only person who knows whether or not you should be with him… is you." She touched Sam's necklace. "I see your necklace was returned to you."

Sam smiled and took the small cross between her fingers and ran it back and forth along the chain. "Yes. Just like you said it would be." Sam paused for a moment. "Malcolm found it and brought it to me."

"Mmm hmm." Nonie gently patted Sam on the shoulder and moved to the window.

She could tell that something was on Nonie's mind, but knew she wasn't in the mood for sharing it. "Nonie, how well did you know my father?" Sam saw her stiffen. She stood there silently, her hands gently splayed on the windowsill. They were interrupted by the shrill ringing of the telephone.

"I'll get it," Nonie said.

"Hello? Hi, Millie. What? Oh, sure I can. It's no trouble at all. Fine, fine, see you later." Nonie hung up and headed out of the room. "I've got to go dear. We've got another game tonight, and Millie said she wants to have it here. I have a feeling she's going a little stir crazy with Billy's family staying at the house."

"I know. She was down at the beach this morning with Billy and the baby. The sun was hardly even up yet, and they looked like they'd been there awhile." Sam smiled. She gave her hair a few last strokes. "Do you want me to help you get things ready?"

"No, no. Thank you, dear, but I'll give Davis a ring and have him come over and help me." She stopped at the doorway and turned back to Sam. "Samantha…"

"Yes Nonie?"

"Nothing, dear." She smiled and waved.

She watched her grandmother leave the room and felt an ache in her heart. She could actually feel Nonie's pain as though it were her own. It wasn't just empathy. Sam could feel it in the air. It was a tangible and very unsettling sensation. She had to take a couple of deep breaths to calm the panic that began to bubble up.

What's wrong, Samantha? Malcolm's voice flowed in her mind like a soothing caress.

It instantly calmed her and made her at ease. *How did*

you do that? How can hearing you in my mind instantly make me feel better? Is this part of the whole Amoveo mate thing?

Yes, this and more.

She could swear she actually felt his hands run down her back, sending delicious shivers through her. *Get out of my head... you're... distracting me. I'll be there soon.* She smiled. She heard him growl in response and knew she was in way over her head.

Sam came downstairs to find Nonie and Davis rearranging the kitchen table and chairs in preparation for their bridge game. They really did look adorable as they danced around one another. She saw how completely comfortable they were together. She gave them each a kiss on the cheek and grabbed the flashlight and her black wrap from the closet. She gave a quick, "Don't wait up," over her shoulder and headed out into the cool summer evening. Sam closed the door behind her, threw the wrap around her shoulders, and made her way toward the beach steps. Just like Kerry's house, it was much quicker to get there via the beach.

She went down the steps, the flashlight beam bobbing along with her. Out of the corner of her eye, she saw movement. She shone the beam over the grass and caught a glimpse of something furry. A dog maybe?

When she reached the bottom of the steps, she stopped to take off her strappy sandals. This time she heard something and froze. Sam had never been afraid on this beach in her life. Something inside of her made her move a little faster. She had the overwhelming feeling that she was being watched. She ran up the steps to Malcolm's house, taking them two at a time. She got to the top and ran straight into Malcolm. Thankfully, he grabbed her before she could plummet down to the beach below. He pulled her close, his mouth inches from hers.

"We're making a habit of meeting like this," he purred, then placed a soft kiss on her slightly parted mouth.

Now she definitely couldn't catch her breath. Her entire body came alive with that one touch. Malcolm's lips were warm, and he tasted like the sea—salty and unpredictable. She kissed him back, and the intensity grew quickly.

She figured he'd meant to give her just a sweet kiss, a welcome only. No dice. The desire between them flared brightly and threatened to boil over. She stood on her tip toes, wrapped her arms around his neck, pulled him close, and deepened their kiss. She swept her tongue along the edges of his. His strong hands wandered down to her hips and held her close, his need for her hot, heavy, and pressed against her. The wind raged around them on the bluff, lips mating and tongues dancing. Their bodies pressed against one another, desperate to get closer.

Malcolm reluctantly broke their embrace and suckled her bottom lip. He held her head in his hands and rested his forehead against hers. "You're making it very difficult for me to be a gentleman," he said between ragged breaths. "I think we should go in the house before you make me completely lose all of my senses, and I take you right here on the railing."

Sam smiled coyly, looking up at him beneath long eyelashes. She was in uncharted territory across the board. She'd never felt any kind of sexual power. She'd never felt sexy. However, she definitely liked the effect she had on him. It turned her on. "I have to admit." She leaned into him as they walked. "You shapeshifter boys sure can kiss. Tell me something… are all Amoveo as good at this as you?"

"No. I am the best," he said with complete seriousness. "At least, as far as you are concerned."

"Really, well I don't know." The pitch of her voice rose to a teasing tone. "Maybe I should try dating a couple other Amoveos, you know, to make sure. Let's see, what other animals are there? I've always liked cats." She continued as they walked onto the deck.

Malcolm reached the door first and blocked her path. "That's not an option." He looked down at her. "You'll find that I don't share well." His features grew dark, and his eyes shifted, creating two glowing yellow slashes in the night.

Sam laughed out loud. "Wow. Doesn't take much to get you riled up, does it? Relax, Conan. One shapeshifting man in my head is about all I can handle."

"Good." With a curt nod, he opened the door for her. "I'd hate to kill one of my own people."

Before she could respond he slipped behind her and covered her eyes with one of his strong hands. He smelled like the ocean. He wrapped his other hand around her upper arm and pulled her back against his firm, long body. Sam sucked in a shuddering breath and held it. He leaned down and nudged her hair away from her ear. His warm breath fanned deliciously down her throat. It was intensely erotic to be blind for that moment. Her body seemed even more in tune with every single spot his body touched. Her hands hung at her side. She reached back and placed them on his rock hard thighs, clothed beneath linen trousers. He placed a delicate kiss on the edge of her ear and whispered wickedly, "I have a few surprises for you."

"I bet you do," she breathed.

Eyes covered, he led her inside. The moment she stood inside the house a sense of familiarity washed over her. Any apprehension she'd had about being here melted away. She heard the door close behind them as he steered her along. Sam could tell they were maneuvering around some furniture on their way to the mystery destination. Sam laughed and kept her hands out in front like a blind old lady.

They stopped, and Malcolm once again pressed himself right up against her. She shivered as his left hand slid down her arm, and he tangled his fingers with hers. He nuzzled her ear again and murmured seductively in her ear, "Are you ready?"

Sam leaned her head back against his muscular chest and squeezed his thigh with her free hand. "If you keep this up I'm going to be ready for a lot more than dinner," she said huskily.

"You're making it next to impossible for me to behave myself," he growled. Before she could respond he uncovered her eyes and pulled her long blonde hair over her shoulder.

Sam smiled and opened her eyes.

The sight in the dining room took her breath away. The enormous dining table had a spectacular place setting for two. There were two gleaming silver candelabras with unlit white tapered candles and two gorgeous china and crystal place settings. They both held fresh, colorful salads. Several other covered dishes adorned the table. A magnum of champagne, chilling in a silver cooler, was in the center of it all.

Sam walked slowly into the dining room, taking in every detail. It looked beautiful, smelled delicious, and she could practically hear the crackling of the champagne chilling. It was a veritable feast for her senses. Never in her life had anyone put together something like this for her. Tears pricked at the back of her eyes, stunned by the spread he had put together for her. She was brought out of her thoughts by the pop of the champagne cork.

Malcolm was filling their flutes with a satisfied smile on his face.

"You did all of this for me?" she asked in disbelief.

"You find it so shocking that I would make you dinner?" He handed her the ornate crystal glass.

"This is more than dinner. I feel like I'm on *Lifestyles of the Rich and Famous* or more likely *Punk'd*. Is Ashton hiding under the table or something?" She looked around.

"I don't know who that is, but I can assure you, no one is under the table." He put the bottle back in its icy bath.

"You don't know who Ashton Kutcher is?" She raised her eyebrows. "Do you live in this house or under a rock?"

"You deserve to have every meal this way, Samantha. Nothing is too good for you." He raised his glass to her and stepped closer. "To you."

"And to you," she whispered. She sipped the champagne and eyed him over the edge of her glass. He looked at her with an intensity that forced her to look away. She was afraid she might lose herself completely and jump his bones right there on the table.

Malcolm smiled as he received the various images that had run through her mind. He knew she had to learn to protect her thoughts, especially around other Amoveo. Tonight he had put up a mental shield so their guards would not hear them. This was one of the skills he wanted to teach her. She would've learned this as a child if she'd she been raised in their world.

"Do you have a match so we can light the candles?"

"No." His smile was cocky. With a wave of his hand, little flames danced before her eyes.

"Show off." She smiled. "Okay… Now I have to admit that's pretty cool."

Malcolm pulled her chair out for her.

"Can all Amoveo do things like that?"

"Yes. We all have the power of visualization. Our abilities grow as we age, especially once we find our mate. The old ones are quite powerful." He sat with her.

"How long do you live?"

"Well, Richard and his mate Salinda are over two hundred years. They are among the oldest."

Sam almost choked on her champagne. "Two hundred? Holy shit! You mean that guy on your deck… Wow, you don't age much do you?"

"No." He smiled. "Not much. If we've found our mates." He held her gaze for a moment, but she quickly looked away.

She placed the pure white linen napkin in her lap and sat quietly, surveying the sight before her. Eventually, her gaze landed on Malcolm, who had begun to enjoy his salad.

"Aren't you going to eat?"

"So you're telling me I can learn to do that candle thing?" She raised an eyebrow.

"Yes. Tonight after dinner, we'll begin. You have a lot of catching up to do." He gave her a devastating smile.

"Right." She had to focus on her salad.

After the spectacular first course, they enjoyed mammoth steamed lobsters smothered in warm drawn butter. Their feast continued with sweet corn on the cob and soft Italian bread. It was topped off by a tower of fresh fruit with warm chocolate fondue. She was grateful that he liked a woman with an appetite and a little meat on her bones.

Conversation over dinner focused mostly on Amoveo history. He told her the legend that shaped the fate of their race. She listened intently as he told her about the star-crossed lovers from so long ago. Lucia of the Lion Clan had been pursued relentlessly by a young human named Victor Caedo. Unbeknownst to him, she was Amoveo and mated to Antonio of the Tiger Clan. However, Victor was obsessed. She spurned his advances repeatedly, but he would not relent. One night he saw the young lovers sneak into the woods. He followed them, planning to tell their parents of their secret tryst. Then, under the canopy of the moonlit forest, he saw them shift. Unable to understand what he'd seen, he allowed his fear to turn to hatred. Eventually, he hunted them down and killed them. Victor Caedo then made it his family's legacy to wipe all of the Amoveo from the planet.

Malcolm didn't want to spoil their evening by revealing the current danger so he turned the conversation to stories of her clan. He explained that her father had been the last of his line in the Wolf Clan and that she was now the last.

By the end of the meal, Sam was stuffed. Her belly was filled with food, and her brain was loaded with information. She sat back and looked at Malcolm draining the last bit of champagne from his glass.

"So obviously Amoveo from different clans can mate with each other. Right?"

"Yes. My father is of the Eagle Clan, and my mother is of the Bear Clan."

"So why are you an eagle? Is it because your father was, and you're a boy? I mean, if we had children, which clan would they take after? They wouldn't be some kind of weird gryphon creature or something, would they? Because that could be a deal breaker on the whole baby thing." Her brow knitted. She tried to act like the conversation was normal. "Not that I'm thinking about having babies…I just…well, would they…if we did, I mean?" She felt like a bit of an idiot.

"No." He shook his head with a small chuckle. "It is unknown which clan a child will favor until adolescence. We don't go through our first shift until we reach puberty. That is when we are able to walk in the dream realm. Our powers of visualization begin to appear then as well."

"So let me get this all straight." She stood from the table and went over to the window. "There are ten different shapeshifting animal clans. I am a wolf. Is that right?"

"Yes."

"You can only have children with your 'soul mate.'" She made air quotes with her fingers.

"Correct."

"You find this mate, who is, by the way, prechosen for you by the universe, in dreams. How am I doing so far?" She faced Malcolm, still seated in his chair.

"Excellent." He sensed her anxiety and subtly sent her waves of reassurance.

"But if you don't find your mate, then you lose your powers and die a slow painful death."

"Correct."

"Oh wait... I almost forgot the best part," she said dramatically. "The crazy zealot Caedo family hunts you down as part of their family tradition."

"They have in the past, but it's been many years since we lost any of our people. Samantha, please." He went to her, putting his hands on her shoulders. *Let's take it one step at a time,* mia piccola lupa.

His voice once again soothed her as it floated into her mind. "How do you do that?" she asked, wide-eyed.

Do what? He looked at her with that knee-buckling smile.

"That." She smacked his hard chest. "Physically put me at ease with your voice. Is it because I'm supposed to be your mate?"

"Yes and no." He took her hands. "All Amoveo are very sensitive to human emotion. We feel it in the air. Similar to the way a bat can see with radio waves or how dolphins use sound. We can navigate human emotions. However, since you are my mate we are even more connected to each other than we would be with anyone else."

Sam's eyes widened with comprehension. "Tonight, in my room, I actually *felt* how upset Nonie was. I mean it wasn't empathy… it was more than that… it was a physical reaction. I got kind of dizzy and a little nauseous. But then when you spoke to me in my mind, it made me feel better. Kind of like telepathic Tylenol." She smiled.

Malcolm laughed at her clever analogy. "Yes, I suppose you could say that. You need to learn to tune out human emotion, filter it so that it won't impact you like that. It's going to happen more and more as your abilities continue to develop."

"Jeez, I can't imagine how hard it would be to be in a crowded place like a mall if I couldn't tune that stuff out." She tried not to be distracted by the soft strokes of his thumb along her hand. She was mesmerized by the little trails of fire he left behind with each touch.

It set off a series of pornographic images in her mind, which Malcolm received loud and clear. *You're killing me, woman,* he growled.

Sam's head snapped up. She felt the color rise in her cheeks.

"First, you need to learn to guard those thoughts of yours. You might just drive me insane, sending me images like that. I would imagine you wouldn't want anyone else to see them either?" He raised an eyebrow.

Sam was horrified at the idea that anyone but Malcolm would hear her thoughts. Especially the ones she had recently. "You mean any one of your people… your mother?"

Malcolm laughed and pulled her to him in a welcome and reassuring embrace. "Not to worry. Most of our people have very good manners and do their best not to intrude on the thoughts of other Amoveo, but if you're shouting, how can they help but hear you?" He stroked the back of her head and rocked a bit as he held her.

Sam stayed there for a moment, allowing herself to sink into the warmth of his embrace. She loved the way his heart beat against her cheek and how his muscles rippled under her hands. He tenderly played with the ends of her long hair, and it was almost hypnotic. *I could stay here forever.* She sighed.

"So could I," he said. "But we have work to do."

Malcolm led Sam into the cavernous living room, and she whistled at the vast cool space. It was not what someone would expect in a beach house, more like something in an old English castle. The furniture was covered in heavy brocade or leather. The wood was dark mahogany with intricate carvings along the edges. The ivory walls had various portraits hung around the room. All of them were of different animals, mostly birds of prey. On the opposite side of the room and to the right were huge archways, which led to the front hall with a sweeping staircase and into the equally large dining room. At the center of the far wall was a massive fireplace framed by a Gothic marble mantle, and Sam just about fainted when she saw what hung above it.

It was her painting. *Woman and the Wolf.*

Chapter 16

"YOU," SHE BREATHED IN A RUSH. "YOU BOUGHT IT." Tears stung at her eyes, and her throat tightened with the sudden onslaught of emotion. A strong wave of relief washed over her. Thank God Roger hadn't been the buyer. The idea that he would've had such a personal part of her had turned her stomach. But Malcolm, now that was a whole different story. She turned and looked up at him expectantly. "Why?"

His eyes crinkled at the corners, and his lips curved. "Well, to be honest, I thought it would make you happy." He cradled her face with both hands and wiped one big fat tear away with agonizing tenderness. "Apparently, I misjudged the outcome," he said with a fading smile.

Sam sniffled and placed her hands over Malcolm's. "It does." She laughed.

Malcolm cocked his head and gave her a questioning look. "Then why are you crying?"

She kissed his palm, linked his fingers in hers, and turned back to the painting. "It makes me happy that you were the one to buy this, and to be honest, I'm thrilled it wasn't Roger."

"Roger," he glowered. "Why would you think that he bought your paintings?"

Sam shook her head slightly at his jealous reaction, wrapped his arms around her waist, and leaned back into his hard, warm body.

"Paintings? You mean you bought this one and…"
Her voice trailed off as she started to put the pieces together. "You're the hottie," Sam mumbled.

"It most certainly was not Roger. I went to the city and purchased this one myself. I knew it was yours the moment I set eyes on it. That Gunther fellow was very helpful. He's a big fan of your work."

"He's a big fan of yours too," Sam chuckled. "When Gunther called and told me that this Barkley guy came in and asked for my work in particular… well, after all of Roger's obsessive behavior…" She let her words trail off and shrugged her shoulders.

Malcolm squeezed her tightly and let out a growl of frustration. "How could I be so stupid?" He kissed the top of her head. "I was so excited to have your work, such an intimate part of you, so close to me." He sighed and rubbed his chin gently on her hair. "It never even occurred to me that you'd worry about Roger buying it," he said quietly, almost contritely. "I'm sorry if my intended surprise caused you any discomfort."

"Don't you dare apologize for buying my work." Sam leaned her head back and craned her neck to look up at him. "Before this, I only sold a few other paintings."

"I will have to find out who has them and buy them back."

"You do know just what to say don't you?"

He squeezed her tightly and placed a warm kiss on her cheek. "I want to have every single one of them. Maybe it's selfish, but I don't want to share you with anyone."

Sam turned her gaze back to the painting. She thought of all of the pieces she'd painted. Many of them were of the ocean or the seashore. There were even two that had wolves in them. "Why did you choose this one to hang here?"

"It's you," he whispered softly into her ear and pulled her closer. "It's the two halves of you."

Sam stilled, and her breath caught in her throat. Of course! All this time, she'd thought the painting was of her mother, but really it was of her mother *and* her father. Her father—Lucas Logan from the Gray Wolf Clan. Tears filled her eyes again, and she let out a small laugh. "Oh my God! You're right. It's my parents... the two pieces of me."

"I have to be honest. I didn't purchase these paintings and put them here just to make you happy."

Sam turned in his embrace and placed her hands on his chest. His strong hands slid down her sides and rested lightly on her hips. She adored the way his muscles rippled ever so slightly beneath her fingertips and how his hands fit so perfectly... everywhere. She looked up at him through narrowed eyes, trying to concentrate on forming a sentence and not jumping his bones.

She cleared her throat and flicked her gaze back up to those spectacular golden eyes. "Okay... why, then?"

He took a deep breath, and his fingers gripped her hips. He kept his now serious gaze fixed firmly on hers. "I knew that they would make you feel comfortable in my home."

"What does that mean?" Sam cocked her head at him and raised one eyebrow.

He licked his lips, and his gaze slid over across her face as if he was memorizing every curve. "Your energy signature emanates from all of your work," he murmured and dug his fingers slightly into the flesh of her hips.

Sam swallowed hard and suddenly became acutely aware of every single spot where their bodies met. Heat flared low in her belly, and his eyes wandered down to her lips. She flicked her tongue out quickly and nibbled her lower lip. "My energy signature," she said absently. She couldn't think clearly with his body pressed up against hers. "What's an energy signature?"

Malcolm leaned down and placed small butterfly kisses along her neck. "It's the very essence of you. All Amoveo have one. It's how I can find you." He paid thorough attention to the soft flesh along her collarbone and pulled her hips tightly against him and the hard evidence of his desire. "It's how I was able to come to you at the diner so quickly."

Sam moaned softly and closed her eyes, allowing herself to float in his arms. "Can I learn to do that?" she breathed softly.

Malcolm let out a low growl and buried his face in the crook of her neck. *See what you're doing to me woman?* His dark velvet voice slid into her mind seductively. He pulled back and placed a tender kiss at the corner of her mouth. "You'll be able to do that and so much more, *mia piccola lupa*." He let out a sigh and released her from his warm embrace. "Let's get started."

They spent the next couple of hours in the living room while Sam practiced her *telepathic tune-out*. The first several tries at guarding her thoughts were comical. She couldn't even get through a word or two without

Malcolm blurting, "I hear you." All of this promptly caused Sam to burst into hysterical fits of giggles. Occasionally, she would lose her sense of humor, getting frustrated when she couldn't get it exactly right.

She knew that he was pleasantly surprised that she was such a quick study. She made astounding progress, considering her abilities had just begun to manifest over the past couple of days. She loved the way he watched her fierce concentration as she focused on protecting her thoughts. She could tell that he admired her feisty determination and tenacity immensely.

Once she got the hang of guarding her thoughts, they moved on to visualization. Unlike telepathy, visualization did not come to her easily. She tried to light a candle for over an hour. Her only glimmer of progress was a single wisp of smoke that rose up from a blackened wick. It made her want to scream with frustration, especially since he was completely unfazed by the entire thing.

"Jesus Christ. Forget it. I'll just use a match." She flopped on the sofa, rubbing her temples.

Be patient, mia piccola lupa, *it will take time,* he whispered in her mind. The tension melted from her head and shoulders. He reached over to toy with strands of her hair.

She looked at him next to her on the couch. He sat there easily, his leg splayed in casual confidence. He was amazing. His wavy, chestnut hair was brushed back off his chiseled masculine face. Her eyes feasted on the length of him. His Levi's fit him perfectly in all the right places, and the long-sleeve green V-neck sweater hugged every muscle. Her gaze made a slow journey back up to his now smiling face. That grin made her stomach flip-flop. He was truly stunning.

The reality of his situation hit her for the first time. He was a pure Amoveo being, and she was only half. She wondered how he would ever be satisfied with her. How would she ever be good enough? She couldn't accomplish a simple thing like lighting that candle. Tears stung at the back of her eyes. She was frustrated, overwhelmed, and disgusted with herself at the same time. Sam rubbed her eyes and sat up quickly. "I should go. I think I've had enough supernatural weirdness for one night." She stood, avoiding his gaze. "Thank you for dinner."

"You have guarded your thoughts very well, but I can still feel how upset you are, Samantha. What's wrong?" He took her hand, trying to get her to look at him.

"Nothing." She took her fingers from him and walked over to the windows. She stared out into the inky black night.

Malcolm didn't move from the couch. He was afraid he would end up chasing her right out the door. He felt so completely uncertain of what to do next. He knew that if he pushed her too hard she'd run. Her energy wave, thick with her insecurity, pulsed over him and gave him pause. "Sam," he began gently. "I know that when a woman says *nothing* it definitely means something… and that's true if she's human or Amoveo." He smiled. "Or both."

"That's just it. I'm not Amoveo or human, am I? I'm some kind of bizarre mutant, a hybrid. I don't have the same strength as a regular woman in your race." She faced him. "Are your people even going to accept me? I can't even light the stupid candle." Her voice rose with fear and frustration. "I'm some kind of freak," she shouted with a broad sweep of her hand.

The next instant a huge fireball exploded in the fireplace.

Sam slapped her hands over her mouth and froze. "Holy shit," she whispered through her hands. She gaped at the flames, which burned brightly.

Malcolm stood and walked toward the flickering light. She moved cautiously closer to her creation.

They both stood silently, staring into the fireplace.

"I don't think we need to worry about the strength of your abilities, Samantha," Malcolm murmured, looking into the dancing flames. "It's the control I'm concerned about." He looked at her with something that looked a lot like love. Sam knew that she was different from a traditional Amoveo woman, but she was his.

His mate.

She knew in that moment that he loved her.

Sam swallowed hard. "Wow," she said, awed.

"My feelings exactly." His voice was low and laced with desire, and he looked at her through slightly hooded eyes. He reached out and took one long strand of hair between his fingers. "It glints like spun gold in the firelight."

She watched the flames reflected in his golden eyes and sensed his desire for her in the air. It was as if the humidity skyrocketed in the living room. Sam's skin felt too small for her body, and she could swear that it practically screamed to be stroked and kissed. She moved toward him almost imperceptibly. She knew that her hips and ample breasts were shamelessly outlined by her body-hugging sundress. Samantha had an overwhelming urge to have Malcolm peel it off of her.

His desire for her slammed into her and stole her breath. Her eyes tingled and shifted with a ferocious intensity.

She could feel the weight of his gaze on her. She couldn't tell if the heat was from the fire or from them. He moved closer to her. In one slow movement, he brushed her hair back, which exposed her shoulder.

"You are perfect, Samantha. Do you not see how amazing you are?" he whispered. He stroked her skin softly and placed a butterfly kiss in its wake.

Her eyes fluttered closed as he traced a deliberate line down her arm with his knuckles. He barely grazed her skin, but she felt his touch in every cell of her being. His massive body was just inches from her. She could feel his warm breath as it bathed her shoulder. She finally opened her eyes and turned toward him ever so slightly. They stood face-to-face beside the roaring fire.

He tilted her face up to give him access to her lush mouth. He smiled when he looked into her shifted blue eyes. "Mate," he whispered as he claimed her mouth with his. She tasted of champagne and spice.

He sensed heat as it pooled low in her womb and their tongues danced and dueled. She gripped his arms for balance as he rained kisses down her neck and breathed in her scent. He pushed aside the delicate strap of her sundress, trailed little kisses along her shoulder. He undid the tiny buttons down the front of her dress, needing to touch her, needing to claim her. One by one, he popped them open as he paid thorough attention to her mouth once again, trying to take his time and make this night perfect for her.

Every time he touched her, he branded her as his. The front of her dress now gaped open and exposed her full round breasts. He looked down and feasted on the sight of her. Taking one of the creamy mounds in his hand, he almost came apart. He felt her nipple harden under his palm. He pushed the other strap from her shoulder, leaving her bare from the waist up, open for him to devour. He quickly bent down and took her other breast in his mouth, suckling on the rosy peak as he held her close.

Her bosom pushed against him as she sucked in her breath and tangled her fingers in his hair. His lips seared her breast. He couldn't get close enough. He wanted to feel his body, feel his flesh against hers. Knowing exactly what he needed, Sam grabbed his sweater and hastily rid him of the offending garment. She sighed with delicious relief as his chest pressed up firmly against her breasts as they clung to one another desperately. He claimed her mouth while he toyed with her nipple, rolling the pebbled bud gently between his fingers.

Samantha held him close to her as lightning bolts of pleasure raced along the edges of his mind and every nerve ending. He practically drowned in it. Her breath was coming in quick gasps, driving him closer to the edge. He pressed the hard length of his erection insistently against her lower belly. He smiled against her lips as she brazenly rubbed the bulge between them, which strained to be released. He moaned his pleasure into her mouth. She swiftly removed him from the confines of his jeans and wrapped her warm hand around the length of him.

Malcolm almost lost his self-control as she wrapped her delicate artist's fingers around him. He groaned as he nipped and suckled at her breast. Growling deep in his throat, he lifted her off the ground, and she wrapped her legs around his waist. He wasn't sure he could wait one more minute to be inside of her. He needed her now. He kissed her ferociously as he pinned her up against the wall beside the fireplace. He held her there, her dress around her waist. The surge of passion rose insistently between them. Their eyes locked as he slid his fingers beneath her damp panties and sunk two fingers into her hot, wet channel. He stared into her luminous wolfen eyes, which glowed with her pleasure. He loved the way she looked, wanton and lustful. Her lips parted in ecstasy as he rubbed her sensitive nub in slow torturous circles, all the while his fingers moved inside of her.

Her pleasure was evident in each ragged gasp as he massaged her to the very brink. He felt a new surge of wetness in his hand and knew she was ready. He pushed aside her thin silk panties and drove himself deep inside of her. Slow and deliberate, he kept his gaze locked on hers as he sank himself into her stroke after stroke.

With every fiery stroke of delicious friction, she felt the orgasm build. He was hot steel covered by silk. Each time he filled and stretched her, it brought a new wave of pleasure rolling over her. With every thrust, she hungered for more. She tangled her fingers in his hair and called out his name as he increased the tempo. He drove into her again and again. Just when she thought she would weep from pleasure, the orgasm exploded over both of them. They cried out in unison, and with one final thrust, he buried himself deep inside of her.

They stayed there for several minutes. Their bodies locked together, breathless, neither one wanting to break the embrace. They were completely and utterly spent. Samantha had heard about sex like that. Seen it in the movies, but *never* had she experienced anything even remotely close to what had just happened. He was breathing heavily and had his face buried against her neck.

Finally, in a muffled voice, he said, "I'm sorry."

Sam swatted his shoulder as her legs dropped from his waist. "What on earth could you be sorry for?" Her legs wobbled a bit under her.

Malcolm stepped back as she tried to put her dress back in its place. He took her face in his hands. "I wanted our first mating to be perfect," he murmured against her throat. "To take our time."

She smiled at him as he kissed her tenderly on the lips.

She was surprised to feel him stir so soon, but then again, she had never been with her mate before.

Her mate. It sounded odd and familiar at the same time.

Sam smiled, and she slowly ran her tongue along his lips. That was all the encouragement he needed. Malcolm picked her up effortlessly in his arms, as if she weighed nothing at all, and carried her toward the front hall.

She shrieked in surprise and instinctively threw her arms around his neck. "What are you doing? I'm half naked. Put me down. You're going to hurt yourself. I weigh a ton."

He sent her a look of doubt as he went up the grand staircase. She continued to protest all the way into his bedroom. Gently, he laid her on the massive four-poster bed. "Now, *mia piccola lupa*, we will take our time," he whispered with a wickedly sexy smile.

She watched with unusual boldness as he stripped off his jeans and tossed them onto a chair in the corner. All the while, his gaze stayed transfixed on her. Her eyes widened at the magnificent evidence of his arousal. She felt a surge of wetness as raw carnal lust flared through her body. She began to remove her dress, but he tenderly pushed her hands aside. He peeled it from her hot sensitive skin. She was surprised by her shocking lack of modesty. She felt completely comfortable as she lay naked before him. *Definitely a first.*

He stretched the length of his body next to hers. They let their hands explore as they savored every kiss. They stayed there, touching and tasting, for what felt like hours, slowly enjoying every inch of one another. Finally, he propped himself up on his elbow so he could take a loving look at her. Her long flaxen hair splayed around her head like a halo, and her pale blue wolfen eyes stayed locked on his. Her lips parted with panting breath as her passion grew.

He trailed his fingers down her lovely neck as her pulse beat enticingly under the surface. He feasted on the sight of her pale breasts with rosy pink buds, thrusting up at him with every breath. Eventually, he splayed his hand across her flat belly and felt the little muscles as they quivered under his touch. His long fingers stroked lower still, to reach the treasure between her thighs. He dipped one finger into her hot depths and took her nipple into his mouth.

Sam cried out with pleasure. She held his head to her breast, her fingers entwined in his hair. She rubbed up against his hand as he worked her most sensitive spot. He loved the way she reacted to his touch and almost lost his resolve completely as he felt another gush of wetness in his hand.

He covered her with the length of his body and settled between her legs. He studied her, wanting to brand this image of her in his memory forever. Her lips were pink and swollen from his kisses, and her Amoveo eyes held nothing but trust. He trailed kisses down her breasts, along the middle of her belly, and lower still to the glistening mound between her legs. He feathered small kisses on her inner thigh and breathed in her musky scent, which added to his arousal. His strong arms anchored her to the bed, leaving her open for him to devour. He leaned in and took one loving taste of her.

When he put his mouth on her, Samantha almost came off the bed as a lightning streak of pleasure shot through her entire body. He was merciless as he continued his assault on her. His devilishly talented tongue sent shock waves through her with every lash. Her head thrashed back and forth. She bucked her hips and writhed against him, mewling small sounds of pleasure.

He sensed she was reaching her breaking point. He smiled and moved over her. Settled at her entrance, he eased himself inside of her, inch by inch. She raised her hips to meet him and urge him faster, her passion driving her to impatience, but Malcolm wouldn't hear of it. He held her hands over her head, looking into her eyes as he slid inside of her with lingering, hot strokes time and time again.

She wrapped her legs around him and locked her ankles, giving him even deeper access to her molten chamber. He drove into her relentlessly as the sweet torturous passion rose between them.

Malcolm locked his eyes on hers, whispered the ancient mating words in her mind, and buried himself in her with one last thrust. *Nos es unus. Materia pro totus vicis. Ago intertwined. Forever.*

The words spilled into her mind, filling every cell of her being. Stars burst behind her eyes as she cried out his name, her body inundated with both her pleasure and Malcolm's. Wave after wave crashed through her, the colors bursting and swirling like the aurora borealis in the air around them. They were completely connected in mind, body, and spirit.

The waves of pleasure subsided into tiny aftershocks. They lay there, entwined bodies shaking and breathless. Samantha realized that life as she knew it was gone. Wrapped in Malcolm's arms, she knew there was no going back.

Chapter 17

SAMANTHA AWOKE THE NEXT MORNING TO SMALL KISSES on the back of her neck—their naked bodies spooned together, skin to skin. The early sun streamed in through the large bay windows, casting golden beams of light around them. She smiled with contentment as his arm tightened around her. She placed a small kiss on his fingers as he nuzzled. Memories of last night flooded back to her in full color. They had made love several times, and she was gloriously exhausted, but she could be convinced to go another round. He was the only man to make her feel completely and utterly cherished. *Not to mention the mind-blowing sex.*

"It was rather mind-blowing, wasn't it," he whispered in her ear.

She jabbed him in the ribs. "Hey. I thought I was saying that to myself. I guess I'm not as good at guarding my thoughts as I'd hoped."

Malcolm chuckled softly and kissed her earlobe. "Now that we are mated, you have to intentionally shut your mind from me entirely if you don't want me to hear you. It's even more than just guarding your thoughts. I hope, however, that you'll never do that."

Sam turned over so she lay face-to-face with him in the soft, warm bed. "What do you mean, *now that we are mated*?" Wary, her brows knitted together.

"Last night, I said the ancient words of our mating

ritual. We are bound, now and forever." He brushed her cheek gently.

She remembered exactly what he was talking about and what happened after he said those words. She sat straight up in bed, holding the covers to her naked breasts. "What do you mean bound? I mean, come on, we had sex. I know it was pretty amazing, and rest assured, I don't run around doing that with just anybody... but... what..." Her voice rose to something that resembled panic.

Malcolm propped himself up on his elbow and looked at her with a puzzled smile. "Samantha, you knew that we were destined. All we did last night was confirm that. I don't see what you're so upset about."

"So what... that's it?" she sputtered. "We're married?"

"Well no. We do have a formal celebration ceremony that is done by Prince Richard."

Sam let out a sigh of relief. "Well, thank God."

"But really, that's just a formality. For all intents and purposes, we are mated. You will feel what I feel and share my thoughts as I share yours." He brushed her tousled hair off her shoulder and trailed his fingertips down her back.

A delicious shiver went throughout her body. Desire flared deep inside of her. Sam jumped out of bed, taking the comforter with her as a makeshift wrap, leaving him with just the sheet. "Stop that." She pointed at him from the bedside. "I can't think straight when you do that."

Malcolm said nothing. He simply smiled that sexy smile and kept his eyes locked on hers. She looked absolutely gorgeous. Her golden hair in complete disarray and that determined look on her face made him want to eat her up. He sent wicked images to her.

"Ooohhh. Stop that too." She clapped one hand over her eyes. "That's not fair. I mean it."

Malcolm chuckled and raised his hands in defeat. "Okay. I'm sorry. I'll stop." He lay back in the bed, both hands behind his head. Only the thin white sheet covered him from the waist down.

She looked away, afraid she'd actually start to drool. Sam paced back and forth trying to wrap her brain around what he was telling her. "So... last night... after you said... wait... what did you say exactly?" She stopped pacing for a moment.

"*Nos es unus. Materia pro totus vicis. Ago intertwined. Forever.*"

"Isn't that Latin? I got the last word, but what does the rest mean?"

"Loosely translated it means: *We are one. Mates for all time. Lives intertwined. Forever.* And yes, it's Latin. That is the language of our people."

She wanted to strangle him. She stood there with her arms crossed, scowling. "Right, so now you'll be able to hear everything I think?"

"Basically, yes."

"Well, brace yourself, buddy. You probably won't like everything you hear."

"I don't doubt it." He then heard some colorful language going off in her mind in rapid succession. "It's the most intimate form of communication, Samantha." He smiled suggestively.

"Uh-huh. Well, I'm sure that's another reason you people don't want just anyone hearing what's rattling around in your brains. It would certainly air everyone's dirty laundry."

"Actually, all communication between mates is protected. Think of it as encoded. Like a private telephone line."

"Okay," she said slowly. "And you said we'll also feel what the other feels?"

"Yes." He nodded. "Last night…" He trailed off hoping she'd be able to finish the thought.

"Last night… after you said those words… I actually saw and felt everything that you did as well as what I… oh boy." Realization moved across her face. Her eyes grew wide, and she blushed at the memory of their shared experience. "Well, that would probably be considered one of the perks."

Malcolm sat up and took her hand, pulling her to him. "I know that you've had many things to accept over the past couple of days, and I will do my best for the rest of our lives to help you through all of it."

Sam looked down at her hand, which had never seemed small to her, and saw it was completely engulfed by Malcolm's. *Is this it? Am I going to lose myself completely and simply be absorbed by him?*

Malcolm heard her but said nothing. He pulled her next to him on the bed and rearranged the covers over both of them. "I promise you, Samantha, everything will be all right." He placed a kiss on top of her head. Samantha felt and heard his reassurances but still remained uneasy. She wondered if she would have a normal life ever again.

"We do live normal lives, Samantha, with a few small exceptions."

"Turning into an animal is hardly a small exception." She laid her head on his chest.

"Now that we are mated—"

"Do me a favor." She put her hand up in an effort to silence him. "Stop saying that. You're stressing me out."

Malcolm sighed and continued. "At any rate, after last night, both of our abilities are heightened. We have not only our own strength, but each other's as well. It's a benefit on many levels." His mind wandered to the Caedo.

Sam lifted her head and looked at him through narrowed eyes. "What's that about the Caedo?"

He looked away from her and got out of bed.

She watched him and couldn't help but notice that he looked as good going as he did coming.

He stepped into jeans that had been cast aside quickly last night.

"Guess that whole *connected* thing works both ways, doesn't it, big guy?" She smiled with satisfaction. "So why are you worried about the Caedo? And don't bother trying to lie to me because, as you know, I now have an inside track to what's going on in your head. So spill it."

Malcolm stood there, his hands on his hips. The muscles in his chest flexed with tension, and he cursed under his breath. "I didn't want to worry you or upset you."

"Uh-huh... well, too late."

"A Caedo hunter has been tracking you. I had hoped to eliminate him before you even had to find out about it, but he's been elusive to say the least."

"What?" She clutched the sheets to her chest. "I thought you said they haven't done anything for years."

"They haven't. That's true."

"Well, why me? I'm not even a full Amoveo."

"We are sure they've watched you all of your life

to see if you showed any of our people's traits. We are quite certain they know that you and I have found each other. As far as the Caedo are concerned, you are Amoveo and now fair game."

"How long have you known about this, Malcolm? What about Nonie? Is she in danger? Or Kerry? Jesus, Malcolm, are you telling me some psycho out there wants to kill me?" Her voice was slightly hysterical.

"He was at Paddy's the other night, and no, I don't think they are in any danger."

"That was why you dragged me outside. Well who is this guy? Jesus. Why didn't you tell me?"

"He's definitely Caedo, but I had never seen him before. He was able to block his thoughts from me." He felt somewhat ashamed. Unable to face her, he turned to look out the window. "With everything else you've had to accept, I didn't want to add to it."

"Wait a minute. Aren't the Caedo human? How could he do that? I mean, block you?"

"Yes, they are human, but as you know…" He looked back over his shoulder. "There are humans with psychic ability. Obviously, this fellow has some."

"That's why you were worried about me running on the beach." The pieces came together.

"Yes. You have been protected all along. I enlisted the help of three Amoveo warriors to aid in our defense. They were here to ensure we were undisturbed last night."

Sam's eyes grew wide. "Here?"

"Yes. Dante, Steven, and William watched over the perimeter of my home. They are three of our fiercest warriors. Dante has a private security firm. Steven is a very gifted healer."

"You mean like a doctor?" Sam asked curiously.

"More than that. He can use visualization to heal most wounds," Malcolm said quietly.

"So… are they here now?" She prayed the answer would be no.

"Yes," Malcolm said. "In fact they are outside right now."

"This whole thing just keeps getting weirder. So what's the bottom line? Some guy is out there and wants to kill me?"

"Us, actually." He faced her.

"Right." She jumped from a knock at the bedroom door, which was immediately followed by Davis's muffled voice.

"Coffee, sir."

"Holy crap," she whispered. "I do not want to get caught in your bed." She dove under the covers, hoping the giant fluffy comforter would hide her presence. Malcolm smiled and, shaking his head, opened the door.

"Morning, sir." Davis walked in and placed the large silver tray on the dresser.

"Thank you, Davis." Malcolm retrieved his coffee.

"Your uncle Brendan is downstairs, sir. He said he needs to speak with you right away."

"Really," Malcolm said with concern. "Please tell him I'll be right down."

"Yes, sir." With a small smile, Davis added, "I brought tea for you, Ms. Samantha. It's on the tray."

Samantha cringed under her ineffective hiding place and uttered a muffled, "Thank you." She heard the door shut, came out from under the covers, and shot Malcolm a withering look. "You might've mentioned that he comes in here with your coffee every morning. And what's this about your uncle being downstairs?" She got out of bed and began to dress.

Smiling, he leaned one hip against the dresser and sipped his coffee.

That only served to piss Samantha off even more. "I don't think it's funny." She buttoned her sundress in a panic. "Jeez, how about your mom and dad? Maybe they can pop in and catch me in your bed too." The very idea of it made her blush right down to her toenails.

Malcolm walked over and tried to pull her into his arms.

She pushed him away. She brushed past him without saying a word, went into the bathroom, and slammed the door. He went over and knocked gently. "Samantha," he said softly.

He was met with the sound of the water running in the sink as she continued to ignore him.

Please don't be angry, mia piccola lupa.

His voice slid easily into her mind, like ribbons of silk along her soul.

Samantha remembered what he'd said and slammed her mind shut to him. It was a lot like the way she slammed the door. Gratefully, she was met with silence. She finished washing the sleep from her eyes, but was unable to rid herself of the now familiar frustration.

Although she had closed her mind to him, she could still feel him there, waiting. She hated to admit it, but she felt like a part of her was missing. Not having that mental connection left her with an unsettling emptiness. After ten minutes or so, she finally opened the door. She knew he was standing on the other side waiting.

When Sam had blocked him from her thoughts, Malcolm was left with a black void where their connection normally was, and it terrified him. He'd never been dependent on another person until now. When she finally opened the door, Malcolm let out the breath he didn't even realize he'd been holding. She stood there in the doorway for a few moments without saying anything. His eyes searched hers for something, anything.

Finally, she went to the dresser and poured the tea, grateful that Davis had left it for her.

"I'm sorry that you were upset this morning," he said quietly as she sipped her tea.

Sam looked at Malcolm over the edge of her teacup. She saw that he was pained by her unhappiness and that he *felt* everything that she did. It made her feel better that she wasn't the only one trying to figure this all out.

"Apology accepted." She placed her teacup back on the tray. "Now, shall we go downstairs so I can meet your uncle?" He pulled her to him, and this time she let him.

He held her tightly against his chest and placed a gentle kiss on her hair.

"I just hope he doesn't think I'm some kind of tramp," she mumbled against his chest.

"You are my mate, and he will treat you as such. If he treated you as anything less, uncle or not, it would not be tolerated." His eyes shifted into two yellow slashes.

Sam smiled at his protective bluster as he took her hand and led her toward her future.

—◇◇◇—

Samantha and Malcolm walked hand in hand into the living room. She was relieved to see evidence of their activities from the last night was gone. Her wrap and her sandals were neatly waiting for her by the deck doors. She was, however, stunned by the man who stood waiting for them by the fireplace. He could've passed for Malcolm's brother. His uncle Brendan was the same towering height as Malcolm. He was dressed in an impeccable black suit with a bright pink shirt and matching handkerchief in his breast pocket. They had similar builds and hair color, but his eyes were almost jet black.

This is your uncle? He looks more like your brother. Only he's a snappier dresser, she teased to Malcolm.

We don't age the same way humans do, remember? I assure you he's much older than me. Anyway, I thought you liked me better without clothes, he thought wickedly.

Brendan turned to greet them, and his gaze instantly landed on Samantha.

She felt like a bug under a microscope.

"Good morning, Nephew." The two men shook hands. "I hope I haven't disturbed you too early." His eyes went back to Sam's face, which had visibly reddened.

"You must be Samantha." He took her hand and gave it a chivalrous kiss. "You are even more beautiful than Malcolm let on."

"Don't go flirting with my mate, you devil." Malcolm took her hand back and held it gently in his. "Careful, Sam, my uncle had quite a reputation with the ladies, until he connected with his mate of course," he said with good-natured teasing.

"It's very nice to meet you. Are you of the Eagle Clan

as well?" She hoped she didn't sound like a big idiot, because at the moment that's exactly how she felt.

"No. I am of the Bear Clan, like my sister." His eyes glittered like two black diamonds.

"I see." She tried not to squirm under his continued inspection.

"Malcolm tells me you are involved in finding other humans. Special ones like my mother," she said with a wave to her painting.

"Yes. If there was one, well, then there are more to be sure. Humans who are able to mate and breed with us would certainly have a major impact on our race." He smiled.

I don't know what to say to him, she thought with palpable nervousness. *I feel like I'm on display or failing some test I didn't know I was taking.*

Don't be silly. He's family. Malcolm gave her hand a reassuring squeeze.

Right, family that can turn into a mammoth bear.

"So what does bring you here this early, Uncle," Malcolm said as he and Sam sat on the large leather sofa.

"I have excellent news, and I wanted to deliver it to you in person." Brendan settled himself regally into the chair by the fireplace.

"It seems they've captured the Caedo hunter that has been tracking you and Samantha."

"What? When?"

"Late last night. We have him at a safe house, and he's being interrogated by some of our warriors as we speak."

"This is outstanding." Malcolm smiled. "Does Richard know?"

"Yes of course. He's asked that we not disturb his interrogation of the suspect. I think he was thrilled to get the first crack at him."

"Well, I'd like to have a crack at him myself. I should come to the safe house." Malcolm rose swiftly.

"Not yet." Brendan held up his hand. "All in good time, my boy. He is being guarded by some of our fiercest men. Not to worry, you'll get your chance." He smiled wickedly.

"This is wonderful news. Thank you." Malcolm gave Brendan a hearty handshake.

"You're more than welcome. This should give you and your mate ample time to... get acquainted." He smiled knowingly with a wink to Sam.

Her face reddened, and she looked at Malcolm for backup.

"We've already completed the mating rite," Malcolm said with pride.

Sam's mouth fell open in utter mortification. She wanted to crawl under the table or do that disappearing act that Malcolm could do. Not Malcolm. He stood there proud as a peacock. She could swear she saw feathers sprout right out of him. Sam snapped her mouth shut and managed a weak smile at Brendan.

"Really," Brendan said with surprise. "Well, that's good news indeed." He looked at his watch. "I'd better be going. I don't want to miss too much of the interrogation back at the safe house. By the way, I took the liberty of releasing Dante, William, and Steven from their duties this morning."

"I see," Malcolm said with raised eyebrows. "Well, I suppose that we don't really need their protection anymore, do we?" He cast a glance to Samantha. It was meant to comfort her, but his energy waves rippled with his lingering concern.

"I'll be in touch." He turned to Samantha. "It was lovely to meet you, my dear. I'm sure we'll be seeing each other again." Then he uttered the ancient language and vanished into the air.

Malcolm said nothing after Brendan left and went out to the deck.

"I am never gonna get used to that disappearing act," Sam mumbled as she followed Malcolm outside.

The rumbling energy waves that rolled off him made her a bit dizzy. Breathing deeply, she wrapped her arms around his waist and rested her head against the warm expanse of his back. She hoped she could comfort him as easily as he did her. "What is it, Malcolm? I can feel how worried you are. I would think you'd be relieved by this news."

"I know." He scanned the beach below and placed one strong hand over hers as it rested on his lower belly. "I'm sure I'll feel better once I see this fellow for myself. I'm sure Brendan and the others will handle things properly. They're good friends."

"Friends? Oh shit! Oh my God, what time is it?" Sam grabbed Malcolm's wrist to look at his watch. "Jeez. It's almost ten o'clock. I've got to go. I'm going shopping with Kerry in town today." She frantically ran back inside, grabbing her shoes and wrap. She dashed over and gave Malcolm a quick kiss on the cheek.

Before she could escape, he hooked his arm around her waist, pulled her to him, and captured her mouth with his. She loved the way he kissed her. It spread delicious warmth through her entire body. He didn't just kiss her… he devoured her. She wrapped her arms around his narrow waist and responded with equal fervor. Finally, he released her, leaving them both breathless.

"Now, that is how mates say good-bye," he whispered wickedly against her lips.

"Right." She tried to catch her breath.

"Come back tonight," he said between little kisses at the corners of her mouth. "You still have to learn to shift… and other things." He gave her that knee-weakening smile. "Besides, as my mate, this is your home as well."

Sam looked up at him with skepticism. "I'm not moving in here."

"Well, not today, but eventually."

Sam patted him on the chest and took a step back. "Let's just take it one step at a time. Okay, let's recap, shall we? Today I'm going shopping with my best friend, you know, something *normal*. Then tonight, say around seven, I'll come here and learn how to turn into a wolf. *Not normal*."

"It's normal for you."

"No, Malcolm. No, it's not normal for me." Her frustration rose. "That's what you don't seem to get. Until a few days ago, my biggest problem was getting my art to sell. Now I find out that I'm only half human. I've got to learn how to turn into a wolf *and* avoid crazy psycho killers. Oh… and let's not forget that apparently last night, I got married or whatever, to a guy who's actually a bird."

"Do you feel better?" Malcolm stood, his arms crossed, leaning against the deck railing.

Sam puffed the hair out of her face. With her nose pointed slightly in the air, she responded. "Yes actually."

"Good." His smile was self-satisfied. "So I'll see you this evening at seven?"

"Fine. I'll see you at seven." Sam got about halfway down the steps and turned around. "By the way... you're not going to spy on me again today. Right? Remember that whole *giving me space* thing?"

Malcolm raised his hands in defeat. "You have my word. Since it seems that they've captured our Caedo hunter, I don't think that's necessary."

"Good." She nodded and continued down the wooden steps.

"Besides," he yelled after her. "Now that we're mated, I would know right away if you needed me."

Samantha rolled her eyes and waved without turning around. "Oookay. Bye," she called ever so sweetly. A smile spread slowly across her face as his voice rippled like a whisper of satin inside of her.

Always.

Chapter 18

WHEN SAM REACHED THE TOP OF THE STEPS AT HOME, she was relieved that Nonie's car wasn't there. She had been dreading finding her at the kitchen table with two cups of tea and a look of disapproval. Gratefully, she had the house to herself and got ready for her shopping date with Kerry in record time. She threw on her pink Capri pants and a crisp white T-shirt. Sam's favorite fashion was easy and comfortable. She was about to walk out the door and the phone rang. "Hello?" She ran her fingers through her hair a few times.

Kerry's voice came brightly across the line. "Hey, woman. Nice walk of shame this morning."

Sam cringed visibly. "Jeez. You saw that, huh?"

"Oh, yeah." She chuckled. "Listen, we've got to take your car. AJ and I are sharing a car while I'm here, and that dork currently has it. He must've had a date with his fish," Kerry said with irritation.

"No problem... if you don't mind riding in the old bug."

"Great! Pick me up in five minutes, and by the way, I want all the racy details. Bye."

She hung up before Sam could retort. Sam smiled, put the last finishing touches on her makeup, and headed out.

Sam pulled up in front of the Smithson's massive contemporary home and honked the horn for her friend.

It loomed largely over Nonie's house. It was all glass and sharp angles, and to Samantha it always seemed cold. Kerry's parents weren't very involved with their only child's life. They ran in the ultra-wealthy crowd, jet-setting all over the world. Kerry used to joke that her mother and father adopted her so that they could have a picture of *The Smithson's* in front of the fireplace every Christmas. Kerry said she felt more like an acquisition for their business, rather than a daughter. Sam thought Kerry's phobia about touching people came from growing up in such a cold family. It broke Sam's heart. Her parents were missing out on an incredible woman.

Within minutes, Kerry came sweeping out the front door with supermodel flair. Sam always felt a little less put together when Kerry was around. She had on white linen pants with a black halter and adorable strappy sandals. It was an outfit Sam would've felt overdressed in, but for Kerry it was breezy casual. Her long black hair was swept up gracefully in a clip. Her oval face was framed by her movie star sunglasses, and a white Chanel bag draped elegantly over her arm. Sam smiled as Kerry slid easily into the front seat next to her. Sam was certain that if you looked up the word *statuesque* in the dictionary, Kerry's picture would be underneath it. "You look too nice to be in this car. I feel like you're going to wilt or something." She pulled out of the driveway.

"Oh, please." Kerry waved it off. "Let's move on to more interesting topics like… oh, I don't know… the little sleepover you had with the hot, mysterious neighbor?"

"His name is Malcolm," Sam corrected.

"Okay. Malcolm. So…"

Sam tightened her grip on the steering wheel. She

wanted to share everything with Kerry, but would she believe it? Sam decided to take it one step at a time. Malcolm was probably right about people needing to see for themselves. "So… it was… well… he made me a beautiful dinner. Salad, lobster, and champagne—you know the works. All of it by candlelight, by the way. It was quite romantic." She continued to rattle off details of the evening as the scenery whizzed past them on their way into Watch Hill.

"Uh-huh. Sounds like this guy set quite the scene," Kerry said quietly.

"What do you mean by that?" Sam felt a bit defensive.

"Did you do it?"

Sam laughed. "Wow. You do get right to the point, don't you? Sheesh."

"We've known each other too long to beat around the bush," she said flatly. "Besides, it's been way too long since I've had sex. I need to live vicariously through others. So humor me." She gave her a friendly swat.

"Yes, you heathen. We did it," she spit out.

"Woo hoo! Samantha got some nookie," Kerry hooted loudly. Then she stuck her head out the window and hooted some more.

"Jesus. Shut up." Sam laughed. "I don't think all of Watch Hill needs to hear about this." She reached over and pulled her friend back in from the window.

"So are you going to see him again?" Kerry inquired as they pulled into the parking lot.

"Yes. I'm going over tonight for dinner actually." Sam shut off the engine.

"Good," she said firmly. "Then he clearly wanted more than a one-night stand. One more question… does he make you happy?" Kerry asked in an unusually serious tone.

"Happy? Well, yes... but it's more than that." She thought as various memories came flooding back. "Since I've known Malcolm, I feel..." She paused, searching for just the right word. "I feel awake... you know... for the first time in my life I am *awake*." She looked over at her friend. "Does that make sense?"

"Not really." Kerry chuckled, her brows knitted together. "But if it makes sense to you, then that's good enough for me." She got out of the car and gave Sam a wicked grin. "By the way, if he hurts you... I'm going to kick his ass."

"I wouldn't expect anything less." Samantha slipped on her sunglasses.

They spent the next couple of hours weaving their way in and out of the little shops along Main Street. The town was made up of one tiny stretch of road along the harbor. The street was dotted with one boutique after another. A few restaurants, the requisite ice cream parlor, and candy shop. At one end was the small harbor with boats of varying sizes and shapes, while the other end was capped by a beautiful old carousel. Year after year children came here to ride the ponies and try to get the brass ring. Sam had many fond memories of riding that carousel herself, but she never did get the ring.

During their shopping excursion, Sam found an adorable little camisole in one place, and Kerry found a sculpture at another. After exhausting every shop on one side of the street, they finally settled in for lunch at *The Olympia Tea Room*. The light and lovely atmosphere was matched only by the incredible food. Over their lunch of lobster salad and white wine, she told Kerry more about her evening with Malcolm. Kerry listened intently and was eager to hear all that Sam had to tell. Samantha still felt the need to hold back. She felt guilty for only telling her partial truths, but she just couldn't bring herself to tell the whole story. Not yet.

After lunch, they perused the remaining shops, finding various treasures along the way. Samantha was picking through a rack of dresses as Malcolm's voice floated quietly into her mind.

Enjoying yourself, are you?

Sam felt delicious little shivers run down her back. *Stop that.* She inadvertently sent him a smile.

Stop what?

At that same moment, Sam actually felt his hands run along her sides. The passion flared hard and fast. With a sharp intake of breath, she steeled herself, afraid the entire store would see her body respond. She yelped when Kerry came up behind her. "Oh. Shit!"

"Sorry. Jeez, you seemed awfully deep in thought about that dress," Kerry said with genuine concern. "Hey! You're all flushed, are you okay?"

"Yes. Sorry." Sam flashed an embarrassed smile. "I was just deciding if I should get this for my date with Malcolm tonight. What do you think?" She held up a hideous brown and white concoction.

Kerry made a face and shook her head. "Jesus. You're out of Manhattan for like two seconds, and already you've lost all sense of fashion. No way." She grimaced and placed the offending garment back on the rack. "Look. I didn't have incredible sex last night, so I need ice cream. One of the benefits of being a model for *real* women's clothing. No need to starve myself. C'mon." Kerry took Sam's hand, leading her out the door.

You told her it was incredible, he chuckled softly.

Sam rolled her eyes. *Good-bye, Malcolm.* She sent him the sternest impression she could muster. She heard his laugh fade into the distance.

They made a beeline straight for the ice cream shop. Kerry opted for rocky road with sprinkles, and Samantha settled on a cone of cookies and cream. They walked quietly for a while as they ate their cold, sweet goodies. Eventually they ended up watching the carousel spin. They watched the children with their jack-o'-lantern smiles reach time and again for the rings. Every now and then you'd hear the victorious shriek of, *I got it, Mommy!* as one of them grasped the golden circle.

Kerry broke the silence first. "You still want kids, right?" she asked, between licks of her ice cream.

"Oh, yeah." Sam smiled. Until Malcolm, she hadn't seriously considered it.

"You want a boy or a girl?"

Human would've been nice. "Oh… it doesn't really matter." Sam smiled. "How about you? Still want kids?"

"I'd love it. But I still haven't found the right guy. Plus… you know that would mean I'd have to find someone I can actually stand touching. Haven't met anyone spookie-free. I could do the whole sperm bank thing, but I still want to have a baby with a guy I'm in love with." She threw her napkin into a nearby trash can. "At least you're on the right track with Malcolm."

"Whoa." Sam made her way back to the car. "No one said anything about us having babies or anything."

"Uh-huh." Kerry eyed her skeptically. "Look, kiddo, I've known you longer than anyone, and I have *never* heard you talk about a man this way *ever*. You'll be married to this guy by Christmas." She casually waited for Sam to unlock the car.

I like her, Malcolm said in his matter-of-fact way.

That's it! You are cut off, bird boy. Sam slammed her mind shut to him. Within seconds, that odd feeling of emptiness began to creep in. She had to steel herself against it. She needed Malcolm to understand and re-spect her privacy. If he couldn't manage it on his own, she'd have to help him.

"Hello? Sam? Wake up. Are you ever going to un-lock the car? These bags are cutting off the circulation in my arms." Kerry waved her fingers at Sam.

Samantha blinked and shook her head with a small laugh. "Sorry. It's just all this marriage and baby talk made me space out."

They filled the little red Bug with their various pack-ages and headed back home. They sang their hearts out to some old eighties tunes, Bon Jovi in particular. Sam loved that liberating feeling of singing at the top of her lungs, belting it out with the windows wide open while the wind whipped her hair in a frenzy. The two friends sang and laughed all the way back home. They got out still laughing and removed all of Kerry's packages from the trunk. Sam pulled out the last bag and noticed move-ment in the tall grasses next to the driveway. Hiding there, stone still, almost completely hidden by the reeds and grass, was an enormous red fox. Its huge amber eyes were fixed on them boldly. It tracked every move they made without the smallest ounce of fear.

"What is it?" Kerry glanced over to where Sam was looking.

"It's a fox," Sam said in a loud whisper. "See, right over there." But when she looked back, it was gone. There wasn't a trace of it. The grass hadn't even wavered.

"I don't see it. Really?" Kerry squinted, trying to find it.

"A fox in the daylight isn't good. Yikes, if you see it again, don't go near it. It's probably rabid." Kerry made a sound of disgust. "I forgot how much I loathe nature." Kerry placed a quick kiss on Sam's cheek. "I'll talk to you later."

"Right," Sam said absently.

"I had a ball, babe," Kerry said, going up the steps. "By the way, we are still on for tomorrow night, right? You, me, AJ, and your... Malcolm?"

"Boy, you never give up, do you?" Sam smiled.

"Nope." Kerry winked. "Have fun tonight, and call me in the morning." Waving, she disappeared into the house.

Sam drove back to Nonie's house. If she had an energy signature like Malcolm said, then it was on fire at the moment. What would it take to make this man understand the word *privacy*? She pulled into the driveway and gravel spit up angrily when she screeched to a halt at the top.

We need to talk, Malcolm, right now.

As the sound of her sweet, but angry voice spread through his mind, Malcolm's body flooded with relief. The moment she'd shut her mind to him, the emptiness came over him like a shroud. The touch of her mind to his was like getting water after a drought. In an instant, he materialized in the car next to her. "As you wish," he murmured.

Samantha jumped several inches out of her seat. "Jesus!" She slapped his arm. "Would you please stop that? You've got to give me some kind of warning if you're going to just pop in and out of places." She clutched her chest.

"I'm sorry. You wanted to speak with me now, so I came as quickly as I could." He trailed one finger along her thigh, knowing it left a trail of pleasure in its wake.

"Stop that too." She pushed his hand away.

He took her fingers and linked them with his. "I like your friend very much. She's quite insightful." He smiled and stroked the pad of his thumb along the inside of her palm, which sent little zaps of lightning over her skin.

"Most men do." Jealousy rose involuntarily inside of her.

"That's not what I meant, and you know it." He turned her face so he could look into her eyes. "She is your friend and means a great deal to you. Therefore, she means a great deal to me."

"You can't tell me that you don't think she's beautiful?"

"She's quite attractive. But *you* are beautiful." He brushed his lips ever so lightly along her knuckles. Her breath hitched in her throat and her mouth went dry.

"There is no one else for me, Samantha." His eyes shifted and locked on hers. "Ever."

She licked her lips and tried to maintain self-control. She closed her eyes and reluctantly removed her hand from Malcolm's. "Do you even know why I shut my mind to you today?" She got out of the car, needing to put some space between them.

"Yes," he said, his voice dropping to almost a whisper. "I invaded your space. I'm sorry, Samantha. It's just that I am so eager to get to know everything I can about you that I suppose I get a little... overzealous." He met her outside the car and took her bags from the trunk.

"Overbearing is more like it." She closed the trunk. "And what's with having that Amoveo fox watching me too? I thought your uncle called off those guys anyway." She took one of the bags from Malcolm, his brow now wrinkled in concern.

"A fox?" A shadow passed over his face. "Are you certain it was an Amoveo and not just a regular fox?"

"Oh no, this was definitely not a normal fox." She led him into Nonie's house. "First of all, it was *huge*. Second, it was watching us. I mean, really watching us, and then when I went to point it out to Kerry, it was gone. Poof. Not even the grasses moved. It was like it just vanished... sound familiar?"

"Yes."

The look on his face betrayed his concern. She also felt it in little waves that made her catch her breath. She wasn't sure if she'd ever get used to having shared emotions; it definitely threw her off balance. They brought her bags into the house and set them down by the stairs.

"Samantha, I need to go speak with my cousin, Dante. I am quite sure he was who you saw today, but I'm unclear as to why he would be here. I'm sure everything is fine, but I would feel much better if I heard that from him." He moved closer, his body just inches from hers. "Would you still like to join me this evening?"

Sam smiled because this time he asked her if she wanted to come over; he didn't assume. "Well." She looked around to see if Nonie was in earshot. "You do still owe me a lesson in shapeshifting, if I'm not mistaken." She looked up at him with a suggestive smile.

"Yes, *mia piccola lupa*, I believe I do," he whispered against her lips and swept her up in one of his devastating, knee-weakening kisses. Her body melded easily against his. She wrapped her arms around his neck, and desire for him warmed her entire body.

He pulled back slowly and placed one last little kiss at the corner of her mouth. "I won't be gone long. I'll see you at seven."

"Oh wait. I almost forgot. Kerry wants to go out tomorrow night so she can meet you. Are you game?" She flashed a mischievous grin.

"I imagine that would be very nice. Will it just be the three of us?" He held her around her waist with one hand and stroked her cheek with the other.

"No." Sam savored the gentle caress. "Her cousin AJ is coming too. He's living there this summer while he works at the aquarium in Mystic," she whispered as he trailed kisses down her neck.

"Whatever you wish," he spoke softly.

Delicious shivers fluttered down her spine. She pulled him closer, wanting to feel his body press against hers.

"Well, don't mind me." Nonie's singsong voice broke the moment like a bucket of water on a fire.

They jumped apart, and Sam wiped at her lips.

"I was just leaving." Malcolm cleared his throat. "Nice to see you again, Nonie."

"Mmm hmm. Good day, Mr. Drew." Nonie brushed past them into the kitchen.

Malcolm went out the door and whispered teasingly

to Sam. *I think you're in trouble. She looks pretty upset with you.*

Sam narrowed her eyes and shot back, *Coward.* She shook her head, smiling after him. Then she took a deep breath and went into the kitchen to receive a good, old-fashioned lecture. She found Nonie rinsing out her teacup in the kitchen sink. "So, go ahead. Let me have it." Sam pulled out the chair and sat at the table, her hands folded.

"I don't know what you mean, dear." Nonie put her cup in the dishwasher, loaded it up with detergent, and set it running.

"You don't having anything to say about what you just saw or the fact that I stayed at Malcolm's last night?"

Nonie turned slowly and leaned against the edge of the sink. She didn't say anything at first, just looked down at her hands as though she was looking for exactly the right thing to say. "You are an adult, Samantha. Next time you plan on staying out all night, it would be nice if you let me know. That's all." Her eyes betrayed her sadness.

Sam could feel how upset Nonie was, it was actually making her stomach hurt. "Nonie, why are you so sad? And don't try to tell me you're not. I can sense how upset you are."

Nonie's eyes welled up with tears, and she hurried out of the kitchen.

Her tears hit Sam like a shock wave. When she stood to follow, she got an enormous head rush. She shut her eyes and steadied herself, leaning on the back of the chair. Malcolm's voice came like a soothing balm into her soul.

Are you all right?

She could hear the twinge of concern, and it made her smile in spite of how she felt. *Yes. Nonie is upset, and it's making me feel sick.* She tried to keep panic from welling up inside of her.

Focus on your breathing, and it will pass. Your body will learn to be more accepting of other people's emotions and will adjust. I promise, mia piccola lupa.

As his words drifted through her mind, her body instantly relaxed. Sam steadied her breathing, and the unpleasant sensation began to subside. She let out a deep breath and whispered back to him in their intimate telepathy. *Thank you, Malcolm.*

Sam found Nonie out on the deck, staring at the rough waters below. Her small body was bundled up in a huge blue sweater, her arms crossed tightly across her chest. She was only a few feet away, but Sam had never felt so far from her. The wind was picking up, and long strands of her silver hair were whipping around her head. "Looks like a storm is coming. You know the sea always picks up like this before a big one." Sam walked over and stood next to Nonie at the railing.

"That's what I'm afraid of." Nonie turned to look at Samantha. "I already lost your mother. I can't lose you as well." Tears filled her eyes.

"Nonie, you're not going to lose me."

Nonie shook her head and turned back out to the ocean. "That's what your mother told me too." Nonie wiped tears away with the back of her time-worn hand. "You're moving awfully fast, Samantha. Do you even know him? I mean, do you know what kind of man he is?"

"Actually, Nonie, I know him better than I've ever

known anyone in my life." Sam wrapped her arms around her grandmother.

"Did he tell you what it really means to be with him?"

She turned Nonie gently so they were face-to-face. Sam looked at her through narrowed eyes, searching for the truth. "What do you mean, Nonie?" Samantha felt Nonie's apprehension rising in unison with her own.

"I—" Nonie was interrupted by the shrill ring of Samantha's cell phone in the front hall.

Sam growled in frustration at being interrupted. They stood there, eyes locked in silence, as the phone continued to ring.

"You'd better get that." Nonie turned back to look out on the sea.

Sam miraculously found her phone on the first dive into her bag. The caller ID confirmed it was Kerry. "Hey, can I call you back? I'm in the middle of something with Nonie." Sam watched her grandmother come back in the house and brush past her to the kitchen.

"I really need to see you," Kerry said through a strained voice. Kerry never cried.

"Hey? What's going on? You sound like you've been crying." An all too familiar wave of nausea came over Sam. *Focus, Sam, and steady breathing, just like Malcolm said.* She held her belly and squeezed her eyes shut. Gratefully, the sensation slowly subsided.

"I can't talk about it on the phone," Kerry said abruptly. "I'm so sorry, but Sam, you have to come over."

Her voice was desperate and scared, which made Sam very nervous. Kerry never let that kind of emotion out... ever. She always used smartass humor to cover it all up. "Okay. I'll be right there," Sam said. The line went dead before she got all the words out. She hung up and heard Nonie going upstairs. "Nonie," Sam called after her. "Kerry is pretty upset and needs me to come over. I've never heard her like this before. I'm worried." She was feeling torn in two directions. She really wanted to find out what Nonie was insinuating, but the fear in Kerry's voice was too alarming to ignore. "I'd really like to continue our conversation when I get back."

"That's fine, dear," Nonie said in a weary voice. She gave a small wave of her hand. "I'm going to lie down for a while." At the top of the stairs, Nonie looked down at Samantha. "You know I love you, Samantha... no matter what." Then she disappeared around the corner to her room.

Malcolm worked in his office and tried many times to reach out to Dante. However, each attempt resulted in silence. His frustration at the lack of contact with Dante grew with every passing moment. Why was he watching Sam if the hunter had been caught? He struggled to concentrate on the tedious emails that glared at him from the harsh light of the computer screen. Moments later his mind was happily flooded with Samantha's melodious voice.

I am going over to Kerry's house. She's very upset and needs to see me.

When she established their intimate mental link, his body was immediately drenched with warmth. An easy smile replaced a look of focused concentration. *Does this mean you'll be late for our lesson this evening?* He put a suggestive emphasis on the word *lesson*.

Well, probably, but I'm also going to cut you off, so to speak.

His instinct was to fight her on this decision. However, he knew she was looking for privacy, which was so dear to her. *As you wish,* he whispered back. Every fiber of his being cried out against this action, yet he relented. It pained him to be cut off from her mentally, but he needed to prove that he could respect her wishes.

Thank you, Malcolm. She let out a great sigh of relief and made her way down the beach steps. *I think it's going to be an old-fashioned girl talk with lots of tears and probably some ice cream. If I didn't close my mind to you, then I'd feel like I was betraying her confidence. You know, letting you in on her secrets, which aren't mine to tell. Do you understand?* She nibbled on her bottom lip.

His next words fluttered across her heart like featherlight kisses.

Promise me that as soon as you're done with your…female bonding… you'll connect with me right away.

Sam laughed softly, and his heart felt a small, unexpected squeeze. *Absolutely… I'll see you soon,* she purred.

Samantha severed their mental link, and he was left with a growing void. As the inevitable feeling of dread began to creep over him, he shook his head and shifted his focus to his work. He reminded himself that Uncle Brendan had the Caedo hunter, and any imminent danger was gone. He repeated it over and over to himself, but couldn't escape the feeling that darkness was coming.

When she shut her mind to Malcolm, a black hole was left in its wake. Sam shuddered and pulled her black sweater closer around her. The winds had picked up considerably. She squinted to avoid the tiny grains of sand caught in the salty gales. She was always amazed at how quickly the weather changed on the ocean. The sky had darkened ominously, which mirrored the shadowy, roiling sea as it crashed onto the deserted shores.

Sam quickly climbed the steps to Kerry's house and was surprised to see the sliding glass doors wide open. As she stepped onto the deck, she was hit with a shock wave of intense emotion. It slammed into her mind violently, like someone drove a spike into her brain. She clasped her head, and stars burst behind her eyes. The crushing pain dropped her to her knees. She knelt there, desperately trying to catch her breath and squelch the panic rising inside of her. Her instinct was to reach out to Malcolm, but she needed to cope with these emotional onslaughts. She refused to be weak. She had to prove that she was able to handle her Amoveo abilities without running to him all the time like a child.

Samantha drew in slow, steady breaths and focused on filtering out the emotion as Malcolm had taught her. Eventually, the crushing pain began to diminish. Shaking, she rose to her feet. She wiped the tears away and steadied her balance on the railing. Something was dreadfully wrong. She had not experienced ferocious emotion like that before. It felt evil. She took a few tentative steps toward the open door. "Kerry?" There was no answer. Sam clutched her sweater around her shaking body. She peered hesitantly into the open doorway and called for her friend again. "Kerry?" To her horror, the entire living room had been ransacked. It looked like someone had fought a war inside the house. Chairs and tables were overturned, lamps shattered on the floor, books and smashed picture frames were strewn about. She was about to run, but a low moaning from behind the couch caught her attention. She quickly climbed over the debris and found a bleeding man. She could tell right away that he was Amoveo. She didn't know how, she just *knew*.

He had several swollen bruises on his face. A huge silver arrow protruded from a bloody wound in his massive chest. Based on his auburn hair, it was likely that this was the Fox she had seen earlier. Malcolm's cousin, Dante, was a Fox… wasn't he? The man stirred slightly. Sam looked him over quickly and saw he was injured badly. Based on the dark stain on the rug beneath him, he'd lost an enormous amount of blood.

"Dante?" she whispered as she brushed hair away from his face. "What happened? Where's Kerry?"

He moved slightly and groaned in response.

"It's okay. Everything's going to be all right," she said more for her own reassurance, trying to keep her fear under control. "I'm going to call Malcolm."

From behind her came a sinister, but slightly familiar voice. "I don't think so."

Something smashed the back of her head, and her entire world went dark.

Chapter 19

NONIE WOKE FROM HER NIGHTMARE WITH A START. She sat straight up in bed. Her heart raced, and she was covered in sweat. Like so many times in her life, this had been more than just a bad dream. She looked out the window at the stormy sky and knew that Samantha was in grave danger. Memories of when she lost her beloved Jane came flooding back and practically paralyzed her. That night she'd been helpless, unable to save her daughter. This time would be different. It had to be. She knew that the one person who could help her granddaughter was Malcolm.

She picked up the phone to call him and was met with a deafening silence. Frantic, she hung it up, silently cursing herself for not getting a cell phone as Samantha had told her to. As quickly as her old body would allow, she made her way downstairs and out into the turbulent night. The wind lashed against her relentlessly, testing her strength with every step down the staircase to the beach. The sands whipped up, stinging her face, but she kept going. After what felt like an eternity, she reached the enormous wooden steps to Malcolm's home.

~~~

Malcolm was seated in his living room, glancing at his watch for the tenth time. It was after eight o'clock, and Samantha was an hour overdue for their date. The inability to touch his mind to hers was torturous. He wanted to reach out and reconnect, but he'd promised her privacy. He wondered how much longer this *girl talk* was going to take. He looked at his watch yet again and cursed silently under his breath as he stalked over to the enormous glass doors. His attention was immediately caught by an intense current of emotion undulating in the air. He went very still, his heightened senses at full attention. His eyes shifted and swiftly scanned the area outside.

Within moments, he spotted Nonie struggling to reach the top of the beach steps. She was exhausted and tremendously distressed. Malcolm dashed out into the whipping wind and rain. When he reached her, she collapsed against him. Her weathered hands clutched his arms as she gasped for air. Malcolm scooped up her frail body and uttered the ancient language. In a flash, they were back in his living room. She was ice cold, drenched, and shaking. With a wave of his hand, a roaring fire appeared in the fireplace, and a dry blanket materialized around her. He wrapped her up. "Davis! Come in here quickly!" He rubbed Nonie's arms gently in an effort to help warm her. "Helen? What's happened?" he asked with pleading eyes.

"I'm not sure," she said through a tearful voice. "I had one of my dreams. Just like the night her mother died. Malcolm, please, you have to go to her. I can't lose her like I lost Jane."

Davis shuffled into the room and came directly to her side.

"Helen? What's happened?"

"It's Samantha." Malcolm helped Nonie sit down.

"Did you call Kerry's house or her cell?" He tried to keep his voice calm. He struggled to dampen the dread rising inside of him.

She shook her head as Davis sat next to her and placed a soothing arm around her shaking shoulders. "The phone lines are down, probably due to the storm." She sniffled. "I don't have a cell phone. Samantha's been after me to get one." She gave a teary smile. "Why don't you just reach out to her Malcolm," she whispered with downcast eyes.

Malcolm froze and peered at Nonie through narrowed eyes. "Helen?"

"She knows all about the Amoveo, sir." Davis tenderly rubbed Nonie's back as Malcolm stared back at him in disbelief. "She has for years."

"And if I hadn't, well, don't you think transporting me in here and visualizing the fire might've been a tip off that you are… different?"

Malcolm wouldn't have been more surprised if Nonie had jumped up and done a backflip. "What? How?"

Nonie silenced him with a glare. "Don't you think we have more important things to discuss? Like finding my granddaughter," she said more sharply than she'd intended. "We can have a history lesson later."

Malcolm nodded somberly. "Samantha closed her mind to me before she went to Kerry's house. Something about privacy for their *girl talk*." He stood. "Well, before I break my word and try to connect with her, I'm going over there."

"Malcolm, please," Nonie said anxiously. "Be careful. I know something is dreadfully wrong."

"I will. I swear to you she will be all right," he said in

earnest. He turned to Davis. "Once she's feeling better, I want you to take Nonie home right away, and stay with her there until you hear from me. Understood?"

"Yes, sir." Davis helped Nonie up from the couch. "First I'm going to get some tea for my best girl."

As Malcolm went out into the stormy night, he heard Davis whispering soft reassurances to her. He shifted. Within moments, he flew through the air, his feathered body pelted by the howling wind and rain. He prayed the quiet promises Davis made were going to be kept.

Malcolm flew over Kerry's house and tried to connect with Samantha, but was met with the same void. He cursed himself for ever agreeing to break their connection. Even before Malcolm landed, he could see that something was dreadfully wrong at the Smithson house. The house was completely dark, and the sliding door was wide open. He landed on the deck and shifted back to his human form, except for his eyes. He needed the special vision now more than ever. Soaking wet, he stepped into the house and was horrified at the scene before him. Evidence of a battle was strewn around the room. A fear greater than any he'd felt before gripped his heart. Panic threatened to engulf him.

He scanned the room and sensed trace evidence of Samantha's energy. What he saw next made his heart leap into his throat.

Blood.

He launched himself over to the sickening stain that seeped out from behind the couch. To his surprise, he found Dante. An enormous silver arrow pierced his cousin's chest. He was unconscious and bleeding profusely. His life force ebbed low. "Dante? Can you hear me?" He was met with only a moan. He knew Dante needed a healer. Malcolm immediately focused on creating a mental link with Steven. Within seconds, Steven answered the call and materialized next to them. He kneeled down to inspect the bloody wound in Dante's chest. "My God," Steven gasped. He closed his shifted green coyote's eyes and placed his hands on Dante's chest.

Malcolm watched the intense concentration on Steven's face as he worked to repair the mutilated flesh. Steven was always known for his smartass humor, but when it came to healing, he was all business. Malcolm wanted to grab Dante and shake him so he could tell them what had happened here. The fear and frustration of not knowing where she was began to consume him. "Is he going to live?" Malcolm asked impatiently. "Why was he even here, Steven? I thought you all were called off because the Caedo hunter had been captured?"

Steven did not answer, but kept his attention fully focused on his patient. *I need to focus on Dante,* Steven telepathed to him in a calm, steady voice. *Why don't you take a look around, and see if you can find anything else that will help us find Samantha?* Through it all, Steven stayed stone still with intense concentration on Dante's wounds.

Of course, Malcolm replied. He felt foolish that panic threatened to overtake him. He went through the first floor, which was littered with broken furniture, lamps, and just about everything else. After finding nothing on the first floor, he made his way upstairs to the bedrooms. The first three bedrooms revealed nothing—no sign of Samantha or her friend, Kerry. Malcolm approached the last room. His hand hit the doorknob, and he was assaulted by an all too familiar surge of evil. His eyes flashed yellow, and he kicked the door down.

His stomach rolled at the sight before him. The walls were papered with photos of Samantha. Her beautiful face with laughing eyes wallpapered the room. There were hundreds of images of Sam in her daily life, doing everything from grocery shopping, jogging, and working in the city, along with several of her here at the beach with Nonie. This sick bastard had been stalking her every move. Rage bubbled up, and the currents in the room shifted dangerously. Malcolm stepped closer to several photos that had huge red targets drawn on them. Bile rose in his throat when he saw that those were of him and Samantha.

There was a photographic record of their time together all around the room.

It made him boil with fury that their privacy was violated. Various notes were tacked along the wall as well, which read things like *Devil Spawn*. Evil permeated the room, and Malcolm couldn't understand how he never noticed it. The Caedo hunter had lived here, next door, right under their noses. How did this hunter not only block thoughts, but create a barrier around this room? Malcolm walked over to the desk where several papers were strewn about. He read quickly through them. They were all from the same person, but they were unsigned. Whoever was writing the letters had been helping with the whole sickening thing. With every passing second, his anger rose higher. His body shook with rage, and he crumpled the papers in a white-knuckled fist. All this time the enemy had been hiding in plain sight.

There were various weapons in the room, as well as night vision binoculars. The last thing that he noticed was a telescope. He looked through it and dread crept up his spine. It peered directly into Sam's bedroom. The rage flared violently and quickly. He knew exactly who had Samantha and had a pretty good idea where she was taken.

Samantha gained consciousness gradually. Excruciating pain radiated through her head. The slightest movement caused the pain to branch out mercilessly in brutal tendrils. Panic and fear threatened to overwhelm her. She focused on her breathing and took stock of her situation. She was blindfolded, and her head wasn't the only source of pain. Her hands and wrists, bound behind her back, throbbed relentlessly. Her shoulder was incredibly sore from having passed out on a cold hard floor. Her entire body ached. Her nostrils were filled with the pungent smell of salt water and fish, which hung heavily in the air. She could hear water swishing around as it echoed in the room. She knew she wasn't alone.

She heard someone breathing and sensed another energy signature that was faint and close to going out altogether. She was about to reconnect her mental link with Malcolm when she heard the door open. It slammed shut and was immediately followed by the sound of a heavy bolt sliding into place. The person who entered brought an undulating wave of sickening energy, which she could only describe as evil. It felt like a thousand snakes were trying to slither into her mind. The bile rose in her throat, and she swallowed hard, forcing it down. She stayed very still in the hopes her captor would think she was still unconscious. No such luck.

"I know you're awake," hissed a slightly familiar voice.

She could feel him and the dark energy that slithered off him incessantly. She steeled herself to withstand the onslaught of his hatred. She fought the urge to shrink away from him. She had never encountered such violence; well, at least it had never been directed at her. His maniacal giggle skittered and echoed around the room.

"I hope you're going to call your boyfriend. The party won't be complete without him."

"How can I call anyone? I'm blindfolded and tied up," she snapped.

He made a scolding noise at her and nudged her leg with his foot. "Shame on you, Samantha. Do you really think I don't know what you are?" He sighed heavily as though bored with her. "You are an animal. Just like him. So you have to die." He practically sang it.

Samantha knew that she couldn't call Malcolm for help. She'd be leading him to his slaughter. She had to find a way out of this, and talking to her captor would buy her some time. "Where's Kerry?" She hoped she didn't sound as scared as she felt.

"Oh, she's passed out and tied up a few feet from you. She put up quite a struggle though. I have to give her that. She's feisty, as you know, Samantha."

She could hear him stalk away from her and over to Kerry's limp body. Fear gripped her heart. She realized the low energy she felt was Kerry. She was dying. Sam licked her dry lips. "You know my name, but I don't know yours." She held her breath, waiting for his response. Would he answer her? Smash her over the head? Kill her?

He said nothing, but moved closer and squatted down next to her. His fetid breath puffed on her cheek. He ran one finger along her jaw and slowly down her neck. She clenched her teeth and resisted the urge to scream. To her surprise, he pulled the blindfold off, causing yet another wave of radiating pain. She thought she might pass out. She steadied her breathing and slowly opened her eyes. Sam squinted as they adjusted to the bright fluorescent lights overhead. Her eyes became accommodated to the light, and she found herself looking into a familiar face. "AJ."

He was dressed all in black, like some kind of ninja commando. In his gloved hands, he held a mammoth black crossbow. He stood up, spread his arms out, and with a perverted grin, took a bow. He postured like some kind of demented peacock in front of a pool of water. The ripples of water were reflected all around them, along the walls and domed ceiling. She figured that they were at the aquarium where AJ worked. It must be some kind of access room above one of the giant tanks that thousands of tourists go by every day. She shuddered to think what was in that tank. She had a feeling it probably wasn't the beluga whales, but something with a little more bite.

Sam glanced to her left and saw Kerry. Her heart sank. She was lying in a puddle of blood, blindfolded, gagged, and bound at her hands and feet. The elegant outfit she'd worn on their shopping trip was torn, dirtied, and stained. Her face was covered by her dark hair, and her breathing was shallow. Was the shopping trip today? It seemed like a lifetime ago. How long had they been here?

"The one and only AJ." He was strutting back and forth across the room as though waiting for applause.

"Why are you doing this?"

"You are a freak just like your father."

"My mother was human." She glared at him, daring him to deny that much at least.

"She was his *whore*!" he screamed, looming over her. "She let herself be touched by one of those… those things." He stuttered, spitting as he spoke. "My grandfather told me all about it. He taught me. He told me that it was all up to me now. I am the avenger now."

"You're Caedo," she whispered. The implications of his heritage dawned on her, and she looked over at Kerry.

"Anthony James Caedo, at your service." He bowed again, and then quick as a snake, knelt next to Sam. He brushed her cheek with his knuckles. "But you can call me Tony."

Sam shrank back from him, and her expression twisted in disgust.

His face grew dark, and he roughly grabbed her chin. "What's the matter? Don't like to be touched by a real man?" Then inching closer, he licked the side of her face.

A rage and disgust that she'd never known before boiled up inside of her. She felt her eyes shift harshly as a guttural menacing growl rose from her throat.

Tony jumped in horror and hid behind the sights of his crossbow. He kept it pointed at her, backed up, and shuffled around the giant pool at the center of the room. He was sweating profusely and breathing heavily as he glared at her with fear and hatred. "See. You are an animal."

Samantha struggled through the mind-splitting pain and forced herself to sit up. She gritted her teeth through dizziness and nausea. She broke out in a cold sweat and leaned against the cement wall.

Tony took a few more steps back and then pointed his crossbow at Kerry. "You come near me, and I'll kill her."

She knew he was afraid of her and had to stop herself from smiling. Good thing he didn't know she had no idea how she'd just done that. She glanced at Kerry and nodded toward her friend. "She's your family, AJ."

"Stop calling me that," he screamed. "I hate that fucking nickname. No one calls me that anymore. It's Tony!"

"Okay. Sorry," she apologized. Sam wanted to keep him as calm as possible, but more than anything she had to keep him away from Kerry. "But she *is* your family."

"*No*," he shouted. "She's not. She's adopted. She's not Caedo blood. Grandfather wouldn't tell her the secret. He didn't even tell her mother or my father. He knew they were weak. He only told me. *I'm* the one he trusted. *I'm* one of God's soldiers. *I'm* his avenging angel, and I'm going to help wipe every single one of you abominations from this earth."

He ranted and punctuated each word with vehement hatred as strings of spittle clung to his chin. She could see why his grandfather had chosen him. He chose Tony for the same reason certain people get sucked into cults. He'd always been a bit of an outcast and considered something of a loser. This was his chance to be special. The fact that he was crazy was probably considered a bonus.

"Now," he hissed. "You are going to call your boyfriend with that special mental telephone."

Sam licked her lips, and she struggled to think of a way to distract him. "From what I understand you have some psychic abilities of your own. Malcolm told me that you were able to block his mental probe. You're obviously talented in your own right." Sam hoped to distract him and appeal to his vanity while she loosened the bindings on her wrists.

His face twisted in a sickening grin of self-satisfaction. "Yeah, that's right." He snorted. "I am special. You know, it's not just anyone that can learn to do that." He puffed up his chest with pride.

"How did you learn how to do it?" Sam continued to work the duct tape around her wrists. The sweat dripping down her arms helped loosen the adhesive.

"A friend," he said smugly. "Definitely not someone I thought I'd ever work with, but it seems we have a common enemy." He glared at her.

"What friend?"

"No more questions," he barked. "Now, call your boyfriend, or I am going to put a nice big silver arrow through her brain."

He calmly pressed the crossbow against Kerry's temple, and she moaned softly.

Sam felt a momentary spike in her energy, and it raised her hopes. Kerry would be okay. She had to be.

"We can find out if there really is a brain in that pretty little head." He taunted, poking Kerry harder, which elicited another groan of pain.

"*No!* No please," Samantha screamed more desperately than she wanted to. Tears welled in her eyes. She squeezed them shut, not wanting him to see it. He was a sick bastard. He was making her choose between her best friend and the love of her life. In that moment, Samantha realized that she was completely and irrevocably in love with Malcolm. The tears flowed now beyond her control, and her breath hitched in her chest. She loved him, and if she called him here, he would probably die. She knew by the violent look in Tony's eyes that he would kill Kerry without hesitation. She lay there helpless and bleeding, unable to fight back. Malcolm, however, was another story. "All right." She sniffed. "I'll call him."

"Good." Tony removed an enormous jagged knife from a sheath at his waist. He placed the crossbow down and leaned it against the wall between Samantha and Kerry. Slowly, he stalked over to Sam with the knife.

She lifted her face defiantly and blew her hair out of her eyes. Her gaze landed sharply on his and with a small smile, she said, "But you know what they say, Tony. Be careful what you wish for."

Chapter 20

MALCOLM WENT BACK DOWN TO THE LIVING ROOM and found Steven with a weak but conscious Dante. He could see the wound in his chest was already starting to heal, but he was extremely pale. Steven looked equally exhausted from his healing efforts as they both sat in the wreckage of the destroyed room. Dante looked up at his cousin with eyes that pled for forgiveness.

"I am so sorry, Cousin," he said weakly.

Malcolm squatted down and laid a hand on his shoulder. "Can you tell us what happened?" He struggled to be patient and fought the urge to shake the information out of him.

Dante took a deep breath, and his face twisted in obvious pain. "I sensed that Kerry was in trouble. When I got here, I found her passed out on the floor." Dante grimaced at the memory of it. "I went to her immediately. She was so fragile, lying there and bleeding."

Malcolm and Steven exchanged curious looks. It was clear that Dante had come here to help Kerry, not Samantha. His gaze flicked back to Dante. Rage filled his eyes as they shifted into the deep amber eyes of his fox.

"I've never been so careless," he growled. "I was so worried about Kerry I didn't even know he was hiding here in the room." Dante ground his teeth against the pain in his chest and the shame of failure. "He shot me from behind and then hit me on the head with something." He touched his head, and his fingers came away bloodied. "That's the last thing I remember," he said quietly with downcast eyes. "I'm sorry I failed you, Malcolm."

"No apologies needed, Cousin. You almost died to protect Sam and her friend. I think I know where he's taken them." Malcolm assured him with an encouraging squeeze to his shoulder and then turned his attention to Steven. "Take him to the Council for further healing, and tell them what has happened here." He stood. "I am going to get my mate." He gave a reassuring glance to Dante. "Her friend as well."

Dante gave a small nod of appreciation, his face still a mask of pain. "Thank you, Cousin."

"You're not planning on going alone I hope," Steven cautioned.

"Oh no." Malcolm gave a smile that promised vengeance. He uttered the ancient language and vanished into the air.

Moments later, Malcolm arrived in the living room of his home. He was about to open a link to his uncle Brendan when his body was flooded with relief. He sucked in a sharp breath as every single nerve ending came alive, and the blood pumped faster through his body as Samantha touched her mind to his.

Malcolm. I'm in trouble. Her voice trembled as it rippled over his soul.

I will come to you, mia piccola lupa. *Are you all right?*

A little banged up, but I'm okay. Kerry is here too, but she's hurt pretty badly. I think she's dying, Malcolm.

Malcolm knew she was trying to be strong, but he

could hear the fear and desperation that wavered under the surface, and it broke his heart.

Kerry's cousin, AJ. He's Caedo. He's the one who's been after us. We're somewhere in the aquarium where he works. He's crazy, Malcolm. I think he killed Dante. He's not working alone. He mentioned having a partner.

Malcolm sent her reassuring energy as he spoke with her. *Dante is going to be fine. You are who I am worried about. I am coming to you now. Keep your mind open to me. As long as you do that, I can always find you.*

When Sam touched her mind to Malcolm's his whole body was reenergized. It was like getting hooked up to a battery for the soul. He could only hope that it had the same effect on his mate.

Malcolm, you shouldn't come. He wants you to come here so he can kill you. Please, I couldn't bear it if you got hurt because of me.

He laughed softly in her mind. *I will be fine, my love.* His voice grew somber. *The only thing that would kill me, Samantha, is losing you. Keep your mind open to me, and I will be there shortly. Be brave, mia piccola lupa.*

He withdrew his mind from hers but maintained a connection to her energy signature. It killed him to delay going to her for one more moment, but he couldn't go in there alone. He needed the help of another Amoveo, one who was older and stronger, someone who could get Samantha and Kerry out of there quickly while he took care of the hunter. He didn't care for his own safety. All that mattered was getting her to safety. He'd finally found her. The fates couldn't take her from him now.

The very thought of losing Samantha brought instant dread. He felt like an elephant was sitting on his chest. No. She would not, could not die.

Malcolm took a deep breath, his nostrils flared, and his eyes shifted brightly. He concentrated on connecting with the one man he knew could help him.

I need your help, Uncle.

Within seconds, Brendan materialized beside the fireplace. His smile faded as soon as he saw Malcolm. He was completely disheveled. His clothing was damp and stuck to his body. His hair was in more disarray than normal, and his eagle eyes were glowing bright yellow. His face was a mask of rage.

"It seems that the fellow you captured was not working alone. He not only captured my mate and her friend, but… Dante came to investigate and was badly wounded in the process."

Brendan's eyes shifted into two glittering black diamonds. "My son," he seethed. "That bastard harmed my son."

"Yes, but he's going to recover," he added quickly. "Steven was able to get to him in time, and he's brought him to the Council for further healing."

Brendan's body relaxed somewhat, but his eyes burned with anger. He nodded his understanding. "Thank God."

"However, Samantha has been taken by the Caedo and so has her friend," Malcolm seethed through clenched teeth. "I need you to come with me. I'm quite sure that he will come after me right away. I need you to get Samantha and Kerry out of there safely."

"I would be only too happy to clean up this mess," he

said in a voice that promised retaliation. "Do you know where they are being held?"

Malcolm nodded somberly. "She opened her mind to me, so I'll be able to find her. But she's hurt and frightened."

"Then we'd better get moving and finish this," Brendan said.

Malcolm whispered to his mate, *I'm coming Samantha.*

The two men grasped each other by the forearms, uttered the ancient language "Verto," and shimmered into the air.

In the blink of an eye, they were standing in the dank cavernous room just a few feet from his mate. Malcolm's heart stopped when he saw Samantha. She was on her knees and tied up. A large purple bruise marred the left side of her beautiful face. The Caedo hunter he'd seen at the restaurant that night was there. He had her by the hair and held a knife at her delicate throat. Malcolm wanted to rip him to shreds, but Brendan held him back.

You won't reach her in time, Malcolm. That blade is right above her jugular. She'll be dead before she hits the floor.

Sam smiled and breathed his name. Tony tugged her hair and pressed the knife against her throat.

"Shut up." He pushed the blade harder still against her.

Malcolm's rage reached a new level as a small rivulet of blood trickled down her lovely neck.

"You are making a grave mistake," Malcolm said in a low deadly voice. He didn't take his gleaming yellow eyes off Tony.

"You're the one making the mistake." Tony laughed. "How do you think I learned how to keep your kind out of my head? How do you think I was able to stay a step ahead of you all the time and keep my plans from you? Huh?"

He yanked Sam's hair viciously. Her frightened eyes squeezed shut, and pain flashed across her face, but she did not cry out.

"My people have captured the one you were working with," Malcolm said steadily.

"Oh yeah," he said smugly. "Not from what I see."

Malcolm's look of confusion only made Tony laugh harder.

"He is a trusting fool. Isn't he?" He giggled.

The air thickened, and Malcolm felt a light breeze next to him as Brendan disappeared. In the next instant, he was standing next to Tony and trained his ebony eyes on him as a slow smile crept across his face. "Not as foolish as you are," Brendan murmured.

With lightning fast reflexes, he grabbed Tony's head and snapped his neck with a sickening crack.

Sam screamed and launched her body away from the violent attack. She landed with a grunt as the breath was knocked from her.

Tony made a gurgling sound as his eyes rolled back in his head. His limp body crumpled in a heap at Brendan's feet.

Malcolm rushed to Samantha, scooping her into his arms. He waved his hand, and the binding at her wrist vanished.

With a soft sob, she gratefully wrapped her sore arms around Malcolm's neck and buried her face in his chest.

He tangled his hands in her hair and breathed her in, as if to make sure she was really there with him. "Thank God. Please never close your mind to me again. I don't know what I'd do if I lost you, Samantha," he whispered into her ear. He rained small kisses all over her face and captured her mouth with his as they knelt there together.

Sam greedily kissed him back.

The sudden sound of clapping echoed through the room, breaking up their intimate reunion. They turned to see Brendan clapping. He walked slowly over to the crossbow that was leaning against the wall. A sick smile spread across his face as their obvious confusion rippled over him. Effortlessly, he picked the weapon up and pointed it at them. His cold black eyes glared at them with a hateful look of disgust.

Malcolm protectively pushed Samantha behind him as they stood up slowly. Sam's fingers dug into Malcolm's arms, and she leaned on him for support, her body weakened and shaky. Realization slithered through her. This was the partner that AJ had mentioned. Her heart beat rapidly, and tears stung at her eyes. Malcolm's uncle, a member of his own family, had been behind all of this.

She gripped his arms tightly as he held her behind him. His entire body had gone rigid, and his biceps quivered beneath her fingers. She could feel his confusion and reached out to him as gently as possible. *AJ said he had a partner, Malcolm. I'm so sorry.*

"Uncle...I don't understand. What..." Malcolm trailed off, unable to wrap his brain around the enormity of the betrayal before him.

Brendan merely laughed.

It was a deep sound that sickened Sam to her very core. He kicked AJ's body toward the giant pool at the center of the room. All the while, he never took his eyes off Malcolm and kept the deadly crossbow pointed directly at them.

Sam noticed that Brendan's eyes had shifted. They were completely black and spoke of nothing but death.

With one last shove of his heavily booted foot, he pushed AJ's body into the massive pool. A flurry of activity followed the splash, and within seconds the water turned blood red. As the body was devoured by the sharks, the entire room became tinted with crimson light.

Sam swallowed hard. *Sharks, great. Can't you blink us out of here now?*

No. Not unless you want to leave your friend behind. I have to be touching her in order to take her with us.

"Well, that ought to give the tourists something to talk about tomorrow," Brendan said in a low voice laced with twisted amusement.

"Brendan, what is going on? Why are you doing this?"

"Did you really think that we would just accept this?" Brendan asked incredulously. "That we would allow it? Let a *human* mate with our people? Breed with us?"

Sam shrank back as he spat the words out. He said *human* as though it was the lowest form of life.

"It's bad enough that you would betray me, your nephew, but your own son," Malcolm accused.

Brendan's face grew dark and somber, his voice dropped. "That was not part of the plan. My son was meddling in something that didn't need to involve him. Perhaps this will teach him a lesson. He was becoming far too fascinated with these humans." He sneered and cast a quick glance at Kerry. "That one in particular." His face twisted in disgust as he continued. "We thought it was a fluke when Lucas mated with that human wretch. At first we let it go, figuring he just had odd tastes, but when she conceived... well, we knew that had to be stopped. I would rather see you both dead than mating with humans and creating half-breeds like Logan did."

A look of horror and realization came over Sam's face. "Oh my God," she whispered as tears blurred her vision. "You... you killed my parents."

"No," Malcolm said with disbelief, shaking his head and looking from Samantha to Brendan. "No. It was the Caedo."

"No, my boy." Brendan laughed a low evil sound. "Oh, we blamed them of course. They are after all the perfect scapegoats. They have killed hundreds of our people over the years, but that..." He sighed dramatically. "That was one they did not do."

Brendan had a smug, satisfied look on his face that was turning Sam's grief into rage.

He let out a sound of exasperation. "Really, Malcolm, you can't tell me you're surprised by this? Did you honestly believe that we would let you breed human weakness into our race?"

"Does Richard know about this?" Malcolm seethed.

"Please," he spat. "He's weak and soft. He's so desperate to keep our race going that he's willing to allow you and others to muddy our bloodlines with humans." Brendan's calm facade disintegrated as he ranted. "You can be assured I am not the only one. There are many of us who want to keep our race pure. If it means that some of our own have to die, then so be it."

"So you teamed up with our enemy to kill and betray your own people?"

"Well, I'd prefer not to kill you," he said casually. "Join us, Malcolm. If you were able to mate with this thing, then you will probably survive once she's dead."

Sam felt Malcolm's body quiver with fury as every fiber of his being tensed. His anger flashed over her with violent intensity, and she steeled herself against the onslaught of the energy. She gritted her teeth and dug her fingers deeper into his arm, hoping to draw strength from him. The last thing she wanted to do was faint like some helpless female in a bad movie. She focused on her breathing the way Malcolm taught her and concentrated on filtering out the hostile energy.

"You are strong and a good fighter. We could use you in our cause. Don't you see? Breeding with humans will weaken our race." He shifted his gaze to Sam, and she could feel his hatred of her as it slammed into her mind. She felt the blood drain from her face. She swallowed back the bile that rose in her throat, but she didn't take her eyes off of his. There was no way she was going to let him get the best of her. "Look at her. She's pathetic. She can barely master simple things that we teach our children. See how easily she's affected by the emotions of others. Is that what you want for your offspring? She's never even shifted to her clan form. She probably can't even do it. Killing her will be a pleasure." He sneered, training the crossbow on Sam.

In that instant, Malcolm's anger boiled over and filled the room. Kerry moaned softly from the corner, momentarily drawing Brendan's attention, which was all Malcolm needed. He shoved Samantha back. A wild scream of fury ripped from his throat and evolved into the earsplitting screech of his eagle. By the time Brendan looked back, Malcolm's massive wings had taken him through the air. His razor sharp talons were clawing at Brendan's face.

Brendan screamed in pain and rage, swatting frantically as Malcolm's talons tore through his flesh and slashed one of his eyes. Bleeding heavily, he clutched at his face and dropped the crossbow. To Sam's horror, he shifted into the most massive black bear she had ever seen. Malcolm flapped his wings and hovered, mercilessly clawing at Brendan's wounded and now furry face. Brendan bellowed a thunderous roar, which rumbled through the cavernous room and shook Sam to her core.

The dark fur on his face was wet with blood. One of his eyes was a sickening clump hanging from its socket. He roared with frustration and continued to swat at Malcolm's unyielding, shrieking attack. Brendan stumbled by the edge of the pool and swatted blindly at Malcolm. Sam's eyes widened with horror as an immense clawed paw connected heavily with Malcolm. A cloud of feathers and blood filled the air. The blow sent Malcolm crashing into the wall. He fell and shifted abruptly back to his human form, landing with an audible thud. Brendan stood triumphant on his hind legs and let out a roar of victory over Malcolm's wounded body. When Samantha saw Malcolm lying unconscious and bleeding, something primal inside of her snapped.

Red-hot fury flashed through her body, and every single nerve ending lit up brightly. Her eyes tingled and shifted fiercely. Brendan took her birthright, he murdered her parents, and now he was trying to take the only man she had ever loved. One image blazed in her mind as she looked at the one who took everything from her.

Wolf.

Flames licked up her spine, lightning flashed across her skin, and she erupted into her wolf form with a vicious snarl. It happened so fast she didn't even realize she had done it. She heard herself growl—at least she thought it came from her. It was a deadly sound that reverberated over her skin and deep into her bones.

Samantha bared her teeth, and with every ounce of energy she had, launched her body at Brendan. He turned toward the unexpected attack just in time for her large paws to land on his barrel chest. She could swear she saw a look of shock on his mutilated face as she sunk her razor-sharp teeth into his thick neck. Blood spurted over her tongue, but the warm coppery liquid didn't repulse her—it only steeled her resolve.

When her body slammed into him and her teeth tore into his flesh, he roared with surprise and stumbled backward. He swatted desperately at Sam, and his claws sliced her flank. She growled as the white searing pain shot through her. His blow knocked her to the side and released him from her grip. She landed next to Malcolm with a yelp.

Between the force of her attack and his wounds, Brendan lost his footing on the slippery cement floor. Sam watched as he bellowed with rage and fell thrashing into the shark tank behind him. He flailed wildly in the water as the sharks got yet another unplanned meal. His blood filled the tank, leaving the room awash in an even deeper crimson light.

Sam lay there, panting for a moment, shocked at what had just happened. Finally she stood, limping on her wounded leg, and let out a low whine. She felt Malcolm stir next to her. He was bleeding from large gashes on his arm and head. She nudged him softly with her wet nose, licking his face, and touched her mind to his. *Malcolm? Can you hear me? Please answer me.* Sam was relieved as his eyes fluttered open.

A slow smile spread across his face as he saw Sam in her animal form for the first time.

Mia lupa piccola, he whispered back, his smile quickly faded as he remembered Brendan. He sat up, wincing at the pain as he looked around the room. *Where is he?*

Sam whined and looked toward the still splashing red waters of the tank. *I'm so sorry, Malcolm.*

He looked over at the bloody water and then knew that Brendan was gone. *No. I'm sorry. I won't let anyone harm you ever again,* mia piccola lupa. He ran his hand along her furred body.

My little wolf, huh? I'm not that little. She sighed.

My little wolf, he insisted with a proud smile.

Well, let's see if I can turn back into the less furry version of myself. Sam closed her eyes and pictured herself as human again. In seconds, she shimmered and shifted back to her human form.

Malcolm's eyes widened in surprise and pride as he witnessed her newly mastered ability. She stood before him, her clothes torn, a bloody gash on her leg, and an ugly purple bruise marring her lovely face. Anger flared deep inside of him at the sight of her wound and the memory of Brendan's betrayal. He softened, however, as he watched her go to her friend. Kerry was still passed out on the other side of the room.

She stepped over the bloody mess by the edge of the pool. Sam knelt down next to Kerry and gently moved the hair from her face. She groaned and moved slightly as Sam looked her over. With a wave of her hand, Sam removed the tape from her wrists and feet. She felt pretty good about her newfound comfort level with her abilities. The moment she'd shifted into her wolf, it was as if every one of her abilities clicked into place and she was finally a puzzle with all of its pieces.

Kerry stirred briefly and let out a soft moan.

"Shhh. It's okay," Sam whispered. "We're going to get you home."

Sam brushed the last few strands from her friend's swollen black eye. Any regrets she had about killing Brendan were gone as she looked at Kerry and then around the room. She went down the laundry list of horrible, hateful things he'd done. Sam saw Malcolm watching her lovingly. She went to him immediately and knelt down to examine his injuries, paying no attention to her own wounds.

Malcolm forced himself to a sitting position and watched his mate with awe. She had shifted instinctively and without the ancient language. She truly was special and had more power than anyone expected. Malcolm interrupted her inspections and took her hands in his. He kissed both of her palms tenderly. Taking her face in his hands, he locked his eyes on hers as his thumb gently stroked her cheek.

Sam looked into his eyes and felt tears of relief prick the back of her eyes. It dawned on both of them how horribly close they'd come to losing each other. She tenderly captured his lips with hers. In her mind, she heard him whisper softly. *I love you, Samantha. Forever.*

Chapter 21

THE NEXT DAY HAD GONE BY IN A BLUR FOR SAMANTHA. It was filled with police reports and a trip to the hospital to visit Kerry. Richard, one of the only people they knew for certain they could trust, helped them get home. Sam and Malcolm were too injured to do it on their own. Once they got Kerry back to the house, Sam called the police and reported AJ's insane attack on both of them. As far as the police and Kerry were concerned, AJ had become obsessed with Sam and attempted to abduct her. Malcolm had heard her screams and come to her aid, fighting briefly with AJ before scaring him off into the night. No one knew about Dante's involvement, not even Kerry.

Their story of AJ's obsession was proven by the photos all around his room; her pictures plastered all over the walls were more than enough to support their tale. Although an all-points bulletin had been released for him, Sam suspected he'd never be found, unless they cut open a few sharks over at the aquarium. Kerry had been passed out through the entire event and luckily had very little memory of anything. She remembered struggling with AJ after he attacked her at the house. Forcing her to call Samantha was the last thing she said she remembered.

Malcolm had been reluctant to let Sam out of his sight again, but she promised to maintain their connection, and there was no way she wasn't going to visit Kerry in the hospital. She knew that the only way he could be sure she was safe was if she kept her mind open to him. So he made her promise she wouldn't sever that connection again. Considering the newly discovered group of Amoveo purists, they both knew her safety would always be in question.

Brendan was not the only one who wanted her dead. The most disturbing part was that these purists were hidden in plain sight among his people. They had proven to be even more deadly and devious than the Caedo. Brendan's betrayal would haunt Malcolm forever. A member of his own family had plotted to kill him and his mate.

Sam pulled her car into the driveway of Malcolm's house—of her house. Her lips curved into a small smile.

Their house.

She grabbed her purse off of the passenger seat and winced slightly at the residual soreness in her shoulder. Most of her injuries had healed quickly over the last couple of days, another perk of being Amoveo.

Sam let herself into the house but still struggled with the urge to knock. She stepped into the spacious foyer and stilled at the sound of voices coming from the living room. She breathed deeply and focused on the energy signatures in the house. There were four other Amoveo in there with Malcolm. She swallowed hard and willed herself to put one foot in front of the other and go in there to meet them, but her feet weren't cooperating.

Malcolm's soothing voice wafted gratefully into her head. *Are you coming in mia piccola lupa? They are eager to meet you.*

Before Sam could answer him, Davis shuffled in from the kitchen with a small package tucked under his arm. "Malcolm and the others are waiting for you in the living room Ms. Samantha." He winked and gave her a gentle pat on the arm. "You'll be fine, miss," he whispered.

Sam gave him a weak smile. "Where are you headed? Aren't you going to come in and say hello?" She hoped so. She dreaded the idea of walking into that room alone.

He held up the small bag and opened the front door. "I'm taking some special tea over to my girl."

Smiling, Sam watched him disappear through the large doorway and tossed her purse on the small side table. As odd as it was to see Nonie with another man, it made her happy to know that she was happy. No one should have to be lonely. She remembered that feeling all too well.

A familiar voice purred against her ear. "I'm the one who's lonely." Sam smiled as Malcolm's strong arms slipped around her waist. Warm, steely strength enveloped her the moment he pressed that rock hard body against hers.

She clasped her hands over his and hugged them against her belly. Sam leaned back and craned her neck to look up at him. She opened her mouth to respond, but his lips were on hers before she could utter a word. She moaned softly and relished the taste of him. His lips were firm and inviting, and his tongue slid deliciously along hers, sending tiny shivers up her spine.

He suckled her bottom lip and pulled back from her slowly, placing a tiny kiss on the tip of her upturned nose. "That's much better," he murmured. "I know you were only gone for a few hours, but it felt like a good deal longer."

Sam opened her eyes and turned her body in his embrace. She placed her hands on the solid muscles in his chest and adored the way his body felt against hers. She fiddled with the buttons on his shirt and gave him a mischievous look from under her lashes. His hands slid down and rested on her jean-clad bottom.

"Well, we could skip the introductions, and I could take you upstairs and ravage you." Sam stood on her tiptoes, placed a soft kiss at the base of his throat, and flicked her tongue along his pulse that thrummed strong and steady.

He groaned and squeezed her ass. "You have no idea how much I want to take you up on that." He ran his hands up her back, over her shoulders, and took her face gently in his hands. His brown eyes stared down at her compassionately. "But we cannot put this off any longer," he said softly. "It's time for you to meet them, face-to-face."

Sam let out a sigh of surrender, and Malcolm linked his fingers with hers as he led her into the living room. Sam wasn't sure what to expect. The only other Amoveo she had actually met—who was supposed to be helping her—had murdered her parents and tried to kill her. Great.

Malcolm, sensing her unease, wrapped his arm around her protectively, and pulled her into the shelter of his body as they walked into the room. She draped her arm around his waist and hugged him. *Don't even think about leaving me alone for one second.* He said nothing, but chuckled and squeezed her back.

The men stood up to greet Samantha. Her eye was immediately drawn to the one with long raven hair who had been seated in the armchair by the fireplace. She recognized him immediately as the man who had vanished from the deck. *Was that only a few days ago? It seems like years,* she mused. Thick, pin-straight ebony hair hung well past his broad shoulders and framed an incredibly handsome face. His sharp features spoke of strength, but his most striking feature were his enormous eyes. His energy signature radiated power and authority, and she could only assume he was Richard, the Prince.

He bowed to her slightly as she and Malcolm crossed the room and closed the distance between them.

Sam steeled herself and extended her hand to him. She swallowed hard. "It's very nice to meet you," she said in a surprisingly stable voice.

He took her hand and kissed it with all the regality one would expect from a prince. "It is a pleasure to meet *you*, Samantha." He released her hand and stood back up to his full height. Sam couldn't help but notice that he was even taller than Malcolm.

Sam turned to the two men who had stood up from the sofa. Both of them were well over six feet tall and looked to be nothing but muscle and bone.

"Jeez, they don't make you guys small, do they?" she mumbled under her breath.

One man remained seated on the couch, his arm in a sling. Sam instantly recognized him. It was Dante. His warm amber eyes smiled at her, and she couldn't help but smile back.

"You'll have to forgive me for not standing up, but I'm still not feeling quite myself yet."

"Please," Sam began quickly, "don't apologize. You wouldn't even be in this mess if it weren't for me. I should be thanking you. Who knows how much worse it may have been for Kerry. If you hadn't shown up, I shudder to think of what else he might've done to her."

Dante's brow furrowed. "I was careless. Believe me, it won't happen again."

The one with shaggy blond hair reached over the coffee table and shook Sam's hand. "I'm Steven," he said with a big smile. "I patched up the tough guy over here." He gave Dante a pat on his uninjured shoulder and flopped himself back down on the couch "Good to meet you, Mrs. Malcolm," he said teasingly.

Sam narrowed her eyes playfully. "Oh, so that's how it's gonna be?"

Steven threw his head back and laughed.

The only other man she hadn't met interrupted sharply. "I don't think there's anything to be laughing about right now, Steven."

Everyone in the room fell silent, and the energy around them rippled. Sam's body stiffened, and the smile faded from her lips as her gaze landed on his deadly serious face. His snow white hair was streaked with brown and pulled back in tight ponytail. He was dressed impeccably in a black suit, which was finished off perfectly with a cobalt blue tie and matching hanky in the pocket. He possessed an icy reserve that set Sam's teeth on edge.

Malcolm held her closer, and his voice slipped into her mind. *That's just William. He's a bit... uptight. You'll get used to it.*

William nodded slightly, but his dark brown, almost

black eyes, remained serious. "I apologize for being so abrupt. It's a pleasure to meet you," he said tightly. "But I do wish that the circumstances were different." He sat stiffly on the couch and smoothed the lapels of his jacket.

"No, you're right," Sam said quietly and looked at each of the faces around the room. "There isn't much that's funny about this situation. Funny-strange, yes. Funny ha-ha, not so much." She looked at Dante because he seemed to be the most accepting and welcoming. Hell, he did almost die to help her. "I do want to thank you. It's nice to know that we have at least a few allies among the Amoveo."

Malcolm kissed the top of her head. "I'm sure there are more of our people who are open to mating with special humans like your mother." He led her to the other chair opposite the couch and motioned for her and everyone else to sit down. He sat next to her on the arm of the chair, and his gaze landed on Richard. "My concern is that there are more than a few Amoveo who share Brendan's prejudice."

"I was horrified by Brendan's actions. I am truly baffled by the violent levels he'd gone to." Richard sat back in his chair, crossed his long legs, and folded his hands in his lap. "There had never been a Caedo assassin captured. That whole thing had been a ruse to leave you both exposed and vulnerable."

"Yes, and unfortunately it worked," seethed Dante. His father's betrayal was still raw, and the pain of it was etched clearly in his features. Sam's heart broke for him. The only person more shaken by the plot than Malcolm was Dante. His father had lied to everyone, including him.

"Samantha, I promise you that we will find the other traitors to our race and protect you at all costs," Richard said earnestly. "Several humans had been identified as potential mates, and Brendan had been in charge of finding them. The next step is to find the list he had developed and be sure they are protected until they find their mates."

"Or their mates find them," Dante said quietly.

They all nodded in agreement.

"Malcolm and I have decided to keep the conspiracy revelation to a select few. I have not even informed the Council. I will tell them the same story you told the humans." His eyes softened, and a look of sorrow passed briefly over his features. "I don't know who can be trusted except for those who are already involved. If word gets out about the purist plot, it will be much harder to ferret out the traitors."

"What about my mother?" Dante asked quietly. "We have to tell her something. She'll be deeply affected by this on many levels."

Richard nodded solemnly. Now that her mate was dead, her own life would be coming to an end as well. "I have been giving that a good deal of thought. As far as anyone else is concerned, your father was killed in an effort to help protect Samantha and Malcolm. No one will know that he was a traitor."

"At least not now," William added quickly.

Dante shot him a look that could've cut through stone. "What does that mean?"

William shrugged casually. "It means that once the purist conspiracy is brought to light, people will have to know the truth." Dante growled, but William remained unfazed by his anger. "The truth always comes out, Dante," he said evenly.

Sam shivered at the harsh reality of that statement. Boy, did it ever.

She listened intently as they discussed the various possibilities. By the end of the conversation her mind was spinning. The bottom line? They didn't know much. The only confirmed purist was dead, and they didn't have any leads on the others.

The men left just as the sun was setting. Sam wanted to spend the evening with Malcolm, but knew she needed to speak with her grandmother. She had been shocked when Malcolm told her that Nonie had known about the Amoveo and her unique heritage. Sam and Nonie talked through the night. It felt so good for Sam to finally tell her everything and share all she'd experienced. She listened with rapt attention to Nonie. She was fascinated that both Nonie and Sam's mother had the same ability. Nonie had always been open with Jane about the gifts that the women in their family possessed. The mothers in their family had passed this gift to their daughters from generation to generation. However, when Jane was killed, Nonie blamed their unique ability. She swore that Sam would remain oblivious to that world. She had hoped it would protect her and save her from the same fate.

Nonie also admitted that she was the seagull from her dreams with Malcolm. She wanted Sam to be with Malcolm willingly. She didn't want her manipulated into it by some archaic tradition like she felt her daughter had been. They cried and even laughed through some tears until the orange glow of sunrise bathed the cozy kitchen. By the time morning arrived, they were mentally, physically, and emotionally exhausted. They hugged for what seemed like an eternity. It was one that wrapped her in pure love.

"Are you coming up, dear? I'm so exhausted from everything I feel like I could sleep for a week." Nonie sniffled as she released Sam reluctantly.

Sam smiled and shook her head slowly. "No. I think I'll go see how Malcolm is feeling."

Nonie nodded. "Yes, of course, dear." She dabbed her eyes with a tissue and started up the stairway. She stopped abruptly and turned back to Sam with a stern listen-here-missy look on her face. "Now, I know you and Malcolm are mated as far as the Amoveo are concerned... but... you are human as well. And you have a human grandmother who would really like to see you married—like a human. You know, wedding, flowers, cake... I can't exactly tell Millie that you are *mated*. Really, what will people think?" She had a twinkle in her eyes, her arms folded, and her heels dug in literally and figuratively.

Sam laughed and scooped Nonie up in another hug. "You are too much. With everything that's happened, this is what you're concerned about?" Sam laughed. "Yes, Nonie. We're getting married."

Nonie squeezed her back with love and a little relief as well. "Good. I was just checking. Night, dear." Nonie released Sam and made her way up the steps.

"Good night, Nonie. Sleep well." Sam watched Nonie go up the stairs.

Malcolm's sexy voice soothingly wafted into her mind. *I'll only sleep well if I have you next to me.*

In the next instant, she felt his warm strong body pressing up behind her. His arms wrapped possessively around her waist, and those sensual lips grazed her earlobe. He whispered softly to her. "I thought you'd like to stay here tonight. So you could be close to your grandmother."

Sam smiled as she melted against him. She tilted her head, exposing her neck, giving him access to her sensitive skin. "I think for her sake we should take this back to your house."

"You mean *our* house," he said softly against her shoulder.

"Oh yeah." She sighed. Sam turned, captured his mouth with hers, and wrapped her arms around his neck. She felt the bizarre momentary displacement that came with the odd form of travel he seemed to like so much. It reminded her of that sense of falling that happens sometimes just before going to sleep, where your whole body startles or jumps.

In seconds, they materialized in Malcolm's bedroom.

"Another perk of being a mated Amoveo," she murmured against his lips.

"Quick healers." He smiled and placed a soft kiss on the corner of her eye where her bruise had all but faded.

They were wrapped up in each other's arms, lips and tongues dancing, and their hands exploring each other with wild abandon. With a wave of his hand and a seductively wicked smile, he divested them both of their clothing.

Sam shrieked at their sudden nakedness and gave him a playful smack on the arm. "Hey, that was my favorite pair of jeans to wear." She giggled.

With a devilish grin, he scooped her up and tossed her on the bed. Malcolm watched her laugh as her hair flowed freely over her shoulders. He hated even that brief moment apart from her and immediately covered her body with his.

"You're my favorite thing to wear," he growled.

Malcolm settled himself between her thighs and slipped inside of her.

Moaning softly, she moved against him. He loved the feel of his body moving in unison with hers. She ran her delicate hands up his arms, and his muscles rippled in response to her silken touch.

He stayed above her, joining his body with hers. He memorized every beautiful detail of her face. He loved that her eyes had shifted blue, revealing her desire for him. He leaned down and kissed the tip of her nose. His fingers tangled in the long flaxen strands, and he reveled in how impossibly soft it felt in his hands. Looking into her eyes, he knew that he was lost to her for all time. Memories of the danger she'd been in flooded back to his mind. A dark cloud passed over his face, and his body tensed.

"I don't know what I would've done if I'd lost you," Malcolm said with a hoarse whisper. "I promise, Samantha, I won't ever let anyone hurt you again. I love you, Samantha, *mia piccola lupa*." He murmured softly against her lips.

Sam savored the tender words with the equally gentle touch. She looked into his large Amoveo eyes and sensed how much he loved her. She knew that he loved her completely, for all that she was, or even what she wasn't. Her heart ached, and joyful tears stung her eyes. She blinked them back and smiled. He kissed away a single salty drop as it rolled down her cheek. That night, he showed her over and over again how much he loved her.

They cried out in unison as the pleasure crested and took them both over the edge. Samantha reached out with her mind in the most intimate form of communication as they joined their bodies and souls.

I love you, Malcolm.

She was his, his Samantha, his mate, forever.

READ ON FOR A SNEAK PEEK AT

UNTOUCHED

NEXT IN THE AMOVEO LEGEND SERIES
BY SARA HUMPHREYS

COMING APRIL 2012 FROM
SOURCEBOOKS CASABLANCA

THE MUSIC FROM THE SMALL BAND FLOWED LIGHTLY around Kerry and the rest of the wedding guests. She sipped the cool, crisp champagne as she watched Samantha dance with her new husband. She could feel their happiness mixed with the late summer breeze. Her gaze drifted over the small group of guests gathered around the bride and groom. They all had that same serene look while they watched Malcolm and Samantha share their first dance as husband and wife. He towered over her as he twirled her around the dance floor and the sound of her laughter peppered the air. The two of them hadn't taken their eyes off each other for one second. If Kerry didn't know any better, she'd swear they were reading each other's minds. She chuckled quietly and sipped her champagne from the delicate crystal flute. The guests were limited to only thirty or so close friends and family members. Her own parents had sent their regrets from Europe, which was something of a relief. Kerry could only handle them in small doses and didn't want their chilly demeanor ruining such a beautiful day for Sam.

"May I have this dance?"

The deep voice rolled over her like sudden thunder in the distance. She jumped with a yelp and splashed champagne onto her deep red satin gown. "Shit," she hissed under her breath. Kerry brushed at the droplets which were now making dark stains on her dress. She shot an irritated glance at Malcolm's best man, Dante. "I don't dance." Something about this guy threw her off balance. Kerry prided herself on her ability to stay in control and this guy rattled her.

"I'm sorry. I didn't realize I'd have that effect on you."

The amusement in his voice made her want to punch him square in the mouth. Or kiss him. She glared at him through narrowed eyes and put on her most stuck up and obnoxious tone, hoping she could frighten him away. "Don't flatter yourself, Tarzan. I was startled. That's all."

He had moved in next to her without a sound. How long had he been standing there? He didn't go away. Instead, he moved in closer, just a breath away from her. She felt the warmth of his body along her bare arm and all the little hairs stood on end. She was terrified he'd touch her and at the same time worried he wouldn't. She quickly turned her attention back to Malcolm and Sam, trying to ignore him, but failing miserably.

He was a difficult man to ignore. At five foot ten, she was usually taller than most men and this guy towered over her, even in her Jimmy Choos. He was massive, well over six and a half feet tall, a solid wall of muscle, and had a handsome, masculine face with the most enormous amber eyes she'd ever seen. His thick auburn hair was almost the exact same color as his eyes. Not that she'd noticed him or anything. Kerry scolded herself. There was absolutely no point in getting all hot and bothered over some guy she'd never be able to touch. *I must be the oldest living virgin that isn't officially a nun.* She drained what was left of her drink. Her goal was to be as horrible to him as possible and get him to go away.

Dante smiled as though he knew she was doing her best to upset him. She could feel his gaze wander down the length of her body.

"You'll dance with me. Maybe not today," he whispered into her ear. "But eventually… you and I will dance."

Kerry turned to give the arrogant bastard a piece of her mind but he was gone. Vanished, it seemed, into thin air. Her breath came quickly and her eyes darted around the tent. Her body still quivered from the soft whisper, laden with innuendo. She was horrified that everyone in the tent would see how he'd thrown her entire body into overdrive. Her cheeks burned with anger, fear, and lust, a potent combination. Kerry straightened her back in an effort to calm her quaking limbs as a welcome voice wafted over her.

"Well now, missy. I hope you're going to keep coming to visit me even though our girl is married off."

Kerry let out the breath she'd been holding and smiled at Sam's grandmother, Nonie. "C'mon Nonie, you're not getting rid of me that easily." Kerry placed the empty flute on a passing waiter's tray and quickly scooped up a fresh glass. Perhaps a little more booze would calm her nerves.

"Well, you know you've always been like a granddaughter to me. You and Samantha are practically sisters. You can't blame an old lady for worrying." She smiled up at Kerry with twinkling eyes that reminded her of the summer ocean.

"Well, since Sam and Malcolm aren't even going on a honeymoon and they're living right next door to you… I don't think you'll be that lonely." Kerry took a fresh swig of the champagne and hoped she didn't sound as jealous as she felt. "I have to leave tomorrow for a photo shoot in New Orleans, but I'll be back after that. To be very honest," she said with a sigh, "I'm getting really burnt out and sick of traveling."

"You're going on a shoot, already? Well now, don't you think you're jumping back into things awfully fast?" Nonie's voice hovered somewhere between panic and anger; Kerry couldn't quite tell which one was going to win out. She couldn't bring herself to look at Nonie, so she kept her eyes trained on the happy couple.

"I'm fine, Nonie. Sheesh, did you and Sam go the same worry-wort school? I'm not in any more danger from AJ. My cousin was obsessed with Sam, remember? I just got in his way. He's long gone from here, anyway. Every cop in Rhode Island has his picture. Westerly is a small town. Millie's even got his picture up at the diner with a big 'DANGER' sign plastered above it. I'd be more worried about Samantha," she said with a nod.

Nonie's mouth set in a grim line. "Samantha will be fine. She's stronger than you think and besides, she has Malcolm. I worry about *you,* Kerry. You shouldn't be traveling by yourself. You just never know what can happen. I would think you've learned that as a result of recent events."

Kerry rolled her eyes at the scolding tone and turned to face Nonie. She looked into her worry-filled eyes set in a soft, wrinkled face and any irritation she felt melted away with the ocean breeze. Kerry had the overwhelming urge to scoop the old woman up in a hug but knew the cost would be too great. Instead she swallowed the lump that had formed in her throat and turned quickly to face the calm, blue sea.

Nonie and Sam were the only two people in the world
she really loved and she'd almost lost them both because
of AJ. He'd been completely obsessed with Samantha
and had coerced Kerry into luring her into his sick trap.
Her mind drifted to that awful night. She had fought
back as much as she could, but he'd overpowered her.
She was disgusted with herself. If she had touched him
before that, just once, she would've seen what he was
up to. She would've seen through the façade to the evil
underneath, but she'd been too weak. Her stomach
roiled at the memory of her cowardice.

Samantha's bright laughter tumbled through the air
and brought a smile to her lips. Nonie was right. Sam
would be fine. If it weren't for Malcolm, AJ would've
killed them both. He'd scared the little worm off and
there'd been no trace of him in the weeks following the
attack. It was as though he'd vanished from the face of
the earth. Samantha had been hurt because of her and
she would never forgive herself for that.

Nonie stood silently by her side as they watched the
waves roll gently onto the sand. Kerry wanted to tell
Nonie and Sam the truth, but was terrified at what they
would think. They were all that she had and she couldn't
afford to lose them. What was she supposed to say? *Hey,
guess what, I have visions when I touch people. Oh, by
the way, it's so painful I want to vomit. How about a
hug?* They would think she was insane, just like her
twisted cousin AJ. She cringed. If she lost them, then
she would really be alone. Kerry pulled the burgundy
wrap tightly around her as the cool ocean breeze picked
up. She shivered, knowing it wasn't from the wind.
Taking a deep breath, she finally broke the silence.

"I'll be careful, Nonie. Listen, I'm going to New Orleans, not Iraq. I'll be perfectly safe."

"Yes, you will." Samantha's all-too-chipper tone came over Kerry's other shoulder. "Malcolm and I have hired someone to make certain of it."

Kerry narrowed her eyes and looked warily at Samantha. "What are you babbling about? Has marriage made you lose your senses already?"

"Oh, I make her crazy. There's no doubt about that," Malcolm said softly. He stood behind Sam with his arms wrapped around her waist and nibbled on her ear.

"Malcolm," Sam giggled. "Cut it out. This is serious." Kerry rolled her eyes but couldn't resist smiling at them and fought the urge to look around for Dante. "You two are gonna frighten the guests. Get a room. Jeez."

"What my lovely bride is trying to tell you, is that we've taken measures to be sure you're kept safe on this next trip. It's only been a few weeks since the unfortunate events of late. We just want to be certain that you have an extra measure of security. That's all."

Kerry eyed the three of them one at a time. Each of their faces held steely resolve and she saw there was no point in arguing. "I can see that I'm being totally ganged up on. Aren't I?"

"Yes!" Samantha wriggled out of Malcolm's embrace, popped up on her toes and planted a quick kiss on Kerry's cheek. The wolf image whisked fleetingly through Kerry's mind, leaving as quickly as it came. Kerry shook her head as Malcolm led Samantha back out to the dance floor. "It better not be some crotchety old cop or something," she shouted after them.

"I'm not crotchety or a cop." Dante's deep, male

voice rolled over her. Instantly she was aware of his body behind hers. So close. Too close. Kerry held her breath and whipped around to face him.

"No way!" She placed her hands firmly on her hips and glared up at him defiantly.

"Inferno Securities has the highest reputation. We've provided personal security for kings and queens. I'm sure I can handle a princess like you." Dante delivered a wicked grin and remained stone still, unwilling to retreat. He smiled as her deep brown eyes flashed angrily back at him. He might be there to protect her, but little did she know, she was the one who would be saving him.

Acknowledgments

"Really great people make you feel that you, too, can become great."

—Mark Twain

This has been such an amazing adventure. I consider myself an incredibly lucky woman to have so many supportive and loving people in my life, both personally and professionally. I couldn't possibly have gotten this book done without all of their love and encouragement.

To my husband Will: Thank you for being so loving, supportive, and understanding. When I said, "Hey, I think I need to go to a hotel—alone—for an entire weekend… to write." You gratefully said, "Okay babe. Whatever you need." There aren't many husbands out there who are willing to provide such unconditional and unwavering support. I love you, and I love being your wife. I'm *your* biggest fan.

To my boys: Thank you for sharing me with the characters in my head and for "suffering" through pizza night on many occasions. I love you all very, very much.

To my Farkle Family: What can I say? Mom, Katie, and Meggie: Thank you for reading various versions of my manuscript and for giving me honest feedback. Dad, I promise I'll black out the sexy parts next time to save you the hassle and weirdness of skipping over "those parts." Charlie—your title suggestions were duly noted, but I didn't think *W.I.L.F.* or *Eagle's Scream: Eww It's in My Fur* would sell to my target market. Thanks to all the Farkles for never letting me take myself too seriously. Love you all!

To the best-beta-reader-ever Sheila: Thank you, thank you, thank you for reading endless scenes, chapters, rewrites, and more rewrites. Your honest feedback has been so very much appreciated. More than anything, thanks for being such a dear friend—dear enough to say, "No. That doesn't work." (But in a way that doesn't make me cry.) Ooooofffa! Love ya, woman.

The College of Westchester: Thanks for sending me to that charity event with Mary Higgins Clark and Carol Higgins Clark! Thank you to my co-workers for cheering me on every step of the way. You guys rock!

Carol Higgins Clark: Thank you for recommending Jeanne Dube!

My patient and tenacious agent Jeanne Dube: You are an outstanding lady and a helluva agent! Thanks for taking a chance on me and for hooking me up with the perfect publisher.

Sue Grimshaw: Thank you for helping spread the good word about my Amoveo series. I don't think we could've gotten this done without you!

My editor Deb Werksman: Thank you so very much for giving me this opportunity. I am so excited to create a home at Sourcebooks. You are a joy to work with!

Amy Petty: Thank you for being my musical muse. *You rock!*

Lauren Markow & Red Pill Entertainment: Thank you so much for allowing me to use Amy's music and for being such wonderfully collaborative and creative folks!

To all my Facebook and Twitter friends: Thank you all for helping me get the word out about this series. (This means you Ellen, Maureen, Lisa V., John C., Joanne K., Lori, and Carrie.) Thanks to the two Marias for helping clarify my Italian dilemma. You'll forever have my gratitude.

Last, but not least… thank you to all of my readers. I look forward to the rest of this incredible journey and sure hope you'll continue to come along for the ride. I'm blessed to be surrounded by really great people.

Dream on.

About the Author

Unleashed is Sara's first published novel and the first book in The Amoveo Legend series. Sara is a graduate of Marist College, with a B.A. in English Literature & Theater. Her initial path after college was a professional actress. Some of her television credits include, *A&E Biography, Guiding Light, Another World, As the World Turns,* and *Rescue Me*. For the past several years Sara has been a professional public speaker and speaker trainer. Her career began with Monster's *Making It Count* programs, speaking in high schools and colleges around the United States to thousands of students. For the past several years, Sara has worked with the College of Westchester in New York as the director of high school and community relations.

Sara has been a lover of both paranormal and romance novels for years. Her science fiction/fantasy/romance obsession began years ago with the TV series *Star Trek* and an enormous crush on Captain Kirk. That sci-fi obsession soon evolved into the love of vampires, ghosts, werewolves, and of course, shapeshifters. Sara is married to her college sweetheart, Will. They live in Bronxville, New York, with their four boys, two dopey dogs, and an extremely loud bird. Life is busy, but never dull.